Road Dogs

ALSO BY ELMORE LEONARD

FICTION

Up in Honey's Room

The Hot Kid

The Complete Western
    Stories of Elmore Leonard

Mr. Paradise

When the Women Come
    Out to Dance

Tishomingo Blues

Pagan Babies

Be Cool

The Tonto Woman &
    Other Western Stories

Cuba Libre

Out of Sight

Riding the Rap

Pronto

Rum Punch

Maximum Bob

Get Shorty

Killshot

Freaky Deaky

Touch

Bandits

Glitz

LaBrava

Stick

Cat Chaser

Split Images

City Primeval

Gold Coast

Gunsights

The Switch

The Hunted

Unknown Man No. 89

Swag

Fifty-two Pickup

Mr. Majestyk

Forty Lashes Less One

Valdez Is Coming

The Moonshine War

The Big Bounce

Hombre

Last Stand at Saber River

Escape from Five Shadows

The Law at Randado

The Bounty Hunters

NONFICTION

Elmore Leonard's
    10 Rules of Writing

Road Dogs

WITHDRAWN

Elmore Leonard

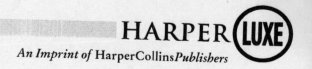

HARPER LUXE

An Imprint of HarperCollinsPublishers

ROAD DOGS. Copyright © 2009 by Elmore Leonard, Inc. All rights reserved. Printed in the United States of America. No part of this book may be used or reproduced in any manner whatsoever without written permission except in the case of brief quotations embodied in critical articles and reviews. For information address HarperCollins Publishers, 10 East 53rd Street, New York, NY 10022.

HarperCollins books may be purchased for educational, business, or sales promotional use. For information please write: Special Markets Department, HarperCollins Publishers, 10 East 53rd Street, New York, NY 10022.

FIRST HARPERLUXE EDITION

HarperLuxe™ is a trademark of HarperCollins Publishers

Library of Congress Cataloging-in-Publication Data is available upon request.

ISBN: 978-0-06-177470-6

09 10 11 12 13   ID/RRD   10 9 8 7 6 5 4 3

For Marjorie Braman

Road Dogs

One

They put Foley and the Cuban together in the back-seat of the van and took them from the Palm Beach County jail on Gun Club to Glades Correctional, the old redbrick prison at the south end of Lake Okeechobee. Neither one said a word during the ride that took most of an hour, both of them handcuffed and shackled.

They were returning Jack Foley to do his thirty years after busting out for a week, Foley's mind on a woman who made intense love to him one night in Detroit, pulled a Sig Sauer .38 the next night, shot him and sent him back to Florida.

The Cuban, a little guy about fifty with dyed hair pulled back in a ponytail, was being transferred to Glades from the state prison at Starke, five years down, two and a half to go of a second-degree murder conviction. The Cuban was thinking about a woman he believed he loved, this woman who could read minds.

They were brought to the chow hall, their trays hit with macaroni and cheese and hot dogs from the steam table, three slices of white bread, rice pudding and piss-poor coffee and sat down next to each other at the same table, opposite three inmates who stopped eating.

Foley knew them, Aryan Brotherhood neo-Nazi skinheads, and they knew Foley, a Glades celebrity who'd robbed more banks than anybody they'd ever heard of—walk in and walk out, nothing to it—until Foley pulled a dumb stunt and got caught. He ran out of luck when he drew His Honor Maximum Bob in Criminal Court, Palm Beach County. The white-power convicts accepted Foley because he was as white as they were, but they never showed they were impressed by his all-time-high number of banks. Foley sat down and they started in.

"Jesus, look at him eat. Jack, you come back 'cause you miss the chow?"

"Boy, you get any pussy out there?"

"He didn't, what'd he bust out for?"

"I heard you took a .38 in the shank, Jack. Is that right, you let this puss shoot you?"

"Federal U.S. fuckin' marshal, shows her star and puts one in his leg."

Foley ate his macaroni and cheese staring at the mess of it on his tray while the skinhead hard-ons made their lazy remarks Foley would hear again and again for thirty years, from the Brotherhood, from the Mexican Mafia, from Nuestra Familia, from the black guys all ganged up; thirty years in a convict population careful not to dis anybody, but thinking he could stand up with the tray, have the tables looking at him and backhand it across bare skulls, show 'em he was as dumb as they were and get put in the box for sixty days.

Now they were after the Cuban.

"Boy, we don't allow niggers at our table."

They brought Foley into it asking him, "How we suppose to eat, Jack, this dinge sitting here?"

Right now was the moment to pick up the tray and go crazy, not saying a word but getting everybody's attention, the tables wondering, Jesus, what happened to Foley?

And thought, For what?

He said to the three white-supremacy freaks with their mass of tattoos, "This fella's down from Starke. You understand? I'm showing him around the hotel. He wants to visit with his Savior I point him to the chapel. He wants a near-death-experience hangover,

I tell him to see one of you fellas for some pruno. But you got this stranger wrong. He ain't colored, he's a hundred percent greaseball from down La Cucaracha way," Foley looking at the three hard-ons and saying, "Cha cha, cha."

Later on when they were outside the Cuban stopped Foley. "You call me a greaseball to my face?"

This little bit of a guy acting tough.

"Where you been," Foley said, "you get stuck with the white-power ding-dongs, the best thing is to sound as dumb as they are and they'll think you're funny. You heard them laugh, didn't you? And they don't laugh much. It's against their code of behavior."

This was how Foley and Cundo hooked up at Glades.

Cundo said Foley was the only white guy in the joint he could talk to, Foley a name among all the grunge here and knew how to jail. Stay out of other people's business. Cundo's favorite part of the day was walking the yard with Foley, a couple of road dogs in tailored prison blues, and tell stories about himself.

How he went to prison in Cuba for shooting a Russian guy. Took his suitcase and sold his clothes, his shoes, all of it way too big for him. Came here during the time of the boatlift from Mariel, twenty-seven years ago, man, when Fidel opened the prisons and sent all the bad dudes to La Yuma—what he called the United States—for their vacation.

How he got into different hustles. Didn't care for armed robbery. Liked boosting cars at night off a dealer's lot. He danced go-go in gay bars as the Cat Prince, wore a leopard-print jockstrap, cat whiskers painted on his face, but scored way bigger tips Ladies Night at clubs, the ladies stuffing his jock with bills. "Here is this middle-age mama with big *tetas*, she say to me, 'Come to my home Saturday, my husband is all day at his golf club.' She say to me, 'I give you ten one-hundred-dollar bills and eat you alive.' "

Man, and how he was shot three times from his chest to his belly and came so close to dying he saw the dazzle of gold light you hear about when you approaching heaven, right there. But the emergency guys see he's still breathing, blood coming out his mouth, his heart still working, man, and they deliver him alive to Jackson Memorial where he was in a coma thirty-four days, woke up and faked it a few more days listening to Latina voices, the nurse helpers talking about him. He learned he was missing five inches of his colon but healed, sewed up, good as new. When he opened his eyes he noticed the *mozo* mopping the floor wore a tattoo on his hand, an eye drawn at the base of his thumb and index finger, a kind of eye he remembered from Combinado del Este, the prison by Havana. He said to the *mozo,* "We both Marielitos, *uh?* Get me out of here, my brother, and I make you rich."

Foley said, "You thought you'd be cuffed to the bed?"

"Maybe I was at first, I don't know. I was into some shit at the time didn't work out."

"A cop shot you?"

"No, was a guy, a picture-taker in South Beach, before it became the famous South Beach. Before that he was a Secret Service guy but quit to take pictures. One he did, a guy being thrown off I-95 from the overpass, man, down to the street, the guy in the air, Joe LaBrava sold to a magazine and became famous."

"Why'd he shoot you?"

"Man, I was gonna shoot *him.* I know him, he's a good guy, but I was not going to prison for a deal this woman talk me into doing, with this dumbbell hillbilly rent-a-cop. I didn't tell you about it? I pull a gun and this guy who use to be in the Secret Service beats me to the draw, puts three bullets in me, right here, man, like buttons. I should be dead"—Cundo grinning now—"but here I am, uh? I'm in good shape, I weigh the same now as the day I left Cuba. Try to guess how much."

He was about five-four, not yet fifty but close to it, his dyed hair always slicked back in a ponytail. "A hundred and thirty," Foley said.

"One twenty-eight. You know how I keep my weight? I don't eat that fucking macaroni and cheese they give us. I always watch what I eat. Even when I was in Hollywood going out every night? Is where I went when the *mozo* got me out of the hospital, to L.A., man, see a friend of mine. You understand this was the time of cocaine out there. All I had to do was hook up with a guy I know from Miami. Soon I'm taking care of cool dudes in the picture business, actors, directors—I was like them, I partied with them, I was famous out there."

Foley said, "Till you got busted."

"There was a snitch. Always, even in Hollywood."

"One of your movie buddies."

"I believe a major star, but they don't tell me who the snitch is. The magistrate set a two-million-dollar bond and I put up a home worth two and a half I bought for six hundred when I was first out there, all the rooms with high ceilings. I pay nine bills for another worth an easy four and a half million today. Both homes on the same canal, almost across from each other."

Foley said, "In Hollywood?"

"In Venice, California, like no place on earth, man, full of cool people and shit."

"Why do you need two homes?"

"At one time I had four homes I like very much. I wait, the prices go up to the sky and I sell two of them. Okay, but the West Coast feds see Florida has a detainer on me for a homicide, a guy they say I did when I was in Miami Beach."

Foley said, "The *mozo*?"

Cundo said, "Is funny you think of him."

"Why didn't you trust him?"

"Why should I? I don't know him. They say one time we out in the ocean fishing I push him overboard."

Foley said, "You shot him first?"

Cundo shook his head grinning just a little. "Man, you something, how you think you know things."

"**What I** don't understand," Cundo said, walking the yard with Foley, "I see you as a hip guy, you smart for a fucking bank robber, but two falls, man, one on top the other, you come out you right back in the slam. Tell me how you think about it, a smart guy like you have to look at thirty years."

Foley said, "You know how a dye pack works? The teller slips you one, it looks like a pack of twenties in a bank strap. It explodes as you leave the bank. Something in the doorframe sets it off. I walk out of a bank in Redondo Beach, the dye pack goes off and I'm sprayed with red paint, people on the street looking at me. Twenty years of going in banks and coming out clean, my eyes open. I catch a dye pack and spend the next seven in federal detention, Lompoc, California. I came out," Foley said, "and did a bank in Pomona the same day. You fall off a bike you get back on. I think, Good, I've still got it. I made over six grand in Pomona. I come back to Florida—my wife Adele divorced me while I'm at Lompoc and she's having a tough time paying her bills. She's working for a magician, Emile the Amazing, jumping out of boxes till he fired her and hired a girl Adele said has bigger tits and was younger. I do a bank in Lake Worth with the intention, give Adele the proceeds to keep her going for a few months. I leave the bank in the Honda I'm using, America's most popular stolen car at the time. Now I'm waiting to make a left turn on to Dixie Highway and I hear the car behind me going *va-room va-room*, revving up, the guy can't wait. He backs up and cuts around me, his tires screaming, like I'm a retiree waiting to make the turn when it's safe to pull out."

"You just rob the fucking bank," Cundo said.

"And this guy's showing me what a hotdog he is."

"So you go after him," Cundo said.

"I tore after him, came up on the driver's side and stared at him."

"Gave him the killer look," Cundo said.

"That's right, and he gives me the finger. I cranked the wheel and sideswiped him, stripped his chrome and ran him off the road."

"I would've shot the fucker," Cundo said.

"What happened, I tore up both tires on the side I swiped him. By the time I got the car pulled over, a deputy's coming up behind me with lights flashing."

"Tha's called road rage," Cundo said. "I'm surprise, a cool guy like you losing it. How you think it happen?"

"I wasn't paying attention. I let myself catch a dye pack in Redondo Beach, something I swore would never happen. The next one, seven years later, you're right, I lost it. You know why? Because a guy with a big engine wearing shades, the top down, no idea I'd just robbed a bank, made me feel like a wimp. And that," Foley said, "is some serious shit to consider."

"Man, you got the balls to bust out of prison, you don't have to prove nothing."

"Out for a week and back inside."

"What could you do? The girl shot you, the chick marshal. You don't tell me about her."

Karen Sisco. Foley kept her to himself. She gave him moments to think about and look at over and over for a time, a few months now, but there weren't enough moments to last thirty years.

Foley's conviction didn't make sense to Cundo. "You get thirty years for one bank, and I'm maxing out seven and a half for killing a guy? How come you don't appeal?"

Foley said he did, but the attorney appointed by the court told him he didn't have a case. "If I can appeal now," Foley said, "I will. If I have to wait too long, one of these nights I'll get shot off the wire and that'll be that."

Cundo said, "Let me tell you how a smart chick lawyer can change your life for you."

"I was told by the Florida state attorney, the federal court in L.A. gave me up 'cause I can get the death penalty here or life with no parole. But this cool chick lawyer I got—and I thank Jesus and Saint Barbara I can afford to pay her—she say the reason L.A. gave me up, they have a snitch they don't want to burn."

"One of the movie stars," Foley said, "you turned into a drug addict?"

"Miss Megan say maybe because they like his TV show. Plays a prosecutor, busts his balls to put bad guys away. You have to meet her, Miss Megan Norris, the smartest chick lawyer I ever met. She say the Florida state attorney isn't sure he can put me away on the kind of hearsay evidence he's got. She believe he's thinking

of sending me back to the Coast. They find me guilty
out there I do two-hundred and ninety-five months,
man, federal. You know how long that is? The rest of
my fucking life. But Miss Megan say they don't want
me either if they have to give up their snitch, the famous
actor. So she say to the state attorney here, 'You don't
want Mr. Rey?' She say, 'Even if he was to plead to
second degree and does a good seven for you straight
up, no credit?' Man, the state attorney is tempted, but
he like me to do twenty-five to life. Miss Megan tells
him she can get that out on the Coast where they have
new prisons, not old joints full of roaches, toilets that
back up. No, she sticks to the seven and adds, okay,
six months, take it or leave it. She ask me can I do it.
Look at me, I already done five years at Starke. It got
crowded up there, the state prison, man, so they send
me to this joint, suppose to be medium security, 'cause
I don't fuck with the hacks or have snitches set on fire.
Ones they can prove. Can I do three more less five
months, all I have left of my time?"

"Standing on your head," Foley said. "What's the
runout for the federal action?" He saw Cundo start to
grin and Foley said, "It already has."

"They have five years to change their mind and bring
me to trial if they want. But I'm doing my time here in
Florida by then, safe from falling into federal hands.

I said to Miss Megan, 'Girl, you could have made a deal, six years, I be almost to the door right now.' Miss Smarty say, 'You lucky to max out with seven plus. Say thank you and do the time.' "

"You get out," Foley said, "you're free, they can't deport you?"

"Fidel won't take us back."

"You glad you came to America?"

"I'm grateful for the ways they are to improve myself since I come to La Yuma. I respect how justice wears a blindfold, like a fucking hostage."

"Where'd you find Miss Megan?"

"I happen to read about her in the Palm Beach newspaper. I call her and Megan come to look me over, see if I can pay her. She like my situation, a way she sees she can make a deal. I tole her I pray to Jesus and Saint Barbara. Those two, man, always come through for me. You ever pray?"

"I have, yeah," Foley said. "Sometimes it works."

"You want to appeal?"

"I told you one guy turned me down."

"Let me see can I get Miss Megan for you."

"How do I pay her, rob the prison bank?"

"Don't worry about it," Cundo said. "I want you to meet her. Ask what she thinks of me, if she goes for my type."

Two

They sat across from each other in one of the lawyer meeting rooms, Foley watching Megan Norris move the tin ashtray aside to place her business case on the table. He thought she'd bring out a transcript of his trial and go over some of it. No, what she took out was a legal pad and spent a few minutes looking at her notes. No rings or nail polish. It was the easy way she wore her blond hair, sort of streaked, and the slim business suit in black that told him Miss Megan was expensive. He thought she'd name her fee and ask if he had it. No, she got right into the case. She said:

"Jack, the judge was out to get you."

And knew he was in good hands. He saw she was comfortable with him and he said, "No, it's the way the man is. Hands out thirty years like he's happy to oblige. It's why he's known as Maximum Bob."

He liked the way she did her hair, only sort of combed, like the girl who used to be on CNN Foley believed he'd fall in love with if they ever met. At this moment he couldn't think of her name, Miss Megan Norris holding his attention. He believed Miss Megan could have her pick of guys; he couldn't see her spending time with a little Cuban who'd come eye-level with her neckline and try his best to look in.

Megan's next question, "Why didn't you fire that dump truck you had for an attorney? He allowed testimony outside Miranda that you'd robbed as many as two hundred banks."

"Every time my lawyer stood up," Foley said, "the judge told him to sit down."

"And he did, never stating his objections."

"Lou Adams, the FBI agent, came to see me when I was being held at Gun Club. First he said we had something in common, both of us born and raised in New Orleans. He had a list of bank robberies under investigation and wondered if he read them off I'd tell him the ones I did. Like I'd want to help him out since we're both from the Big Easy, both love our hometown when it wasn't under water. Special Agent Lou Adams seemed surprised when I questioned his intention. He said it was so they could close any cases I could help him with, file 'em away. I said, 'You're having fun with me, aren't you?' and kept my mouth shut. But once Lou got on the stand he swore I'd robbed a couple hundred banks and believed he could name them. My lawyer raised his voice objecting, but Maximum Bob allowed it. He said, 'Let the witness have his say, this is good stuff.' That's how he talks, His Honor Bob Isom Gibbs. Out of court he's also called Big, but he's a little bitty guy."

"He sits on cushions," Megan said, "behind the bench. What you say is pretty much what I got from the transcript. I think I can get this reversed based on the judge's behavior and the FBI agent's imagination. We either retry it or work out a deal. Your buddy Cundo is taking care of my fee."

"He never told me what you're asking."

"What I'm getting, not asking. Fifteen thousand for this one. But we'll avoid going to trial again. Thirty years, according to sentencing guidelines, is the maximum you can get. I'll ask the state attorney about a deal, consider the minimum sentence less time served, and see if I can get no parole as part of the deal. I think Jerry already sees the problem with the case and will go along with what we want. He's a no-bullshit kind of guy. Why hang you up that long for no reason? One of these days he'll run for judge and make it."

"All that work for fifteen grand," Foley said, "even if it takes you a couple of days."

"It could take twenty minutes," Megan said, "you get back as much as twenty-seven years of your life. Put a price on that." She said then, "You're wondering how you'll repay your buddy, aren't you? Or how he might ask you to work it off."

"It's crossed my mind," Foley said.

"You'll owe him at least thirty thousand before we're through. The next court appearance will be an exam on the escape case. Corrections would simply extend your sentence. But this examination will focus on kidnapping, the abduction of a federal officer you held as hostage."

"Karen?"

It was the first time in months he had said her name out loud.

Foley eased straight up in his chair.

"Karen Sisco," Megan said, "with the Marshals Service. Also an attempted robbery and several homicides the prosecutor in Detroit wants to know about. So there could be more court time up north."

"I have to appear in Detroit?"

"You thought you were getting away with it?"

"Karen *shot* me. What am I getting away with?"

"We'll go over it the next time I see you," Megan said, "later in the week. I want to talk to Karen first."

"I'll tell you right now," Foley said, "I didn't kidnap her or hold her hostage."

Megan put her legal pad away and got up from the table, her expression pleasant enough.

"Let's see what Karen has to say, all right? She'll be a witness for the state. There's also the guard, Julius Pupko, who was injured."

"I forgot about the Pup," Foley said. "I thought 'the Jewel' would be a good name for him, but everybody liked Pup better."

"Well, if you didn't hit him over the head then someone else did," Megan said. "We'll do the escape-abduction hearing first, then appeal the bank robbery sentence. See if we can make a deal. Jerry knows I'd kill him if he retries the case."

Foley said, "Why don't we do it first? Get the robbery appeal out of the way."

"Why don't you leave it to me?" Megan said.

They met in the bare office once more before the escape hearing. The first thing Foley wanted to know, "Did you see Karen?"

"We'll get to Karen," Megan said, wearing off-duty designer jeans today with a narrow navy blazer. "I see the appellate court assigned an attorney"—Megan looking at her notes—"and he told you there were no issues in his judgment worthy of appeal?"

"I never saw him," Foley said. "The guy turned me down with a half-page letter."

"You keep drawing dump trucks," Megan said. "This one is blind or didn't read the transcript, it would have hit him between the eyes. Don't worry about it. Right now I want you to describe the escape, how you got involved."

He told her the muck rats dug a tunnel that went from under the chapel out past the fence toward the parking lot. "I happened to be in the chapel saying my rosary, meditating I believe on the Sorrowful Mysteries. You know there're also Joyful Mysteries you can meditate on."

Megan said, "Yes . . .?"

"When the muck rats came in—that's how I think of the guys that dug the tunnel. They came in the chapel, grabbed me and said I was going first. I get shot coming out, they have to decide if they want to try it."

"Wasn't a guard there, Mr. Pupko?"

"That's right, he was looking out the window, watching 'em play football in the exercise yard. Sometimes a play ends, a guy doesn't get up from the pile. The muck rats sneaked up and clocked the Pup with a two-by-four, put him out."

"They had it with them?"

"There was scrap lumber lying around. Some inmates were doing fix-up work in the chapel. Anyway, I made it through the tunnel and the five rats followed me out."

"At that point," Megan said, "couldn't you have put your hands in the air, indicate you want to surrender?"

"I was about to," Foley said, a Sorrowful Mystery look on his face. "But I saw Karen. Her car's right there and she's getting something out of the trunk, a shotgun."

"She sees what's going on."

"By then the siren's going off."

"Before you could give yourself up."

"Yes, ma'am, exactly," Foley said, starting to fall in love with his lawyer. "Before the hacks could blow us away I got Karen in the trunk."

"Deputy Marshal Sisco."

"That's right."

"You threw her in the trunk."

"I helped her get in. I remember saying something like, 'Miss, this is for your own good.'"

"She still has a shotgun?"

"She must've dropped it. But she had a Sig .38 on her."

Megan said, "If the court believes you took Karen Sisco hostage, you're in here for the rest of your life. I asked Karen if she felt like a hostage. You know what she said?"

He was afraid to ask.

"Karen said, 'No, I was his zoo-zoo.' "

"My treat." Foley grinning now. "She said that?"

"Not until you were in the trunk with her."

"Yeah, I got in to keep from getting shot."

"The car drives off . . . But Karen won't say she was being abducted."

"I never threatened her. She tell you she had the Sig Sauer?"

"She said she was waiting for a chance to use it."

"Maybe at first, before we started talking."

"You're both in the trunk, quite close together . . ."

"In the dark. I must've smelled awful from the muck. We started talking about movies, ones like the fix we were in, and I mentioned *Three Days of the Condor* with Faye Dunaway and Robert Redford. He's hiding out in her apartment and he asks her if she'll do something for him. It's the morning after they'd got it on, even though they only met that afternoon. He asks if she'll drive him someplace and Faye Dunaway says—"

" 'Have I ever denied you anything?' " Megan said.

"You saw it."

Megan said, "When the car stopped she did shoot at you."

"I believe that was nerves."

Megan said, "We don't want the court to think anything personal was stirring between you and Karen."

She looked at her legal pad. "They'll ask who was driving the car."

"Buddy, a friend of mine. He was visiting."

"At night?"

"No, he was dropping something off."

"Get your story straight."

"I'd ask him," Foley said, "but he's out of the country. Took his sister to Lourdes hoping for a miracle."

"She's an invalid?"

"An alcoholic. Her liver's iffy, so she has to pace herself. Two bottles of sherry have to last all day."

Megan was staring at him and Foley began to nod his head.

"I remember now, Buddy was working part-time for a law firm. They must've sent him here to serve court papers, one of the inmates bringing suit against the prison system."

Megan made a note in her legal pad. "That's why Karen was here, serving process. Tell me how she got away from you."

"We stopped, I let her drive off. It was her car."

"Later on she followed you to Detroit. Why didn't you give yourself up when the police arrived?"

"Get sent back for my thirty years. I don't know how to explain what happened in Detroit that would help you."

"Karen doesn't either. From what I understand"—
Megan looking at her notes again—"you took part in a
home invasion for the purpose of armed robbery and
left three homicide victims."

"Two," Foley said. "White Boy Bob tripped going
up that staircase and shot himself in the head."

"If she's subpoenaed, later on in Detroit, Karen will
tell the truth."

"About what?"

"Why you were there."

"What does she say I was doing?"

"Holding a gun in each hand as the police arrive.
They're ready to shoot to kill and Karen put a bullet in
your thigh. She kept you alive."

"So I can limp around here the next thirty years."

"It still hurts?"

"Aches."

"I spoke to Kym Worthy, the prosecutor in Detroit,
I asked if she wanted to wait for you that long. Kym
said thirty years sounds like enough. She sees no need
to bring you up, so she'll pass."

"I see what you're doing," Foley said. "With Detroit
out of it you appeal and get the sentence reduced as
much as you can."

"We'll save that for last and do the escape-abduction
hearing next. Karen's their witness, but her testimony

will have them wondering why they called her. We don't want to indicate you and Zoo-Zoo had anything going, so she won't mention the time you were alone together. She did shoot you, you're a fugitive felon, not to save your life."

"I couldn't believe it," Foley said.

"So I don't want you to talk to each other in the courtroom, if the opportunity presents itself. All right?"

Foley nodded.

"I have your word?"

"I won't talk to her."

"We'll do this one, then the sentence appeal," Megan said, "and see what's next in your life."

Foley didn't see Karen until she was called as a prosecution witness and took the stand. They were in federal court for the escape examination. Karen glanced at him. He smiled and she looked away.

Megan asked if she was placed in the trunk of her car as a hostage.

Karen said the guards were firing at everyone outside the fence. "For all they knew I was providing the getaway." She said, "I have no doubt that Mr. Foley's action was protective."

"But he was escaping from prison," the prosecutor said.

"Forced to go first," Karen said, "a shank jabbing him in the back. I saw he was bleeding from several wounds."

Then Megan asked how she got away.

"Once we reached the turnpike they let me have my car. I asked Mr. Foley if he intended to surrender. He said yes, but wanted to clean himself up before they threw him in the hole. He was saturated with blood as well as muck from the tunnel."

Karen looked at him again, Foley staring at her. She turned her head before he could see what was in her eyes.

More questions from Megan and Karen said that subsequently she arrested Foley in Detroit. "He'd learned a former Lompoc inmate, one he knew, was planning an armed robbery. Mr. Foley saw a chance to stop him."

Rather than call the police, Megan said, and give himself up?

"Jack Foley," Karen said, "also knew that the intended victim of the robbery, a well-known investor, did a year in Lompoc for insider trading. I saw Foley's intention as redemptive. To show, if you will, he's basically a good guy."

He saw her eyes for a moment with a look he remembered.

The state prosecutor asked Karen, "Weren't there homicide victims at the scene in Detroit? You were there. Don't you see this 'basically good guy' as the shooter? Since he's the only one who came out alive?"

Megan stepped in.

"Detroit's bodies," she said, "Detroit's case. We'll see if they want to talk to my client, already doing thirty years for bank robbery."

Foley watched the judge finally look at the prosecutor and say, "I don't see it. Your own witness Ms. Sisco testified that all this happened under extreme duress. I see no criminal intent, therefore no escape, no kidnapping. Case dismissed."

Three

They were taking their walk the day after Foley's robbery conviction was reversed on appeal, Cundo saying, "I don't believe it. She got you off on the escape then got you down from thirty years to a few months? Come on—"

They were passing the chapel—"Where the muck rats found me meditating," Foley said, both of them looking at the chapel, a dismal shade of red, no life to the look of buildings that made a prison. They came to the gun tower on their left. "Where most of the firing came from," Foley said—Foley almost a head taller than Cundo, Mutt and Jeff coming along in their tailored prison blues to the exercise yard.

"'Cause you save this chick's life, Karen Sisco, they cut you a deal because you put her in the fucking trunk?"

"Thirty years reduced to thirty months," Foley said. "That's two and a half years less time served. And no parole. That could've been the deal breaker and Megan got it for me."

"Man, me and you be out almost the same time, but you ahead of me. You always lucky like this?"

"When I have a rich little Cuban paying my way."

Foley was grateful but didn't feel good about it.

"I'm gonna pay you back, but it might take a while."

"Or you do five grand a bank six times in a row and not get busted. Forget about it, we friends."

"I'd rather pay you back," Foley said, "than have you come around later and tell me I owe you one. Okay?"

"We friends or what? You the only white guy in this joint I ever tole about my life. You smart for a fucking bank robber. You and Miss Megan, you both sound like you know what you talking about."

"She never used a tone of voice in court," Foley said, "to irritate the prosecutor. She'd make a remark passing his table and the guy would grin. It was like they're both on the same side. Then she'd look up and toss her hair, but I never once saw her touch it."

"Knows it looks good," Cundo said. "I'm trying to remember how she fix it."

"Like Paula Zahn's on the news. She and Megan have the same style hair when they don't change it for a while."

"She say anything about me?"

"Who, Paula?"

"Miss *Megan*."

"She thinks you'd be fun."

"Yeah . . .?"

"If she ever went for a little greaser."

Foley played basketball every day, nine black guys on the court—they'd flip to see who got Foley—pressing each other, hands in the face, talking trash, Foley showing his moves, his jukes, faking guys out of their jocks, passing behind his back, throwing in swishers, all net, with either hand. Cundo watched.

Foley limped over to smoke a cigarette and Cundo said, "Man, how can you keep running like that? Lose some pounds I get you a job as a lifeguard. There six hundred lifeguards, man, watching thirty miles of beach, Malibu, Santa Monica, Venice, I was buddies with the crew on *Baywatch*, how I know about lifeguards. Man, I believe I can fix you up."

Foley said, "If I lose some pounds, would I have to know how to swim?"

"Tha's the thing," Cundo said, "all you know is how to rob banks. You tell them in court you swear you not doing it no more?"

"Nobody asked me."

"I know you can't rob jus' one. I bet is the same you can't rob a hundred and quit, find something pays as good."

"That was Lou Adams's point, the FBI guy. After his testimony was thrown out and we were done, he came over to me in the courtroom. He said, 'From the day you get your release the Bureau's gonna be on your ass, and I mean every day of your life. You understand? Nod your fucking head.'" Foley was smiling as he said it.

"You think is funny?" Cundo said. "This guy watching you all the time?"

"I think it's funny he believes he can do it. Assign a squad around the clock to watch one guy? They'd never do that," Foley said. "Would they?"

He started telling Cundo a little about Karen Sisco, knowing he'd never see her again, and her part in the hearing: how she told the court she never considered herself a hostage, she was armed the whole time. "She believes I saved her life by putting her in the trunk."

"The fucking hacks shooting at you," Cundo said. "I believe it too."

That's all Foley was going to say. But then he told Cundo he wasn't supposed to speak to Karen in court.

"Megan asked me when I first saw Karen. I said she was coming around from the trunk of her car with a twelve-gauge." Foley paused thinking about it. "But we didn't get to speak to each other in court."

"Why not?"

"Megan didn't want us to show there was anything personal between us."

Foley stopped there and Cundo said, "Yeah . . .?"

"I hadn't seen her since Detroit, months ago," Foley said. "When she was on the stand she glanced at me a couple of times, but that was it. I said to myself, Okay, it's over, not meant to be."

"Wait a minute—you telling me you and this marshal had something going?"

Foley told it because it was an event in his life, one of the best things that ever happened to him.

"See, what we did, Karen and I took a time-out from who we are and spent the night together in Detroit. At a hotel."

Cundo said, "Jesus Christ, you took the chick marshal to bed?"

"We made love," Foley said. "There was nothing else we could do."

"Man, you fucked a U.S. marshal?"

"A deputy marshal. It was real, not like a score. We both felt it, but knew there was no future in it."

"No—but you gonna remember her as long as you live."

"The next day," Foley said, "she shot me."

"Listen, before we get out of here," Cundo said, "I tell you about a woman who came to me and changed my life forever."

By the time Foley was looking at a few months before release, Cundo was telling him he should move to the Coast, have a look at Venice.

"Experience the show it puts on, tattoo artists, fortune-tellers, drummers in a circle beating the shit out of their drums, their snares, congas, tin cans, all these people watching. You know Jim Morrison, the Doors? His ghost live in the hotel where he like to stay. This woman I tell you about sometime, Dawn, saw him one time in the hall." Cundo serious, then grinning, showing his teeth. "You on that walk by the beach, look out. Here comes this chick in a bikini and the longest fucking legs you ever saw, she's Rollerblading through the crowd. Guys step aside and turn to check her out."

Cundo said, "All right, now the real Venice.

"Walk away from the beach. Now is homes, all size homes, old ones, new ones, some new ones so new they don't look like homes. Remember the hippies, how they were? Easy does it, never lost their cool. Tha's how I see the people who live in the homes, hippies who grew up and are good at whatever it is, painting—there lot of artists here—people in the movies, people design homes, own restaurants. You have to be a star at what you do to live here. But they don't care if anybody knows it. They don't make announcements, build high-risers on the beach. They leave the beach to the beach. They like to talk to each other and drink wine."

Cundo said, "You see young gangsters giving each other serious eyes. You know how to talk to those guys. You can buy ganj, blow, whatever pleases you. I can get you numbers to call."

"When you went down," Foley said, "how come they didn't take your property?"

"I don't own any. Listen, when I was making money out there, buying homes, cheap compare to what they worth now? I sign them over to a guy is my bookkeeper, the Monk. We both come out of Combinado del Este in Cuba, the Monk in there 'cause he embessle money from a company, to buy things for himself. You look at the Monk," Cundo said, "you don't see a criminal, not even a white-collar one. He's a good-looking guy, man, but timid, ascared to death in Combinado of these guys want to dress him like a *puta*, put red lipstick on his mouth and fuck him. I work it with the guardias to put him in my cell and the Monk cried, man, he was so fucking grateful."

Foley said, "He was your wife?"

"Once in a while I let him smoke my cigar, sure, but I never care for it much with a guy. The guardias are bringing me ganj and half pints of rum I sell and we split. I tell the cons who want to fuck the Monk, behave yourselves or you don't get stoned no more. Okay, Fidel let us out, I bring the Monk to Miami and get him a job with Harry Arno. Harry use to run a sport book till he retire and marry a stripper, the only one I ever saw wore glasses when she danced, so she don't fall off the fucking stage. Then, after I almost die from being shot that time, we get out of town, move to L.A."

"You bring the Monk along," Foley said, "everywhere you go?"

"He's become a business partner," Cundo said, "for different ways he knows of using money to make money."

Foley said, "Like running a sports book?"

"Tha's one of the business where I'm a silent partner. It goes down, the Monk goes down. You understand he's always been an accountant, an expert with numbers, man. He works a calculator, he don't even look at what his fingers are doing. We in another business called Rios and Rey Investment Company. Is like a bank with numbered accounts, no names of investors."

"A real bank?" Foley said. "Like a Swiss bank?"

"Is it real? It must be," Cundo said, "they's money in it the Monk invests in bonds and real estate. Have it work for me, not bury it someplace, hope nobody finds it. Do you pay income tax on the money you take from banks?"

"Not as a rule," Foley said.

"I do," Cundo said, "I pay my fucking taxes. Maybe you like to rob this bank. How you do it? There's no teller you call sweetheart and ask her for money. The Monk say a time will come we won't use cash no more for most things you want. The Monk knows all this electronic shit with the digits. But I have to remind him also to keep an eye on Dawn for me. See nothing happens to her."

Foley said, "You're full of surprises, aren't you? Who's Dawn?"

"Dawn Navarro, man, the best thing ever happen to me."

For two years he'd been telling Foley his life history and never once mentioned he was married. Cundo said he didn't want people to know she was living alone in Venice, California, the Monk keeping an eye on her.

Foley said, "You trust the Monk?"

"Why you think I call him that? He's like a monk who took a vow never to fuck a woman. He don't even check them out. Listen," Cundo said, "after I was given the sentence I phone Dawn. I say, 'Can you live the life of a saint for seven years or longer? Not fuck any guys, not even an old boyfriend you run into and do it in the car with him for old time sake? Dawn say she would wait for me her whole life. Not leave the house except she's with the Monk."

Foley said, "He can keep guys away from her?"

"He packs, has a guy looks like a fox with a big Dirty Harry gun drives him, he goes anyplace. I was married to Dawn four months before I was return here to Florida. The first time I ever saw her was at a party in the Hollywood Hills. Dawn is laying down tarot cards, telling people their fortune. It becomes my turn and she starts doing my cards. But she don't say nothing to me. I ask her to tell me what she sees. Her eyes raise—"

Foley said, "She tell you you're going on a long journey?"

"How do you know that?"

"Isn't that what fortune-tellers tell you?"

"She say I'm going back to Florida within one year. I say oh, for what reason? She say she don't know, but

I can tell she does and I wonder, why she wants to hide it from me."

Foley kept his mouth shut.

"We left the party. I took Dawn to Venice, to my white home—I won't stay in the pink one—the walls full of pictures of me with various movie and TV stars. We stay three days, man, never leaving, telling each other of our lives, not so much you know *de*tails, but basic shit. How I stole cars at one time and danced go-go as the Cat Prince. She thought that was hot. I ask her what she can see in her future. She say you can't be psychic about yourself, no real psychic can. She say most of the ones who call themselves psychic are frauds, they turn cards and tell you you gonna meet a tall, dark stranger. We drinking wine, smoking some good ganj, I say to her, 'So I'm going back to Florida, uh?' She don't want to tell me why I'm going, but I keep at her and she tells me she sees me in a courtroom on trial for killing a guy. You understand this is four months before I was arrested and then sent to Florida. I say to Dawn, 'Oh, I happen to kill somebody?' In her vision she sees me and another guy one night out in the Atlantic Ocean fishing."

"The *mozo*," Foley said, "who fell over the side and drowned."

"His girlfriend say he went out with me and never came back. I say I drop him off down the beach. No, the point I make, Dawn saw me in the courtroom four months before I was there."

"When'd you get married?"

"The next day after she tole me, we drove to Vegas."

"She's all for it, uh? Once she's seen the homestead?"

"You say something like that—you don't even know her. She say she been waiting all her life for the right guy, wha's a few more years? She looks me in the eye telling me things."

"She ever come to visit?"

"I tole you, I don't want nobody knowing things about her. She sends me pictures instead of coming here. Some of them, she don't have no clothes on."

"Is that right?"

"Keep me interested. She could go in a bank with you, tell you which teller will freak, which will stay calm."

"You little devil," Foley said, "you're gonna use her fortune-telling to tell you where the fortunes are, aren't you, work as a team."

"Is like Dawn tells this woman she's under some kind of spell, like maybe a ghost is fucking with her, hiding her jewelry she can't find."

"You're the ghost?"

"I can do that, sure. Or I go in the house at night and throw the woman's clothes in the swimming pool."

"You've done that?"

"Not yet—we talking about it. See, Dawn gets rid of the fucking ghost she calls an evil spirit and saves the poor woman from going crazy. Charges her ten to twenty-k for it, and the woman is happy again. Is like I deliver a key for seventeen to twenty-k to a famous actor and he gets his confidence back again."

"You and the wife," Foley said, "devoting your lives to caring for people."

"Is the reason we fall in love with each other. We alike in how we know how to make people happy."

"But running a psychic con," Foley said, "doesn't mean she's actually psychic."

"She saw me in the fucking courtroom, didn't she?"

"She as cool as Megan Norris?"

"They both cool, but in different ways. Miss Megan is cool because she smart, man, always knows what to say. Dawn is cool because she knows what *you* going to say."

"They must be a lot different," Foley said, "in how they see things."

"Tha's what I just tole you, they different."

"Megan asked me how could I stand to throw away some of my best years in a dump like this. She wanted to know why I didn't get in a prison rehab program. Learn how to grow sugarcane."

"Burn the field you ready to go in and cut the cane, these poison snakes in there eating rats, man, they come out at you. Hey, fuck that. You tell her God made you a bank robber?"

"I think she knew it."

"The way I see you, Jack, you smart, you can be a serious guy, but you don't like to show anything is important to you. You here, you don't complain—not anymore—you could be an old hippie living here. You get your release . . . Ah, now you get to think what you going to do."

"I've been reading about Costa Rica," Foley said. "Go down there and start over."

"Yes, someday, uh? You want me to tell you," Cundo said, "you leave here, the first thing you going to do?"

"Rob a bank."

"See? Is already on your mind."

"It's on your mind, not mine."

"How you gonna get to Costa Rica?"

"If I make up my mind that's where I'm going," Foley said, "don't worry, I'll get there."

"I see you walking out the gate," Cundo said, "you thinking about the things you miss. Getting drunk on good whiskey for a change. Getting laid as soon as you can . . . How you gonna work it you don't have any money?"

"It's already arranged," Foley said.

Cundo stared at him to see if he was kidding, reading his face, his eyes.

"Is already arranged? How you do that?"

Four

At first, trying to talk on the phone in this prison was work, all the morons in the line behind Cundo telling him what to say to Dawn, knowing he was talking to a woman. That's who every one of them talked to, a woman. These guys talking trash to him, telling him what to say, dirty things the morons thought were funny. He told Dawn, "They say to tell you, I get out what kind of things I'm going to do to you." Dawn said, "Like what?" "They ask me if I ever stick hamburger in your—I think they saying 'twat' and have a pussyburger." Dawn said, "What else?"

This was during his first year of imprisonment at Starke, the state prison, before being transferred to Glades. One week he skipped calling Dawn to get hold of the Monk, Cundo telling him to find the names of the guardia officers running this place and bribe them. "Man, I need space to breathe." The Monk worked the Internet to learn whatever he wanted to know. He sent a ham and a case of whiskey to the home of each guardia on his list and signed Cundo's name to the card that said: "I am hoping because of my poor health, you will allow me to work in a prison office. I can serve as a writer of letters in Spanish whenever there is a need for one." It got Cundo a manual type-writer and a telephone he could use to call Dawn and reverse the charge. In his quiet corner of the office Cundo would hear Dawn's voice accept the charge and he'd ask:

"Are you being a saint?"

Dawn would say, "Of course I am." Or she would vary the answer and say, "Aren't you my love?" Or sometimes, "Aren't you my undying love?"

Cundo believed saints never got laid, so he'd say, "You swear to Almighty God you being a saint for me?"

"I swear to God I'm being a saint."

"For me."

"Yes, for you."

"I want to hear you say it so I believe it."

After several months of this Dawn began to say, without raising her voice or showing any strain, "How

many times do I have to tell you, yes, I'm being a saint
for you?"

"Your tone of voice doesn't convince me."

"Because you make me say it over and over and
over." Now there was a hint of strain. "Will you please
stop asking me if I'm being a saint?"

One day, still during Cundo's first year inside, Dawn
said, "If you ask me that again, I swear I'll hang up the
phone. I won't be here the next time you call. I'll vanish
and you'll never hear my voice again as long as you live.
If you don't believe me, ask if I'm being a saint. I fucking dare you."

He believed her.

But how could she remain a saint living by herself in
Venice, cool guys around, movie guys who were good
with women and would go for her, Dawn Navarro,
man, blond hair and cool green eyes, a hot chick with
a gift.

The Monk swore to it, yes, she was being a saint. He
never got a report of a guy visiting her. They went to
a club, she never spent time with any guys. The Monk
always had a bodyguard along, Zorro. After a while
everybody in the club knew who Dawn was—she
could talk to people, different guys, all she wanted. But
if one of them tried to take Dawn home, Zorro would
step in—Zorro, the Monk's personal bodyguard would

step in and open his coat enough to show his Dirty
Harry pistol.

Cundo decided, okay, she was a saint. Pretty soon he
would be with her—not have to imagine her anymore
with different gringos, all these tall white guys.

Today at Glades talking to Dawn on the phone, his
bodyguard standing behind him, Cundo said, "Jack
Foley got his release this morning."

"Good for Jack," Dawn said.

"I sent him to a guy in Miami's fixing him up with a
driver's license and a prepaid credit card. He's gonna fly
to L.A. and live in my pink home while he gets the feel
nobody's watching him. He don't mind it being pink."

"I'm in the pink one," Dawn said.

"I know you are. I told him to stay in the white one,
but switch with you before I come out, I think the week
after next."

"Why are you so nice to him?"

"I told you he's robbed hundreds of fucking banks.
I like to know does he want to do any more."

"Of course he does."

"But is it something he has to do?"

"I'll let you know," Dawn said.

"I tole him about you, how you can read minds. He
goes, 'Yeah?' and listen to every word."

"He won't believe it," Dawn said, "till I tell him to quit trying to picture me naked."

"Don't say that, please. I don't want to think of him getting ideas. You and Foley going to be neighbors across the canal. You meet and sit down to talk, you can tell him his fortune."

"You mean tell *you* his fortune."

"Look in his eyes, see if they any coming attractions, things you can tell me about. I got money invested in this guy."

"Once he gets the credit card you might not see him again."

"He has to wait two days for the license, but I know he won't run off on me. Jack Foley is the most honest fucking con I ever met, and maybe the smartest. But he's different than the ones here they say have the high IQs."

"What do they do?"

"Have to suck guys off unless they jailhouse lawyers. Foley has his own way of dealing with all the different kinds of bad guys. He's our celebrity, robbed a hundred more banks than John Dillinger or anybody you can name. And, has never had to shoot anybody. He say to a con, 'If you don't understand why I'm proud of that, you and I have nothing to say to each other.' "

"What you don't know," Dawn said, "is how he is with women."

"I know Miss Megan got goose bumps talking to him."

"Who told you that?"

"He did. She calls him Jack in the letter she wrote with her bill for thirty-k. Listen," Cundo said, "when he busted out, there was a woman United States marshal chased after him. They met at a hotel and spent the night together before she brought him back."

Dawn's voice on the phone said, "You're kidding."

"And spoke for him in court, tole what a sweet guy he is. Listen, his ex-wife name Adele? She wrote all the time saying she still in love with him."

Dawn said, "You want *me* to use him."

"With your gift, your spirit guides and ESP shit. I like to see you work Foley into your act, make us some money off him."

"I've got a new client," Dawn said, "another widow in Beverly Hills."

"You and your widows."

"She came to one of my psychic house parties, stayed after to talk and said she'd been seeing Madam Rosa—"

"I remember her, the gypsy queen."

"Rosa has my client believing her dead husband's put a hex on her, the reason she can't find true love."

"Wha's a hex?"

"A curse, an evil spell. My client decided Madam Rosa's a fraud, but still believes her dead hubby's bothering her and wants me to help her."

"You know how?"

"I deal with ghosts all the time."

"I got to hang up—these fucking guys . . . Listen, think of a way to use Foley."

"I'll look him over."

"See if he's any good with hexes."

Five

Lou Adams, the federal agent with "Jack Foley" imprinted on his brain, had called Glades to learn the date and time of Foley's release. They told him today by ten A.M. they'd have him separated out of there. Lou arrived a little after nine to make sure Foley didn't slip out on him. What Lou had in mind, he'd wait in the car until Foley was coming through the double gates. Lou would get out then and stand in plain sight and wait for Foley to see him. Lou believed Foley would stop in his tracks, remembering what Lou had told him thirty months ago: "From the day of your release, the manpower of the Bureau will be covering your ass like a fucking blanket." Not in those exact words—they were in a court of law when Lou laid it out—but that idea.

Lou Adams's buddies in the West Palm field office thought it was something personal with him, the hard-on he had for this bank robber. Lou said, "I know I looked unprofessional in court. I was trying to make the point this guy is not just another fucking bank robber, and I lost my temper. But if the guy robbed a hundred banks, that's who he is. The Man Who Robbed a Hundred Banks. It makes him special. Who else has done that many bank licks that we know of? Nobody. You remember the press he got? The picture in the paper, Foley and that knockout lawyer, that little broad who practically got him off? I bet you ten bucks he fucked her. Where, I don't know, but he's a good-looking guy, he's our star bank robber."

An agent said, "You keep waiting for Foley, you're gonna get Professional Responsibility on you."

"Listen," Lou said to his buddies, "I'll bet you anything that as we're speaking a writer is doing a book on Foley. Gonna call it *The Sweetheart Bandit*, the name we gave him, his note to the teller always saying, 'Sweetheart, give me all your hundreds, fifties and twenties, please.' Some book reviewers will give it their own fucked-up interpretation and the general public will think the writer's calling Foley a sweetheart 'cause he's a nice guy, never threatened or scared the shit out of the teller when he asked for money. No, he says to the teller, 'Do the best you can.' You'll see a bank employee saying in the paper, 'It's true, he was a sweetheart. He took the money, thanked me, and gave my hand a pat.'"

Lou said, "Or you take a guy like Willie Sutton. Willie Sutton became famous for saying he robbed banks because that's where the money was. It didn't matter Willie Sutton never in his fucking life said it. Once the general public believes he did and thought it was a cool thing to say, Willie Sutton's famous. The newspapers loved him: they said he must've made off with a good two million during his career. Oh, is that right? If Willie Sutton spent over half his fucking life in stir, how would he have time to score two million bucks? I say that because I estimate Foley's take—working his ass off, out of action only ten years counting his falls—at half a million for his hundred or so bank licks. Not bad. Foley and Willie Sutton both drew thirty years and both escaped from prison in a tunnel, and that's the only similarity in their careers."

John Dillinger would always be Lou Adams's favorite bank robber. Then Jack Foley because you had to give him credit, he was conscientious, never shot his mouth off, and made sticking up banks look easy. Lou threw in Willie Sutton because he was good conversation, famous for something he never said.

Okay, here was Lou's question to the general public:

"You all have heard of Dillinger, Jack Foley and Willie Sutton. Now let's see you name three agents of the Federal Bureau of Investigation who are as well known."

He'd give the general public J. Edgar Hoover, "And you can have his sorry ass. Now try to name two more. You like Eliot Ness? Me too, only he wasn't FBI. Let's see, how about Melvin Purvis? Your general public thinks about it and says, 'Melvin who?'

"Jesus Christ, he's only the guy who said to John Dillinger coming out of the picture show, 'Stick 'em up, Johnny, we got you surrounded' and Dillinger took off. Melvin Purvis held his fire. Three agents on the scene shot at Dillinger and he went down for good. It was never revealed which agent actually killed him. The same year," Lou said, "1934, Melvin Purvis was named the most admired man in America. It galled Hoover to the point of his forcing Melvin Purvis to resign. It was Melvin Purvis's buddies gave him a chrome-plated .45 as a farewell present, the same pistol Melvin Purvis used in 1960 to blow his brains out.

"And that's where we are," Lou Adams said to his buddies. "Who the fuck's Melvin Purvis? The good guys fade from memory while the bad dudes catch the public eye and become celebrities."

Lou believed with all his heart he should get some attention before he retired. Look here, will you, I'm one of the fucking good guys. Will you watch what I'm doing? I'm gonna dog Jack Foley till he robs a bank. I mean it, take my leave, thirty days is all I need and put that sweetheart away for good.

He saw a prison guard—no, two of them over there unlocking the gates to let Foley out. It got Lou Adams sitting up straight behind the wheel. He watched Foley come through the gates and turn to give the hacks a wave—So long, boys, no hard feelings—showing the kind of ass-kissing sweetheart he was.

Lou got out and walked around the front of the Crown Vic he'd put through a car wash at 8 A.M. Came all the way around to lean against the right-side front fender and fold his arms, the way he'd seen himself doing it all morning, looking directly at the double gates by the administration building, to the right of the cars parked ahead of him in the row nearer the fence. He watched Foley come out past the cars to the aisle where Lou was waiting, watching him from a hundred feet away, watching him stop, Foley looking this way at Lou holding his pose, Lou reading Foley's mind now and saying to him, I told you, didn't I? Well, here I am, buddy. Want me to drop you somewhere? He watched

Foley raise his arm and Lou raised his, a couple of old pros taking each other's measure.

Only Foley wasn't looking at him.

His gaze was down the aisle and Lou turned his head to see a car coming, Lou standing as a Ford Escort went past him, a woman with dark hair in a red Ford Escort, nice-looking. Now he saw the car from the rear slowing down, coming to a stop where Foley was waiting, Foley raising his arm again and looking right at Lou as he got in the Escort. Lou didn't raise his this time, hurrying to get in his car—the Escort out of view circling behind him—but there it was again, leaving the prison grounds. No need to hurry, he could keep it in sight.

The main thing was Foley saw him. It was the whole point of Lou being here this morning. Like telling Foley, See what I mean? Every day of your life I'm gonna be watching you. If Foley ever stopped to talk he'd tell him in those exact words: every fucking day of your life. Foley wouldn't believe him. How could he maintain a watch like that on one man, around the clock?

When he came up with the idea of how he'd work it, Lou told himself, You're a fucking genius, you know it?

He recalled now it was Foley's ex-wife Adele owned a Ford Escort. Divorced him while he was at Lompoc and here she was giving him a lift. The one Foley must've known he could count on. Honey, can you pick me up when they let me out of prison? Why sure, sweetheart. The kind of broad you could talk into doing whatever you wanted. At the office they had pictures of Adele in tights, nice jugs, taken when she was working for the magician, Emil the Amazing, disappeared from a cage and got sawed in half. Nice-looking broad, the dark hair, pure white skin, five-seven and about 140, plump compared to Lou's ex-wife Edie. A year ago divorced him and moved to Orlando with the two kids. Edie said because his job was more important to him than his family, why he was never home, and when he was all they did was argue. Man, women. They all had problems they imagined or made up. They didn't get their way they told you to take a fucking hike.

He'd get his Foley file out of the glove box and look up Adele's address in Miami Beach, on the south end of Collins Avenue, if she was still living there. Stop by and find out what she was doing with Foley, as if he didn't know, the guy fresh out of the can. She must still like him. Lou remembered she was not bad at all; he'd seen surveillance photos of her when they were looking for Foley, but only in person once: at Foley's trial, the first one, this nice-looking woman biting her nails waiting for the verdict.

Six

They were driving south now on the turnpike, Adele telling Foley about the polyp on one of her vocal cords. "The doctor asked me if I'd been screaming at anyone lately or doing a lot of singing. I'm not supposed to raise my voice or talk to anyone I can't touch." Adele turned her head and they were grinning at each other. "So you'll have to hold me while you tell me about life in prison and what the guys are like." She reached over to touch his face and said, "Boy, do you look good. Why don't we stay home, have a few pops and I'll fix us something?"

Foley touched her hair and laid his hand on her bare shoulder in the sundress, Adele holding the Escort at seventy all the way to where they left the turnpike and cut over toward Miami Beach. He told her about Cundo

Rey, the rich little Cuban, about Cundo being funny, Cundo being sneaky.

Adele said, "Don't trust him." This was even before he told about Cundo putting up thirty grand for his appeals lawyer, another few thousand for his ID and the plane fare to the Coast.

This time Adele said, "Why, because you're pals? Come on."

"I'm staying in one of his homes," Foley said, "while I work on an idea. I'm thinking of moving to Costa Rica."

"And do what?"

"Get into something. Game fishing . . . I don't know, maybe land development, real estate."

"Move to Costa Rica and sell condos."

"It's the new place to go," Foley said, "when you aren't making it at home. Get in on the ground floor."

Adele said, "You want me to tell you what you're gonna be doing sooner or later?"

"I've had jobs," Foley said. "I sold cars one time."

"That you stole?"

"You want to nag," Foley said, "or have a nice time?"

They stopped in front of the Normandie and got into another conversation. Foley had to see a guy and wanted to take Adele's car. Drive up to Dania, not far, have his picture taken and meet Cundo's guy who was making him a driver's license.

"Instead of taking the time," Adele said, "to do it the right way. What's the hurry? You went to Lompoc I said that's it, I'm getting a divorce. You said, 'Honey, I can do seven years standing on my head and I'm out.' Remember saying that?" Yes, he did. "Remember what I said?"

"You said you weren't getting any younger."

"I was twenty-nine going on thirty. My husband is about to miss the best fucking years of my life standing on his head. But you can't wait a few weeks to get your own license. You do it the hard way because you've learned to think like a convict. Get it from some guy around back when you can walk in the front door. But you can't help it, can you?"

"I don't think like a convict."

"You don't?" Adele said. "Look at the people you've been living with the past ten years. You ought to be ashamed of yourself. He gives you money too?"

"I'm getting a prepaid credit card."

"For how much? Like it's any of my business."

"Three thousand. He's paying a grand for the license I'll use at the airport for ID. I'll get a regular license once I'm out there."

"He pays your way," Adele said, "he owns you. Don't you know that? Now you want to take my car—a hundred and sixty thousand miles on it I'm driving to Vegas the end of the month. My mom got me a job at the Hilton dealing blackjack. Her boyfriend's one of the executives, an older guy. She tells him, 'I can't lie to you, Sid, I'm no spring chicken, I'm forty-three years old this month.' She was fifty-five when she started working there. Mom got me the job telling Sid I have magic hands with playing cards. I can do the Hindu shuffle, the double lift, the glide—not that I'd use any of them." Adele and Foley smiling again, thinking about her hands doing magic things. Adele said, "You don't have a license but you'll take a chance with my poor car."

Foley got out and went around to Adele's side, brought her out of the car and kissed her on the mouth, mmmm, keeping it tender, not trying to stick his tongue down her throat—and started to grin, feeling good.

"What's funny?"

"I'm trying to show prison hasn't turned me into a sex fiend."

"I don't mind a little rough stuff," Adele said, "as long as it isn't nasty."

Foley said, "I'm coming right back. But I'll call you once I'm up the road. Just in case."

"In case of what?"

"Lou Adams."

He wasn't far behind. Lou circled the block and checked the alley looking for the Escort, came around to the front of the Normandie and stopped between the two no-parking signs. The last time he came by, not more than four years ago, there were old ladies sitting on the porch in a row. They were gone, the porch was gone; the building now had a jazzed-up façade that looked like shelf rock across the ground floor, the Normandie having gone condo. Now you walked into a vestibule of mailboxes and a list of tenants. Lou saw Adele Delisi 208. Not A. Delisi or A. Foley, Adele Delisi, using her maiden name.

Through with being married to a bank robber.

Except he was upstairs with her.

Fresh out of stir and she can't say no.

Well . . . Lou held the door for a couple in their eighties coming out, the woman in a big sun hat and one of those toy Mexican dogs on a leash, the little doggie looking way up at Lou, the couple taking time to have a look at Lou themselves, in his dark business suit and tie, his wavy hair combed and parted, and approved of him on the spot. The woman said, "Dear, can I be of assistance, help you find someone?" in that soft, almost Brooklyn accent Lou recognized right away.

He said, "Katrina blew you all over here from New Orleans, didn't she?" He heard the woman ask how he knew that, surprised, Lou already pushing through the glass door to the lobby inside, letting it swing back on the couple in their eighties and heard the Mexican dog yelp, the sound coming like a tiny scream. Lou heard it, but his mind was set on Adele Delisi now, recalling photos they had of her, zooms, taken on the street, remembering Adele as a good-looking woman and thought of her that way, as a woman with something to her, not just a girl. Though he had nothing against girls. Riding the elevator to the second floor he was anxious to see her up close.

Adele opened the door in her favorite robe, this one a short, silky peach, Adele still wearing her heels to give her long legs another few inches. She'd sipped a vodka martini while she changed, in the mood for some fun with her ex. Why not? They still loved each other and always would.

Only it wasn't Foley, it was the FBI.

Special Agent Louis Adams holding his blue and white Federal Bureau ID in front of her saying, "If I'm not mistaken, you're the former Adele Foley?"

"Yes, I am, Lou. And I believe you're the one who was at the prison. Jack got in the car, he said, 'That's

Lou Adams back there.'" Adele gave Lou a cute shrug. "And here you are. You followed us thinking Jack would be here, didn't you? He said you were out to get him and he couldn't understand why. I can't either, but I can tell you you're wasting your time. Jack Foley swears he won't ever rob another bank, and I believe him."

"I'd be out all night and come home," Lou Adams said, "my wife Edie'd want to know where I'd been. I tell her, Jesus, I was on a stakeout all night and she'd say, 'It seems to me I've heard that song before' . . . half-singing it in her slow, sexy voice. She always had kind of a hoarse quality to her voice, like Janis Joplin. I told her it was from smoking and drinking bourbon late at night."

"Were you on stakeouts?"

"I *was*. I was with the Criminal Division Gang Squad working sixty-hour weeks and she walks out on me."

"And blames you because you worked late," Adele said. "You sure she didn't have a boyfriend? Girls named Edie who drink bourbon late at night have boyfriends." She said, "I'm sorry Jack isn't here. Give you two a chance to talk."

"Edie," Lou said, "did not have a boyfriend."

"You looked for one?"

"I looked into the possibility. And," Lou said, "I'm done talking to Foley. I'll always have him in my sights and he knows it, wherever he goes. No, you're the one I came to see." Lou's gaze moved past her into the apartment. "But I am curious—"

The phone rang.

"If you wouldn't mind telling me where he went—"

The phone rang.

"I'd appreciate it."

"Let me see who that is," Adele said, "excuse me." She turned and stepped to the portable phone on the coffee table, the phone ringing again, twice, Adele taking her time—if anyone cared to notice how cool she was—before picking up and saying, "Yes . . .?"

Foley said, "What were you doing?" and said, "Oh, Lou's there, with you."

Adele said, "Who? No, I'm sorry you have the wrong number."

"He's heard that one," Foley said. "It's okay. I may as well talk to him, if that's what he wants."

Adele turned her back to Lou Adams in the doorway.

"He said he came to see me."

"When he saw I wasn't there. I'm gonna tell him I'm at the airport, about to leave. I'll call to check on you when I'm through here. The guy's almost finished."

"After he talks to you," Adele said, "you don't think he'll want to hang around and talk to me? In my baby doll lingerie?"

"Tell him you have a headache."

She said, "You haven't changed a bit, have you?" turned to Lou Adams and held out the phone.

"It's for you."

Tell me so I'll know," Foley said, "why you're dedicating your career to putting me away. Because you mouthed off and had your testimony thrown out of court? I never scored two hundred banks and you know it."

Lou Adams's voice said, "You through?"

"Is that why you're pissed off? You blame me 'cause you didn't get your way? You start yelling when you were told to step down?"

"Now you through?"

"You have a bug up your ass on account of me, and I'd like to know why. 'Cause you're a hardnose, you're always right? How about if we had a fistfight and I let you hit me a couple times, get it out of your system."

"We could have a gunfight," Lou said, "stead of fists. Yeah, I'd feel better, but I'll settle for putting you away."

"Lou, I did banks. I'm not a desperado, a public enemy. I was convicted and did my time. Why can't you accept that?"

"So what're you gonna do now," Lou said, "get a job at a car wash? Bag groceries at the supermarket? Tell me what you're gonna do, I'd like to know."

"You ought to see a shrink," Foley said. "Find out why you're fucked up."

" 'Cause I'm asking what you plan to do?"

Foley said, "Lou, I'm at the airport, about to get out of town. You understand what I'm saying? You're not gonna ever see me again. Okay? So take it easy and I will too."

"Jack?"

Foley took a moment to settle down. "What?"

"You think I won't find you?"

"Lou, I can go anywhere I want—"

"You're gonna rob another bank. You know it and I know it."

"Put Adele on."

"When you come strolling out," Lou Adams said, "it doesn't matter where the bank is. It could be in fucking Alaska, I'm gonna be there waiting for you."

Foley said, "Will you give Adele the phone?"

Lou handed it to her and Adele turned her back to him saying, "Yes . . .?" Listening for a time and saying all right, okay then, before telling him, "Hon, have a safe trip."

Lou said, "You still care for him."

"Of course I do."

"But glad you're not married to him. Knowing he'll do another bank and end up back inside, 'cause he can't help himself. Am I right?"

"I wouldn't rule it out," Adele said. "It's too bad, you get to know Jack he's really a good guy. Girls love him."

Lou allowed Adele to take him by the arm to the door, still open, Adele saying, "Girls find out he robs banks, they get turned on. And he is good-looking, you have to admit. But say the girls find out he holds up liquor stores? It would turn them off, or they'd be scared to death of him."

"That's true," Lou said. "There's something about bank robbers, the way the general public imagines them as cool guys. Why is that? When nine out of ten are bums, deadbeats, owe car payments or need a fix. Guys who'll never in their life get ahead of the game."

Lou stepped through the doorway and turned to Adele.

"What I'm wondering about now, what kind of ID Foley showed to get through all the airport security." Lou said, "His mug shot? Tell me how he buys a ticket, with a credit card he swiped?" Now he was looking at Adele, almost up to him in her heels. She smelled good.

"I know he's still around here," Lou said, "so I better keep an eye on the Normandie, huh? There's a fella at the airport can look at his computer and know if Foley's on any of the flights going out of Miami International. I can sit home watching TV, Foley's name comes up on a passenger list, I get a call and I know where he's going. I told the security guy, you're working with the FBI, partner. You see Foley going somewhere, you're on the trail of a criminal happens to be America's foremost bank robber."

Adele said, "What do you get out of making his life miserable?"

"I hope that's what I'm doing."

"Give him a break, he's a good guy."

"You picked him up at Glades Correctional," Lou said. "That's where they keep the good guys, uh? I'll bet you a hundred bucks," Lou said, "Foley robs another bank in the next thirty days." Watching her he started to grin. "You can't bet me he won't, can you?"

Seven

There were photographs of Dawn Navarro all over the house, blown-up prints in the front room, Dawn not bothering to smile but patient, blond hair across her eyes lined in black like the eyes of a pharaoh, Dawn the psychic staring at Foley from photos taken more than seven years ago. And yet he had the feeling she was looking at him now. Her Egyptian eyes telling Foley she could see him, Foley standing there in his prison underwear, the room dim. Dawn saying, I can see you, Jack. She even knew his name. He said to her face in the photo, "No, you can't." She kept staring at him and he said, "Can you?"

There were shots of Dawn taken on the walk along the canal, on the patio, on the concrete steps to the second-floor veranda. Foley could see Cundo following her with his camera saying, "Look at me." Saying, "Yes, tha's it, just like that." Dawn looking over her shoulder.

The property, little more than thirty feet wide, ran back a hundred or so feet to Cundo's garage in the alley. Here he had shot Dawn behind the wheel of his Volkswagen convertible, twelve years old but looking good, dark green with the tan canvas top. Or maybe it was hers. But why keep it here if she lived in the pink house? Foley didn't use the car until his second day in Venice.

The first day he drank rum from Puerto Rico and listened to Carlos Jobim until he passed out in Cundo's king-size bed.

There was a painting of Dawn in this master bedroom on the third floor, close to life size, though at first he didn't realize it was Dawn, now with dark hair, no exotic eyeliner, a more natural-looking Dawn than the ones with the eyes in the photos.

The painted Dawn lying in this bed looking at him, her hands at her sides, was a naked dark-haired Dawn on the wall next to the bed. He saw Dawn when he closed his eyes and when he opened them in the morning, Dawn still looking at him now from the painting.

In all the photos of her she was blond.

The next day he put the VW's top down—anybody who wanted to look at him it was okay—and drove through the streets of Venice to see what they had here, all the million-dollar homes that wouldn't sell for a quarter of that anywhere but on the California coast. It didn't matter. According to Cundo everybody living in Venice was happy to be here. "There rich people and not rich people, but they all have class. Everybody is included except the gangs. They here, but not invited to the block parties." Foley didn't see any gangs. He drove around, stopped and walked up one of the streets that was a sidewalk separating front yards facing each other, each house with its own idea of what the landscaping should look like, from tropical plants and palms to thick patches of bougainvillea.

Foley drove along Lincoln Boulevard until the sign ROSS, DRESS FOR LESS lured him to the lot behind the store. He used his prepaid credit card to buy new clothes, the first time in more than ten years: three pairs of faded Levi's, white T-shirts and briefs, tennis shoes, sweat socks, a green cotton sweater, an off-white drip-dry sport coat, limp, no shape to it, for sixty-nine dollars, then had to pick out some dark T-shirts and a couple of silky black sport shirts to wear with the coat. He drove up Lincoln to Ralphs supermarket and bought bathroom supplies, shampoo, a skin cleaner, a pair of flip-flops, in the habit of wearing them in the shower at Glades; he bought four bottles of Jack Daniel's, fifths, a case of Dos Equis he remembered he liked, six bottles of red from Australia, six rib-eye steaks, Wheaties and bananas, a sack of oranges, apples, cheese, popcorn, milk, French bread and real butter. He asked a clerk if there was a sporting goods store around. The clerk said you bet, the Sports Chalet in Marina del Rey, and he stopped there to buy a basketball before going home. There were courts on the beach. He liked feeling a basketball in his hands. He wanted to shoot hoops while the sun was bringing down a red sky to sink off the edge of the ocean.

Cundo owned a pair of Zeiss field glasses he'd told Foley one time he always had with him he went to Santa'nita for the horses. Or when he went up on the roof, three stories high, man, and looked down into these homes so close together, into people's lives and see what they doing. "These glasses, man, you see a guy on his porch looking at a newspaper? These glasses you can read the fucking paper yourself."

Foley used the glasses to look around, see if anybody was watching him. Like the same guy in the same place three days in a row not doing anything. Who knew he was here? Nobody, but it didn't matter, if that wacko fed wanted to find him, he would. What do you do, put up with it? There was no way Lou Adams could get the feds here to put a surveillance on him during banking hours. Or watch to see if he leaves town. They couldn't do it. Could Lou hire his own crew on a government paycheck? Who would he get to work for free? And Foley thought, Jesus Christ, who do you think? Some asshole he'd threaten to put in jail if he didn't.

That was an idea right there. Get some gangbangers to help him out. He wondered if Lou was already here.

During the first three days Foley went up on the roof with the Zeiss glasses that put you wherever you were looking. He checked on who was around all three days, in plain sight working construction, little Mexican guys doing yard jobs, hanging out in the alley. He didn't see anything going on that he wondered about.

Once he swept the places for people who could be watching, he'd swing the glasses over to the pink palace where Dawn had been living the past almost eight years by herself, settle on the roof, adjust the focus and come down to the front yard, the patio, poke around through the shrubbery and try to see in one of the windows. He never saw a soul over there. He was hoping the dark-haired Dawn Navarro liked to lie in the sun.

Cundo called from Glades the morning of the fourth day, Foley about to go up on the roof.

"How you think about it?"

Foley said it was the home he'd always dreamed of.

"You like it, uh? You see Dawn?"

"Not yet. I just finished counting the pictures of her. You know how many you have?"

"Man, I took a hundred. I couldn't stop."

"Thirty-seven, not counting the ones you taped to walls as you ran out of time, thinking of her right up to the end. You're a beautiful guy, Cundo. I saw the shots of you and your Hollywood buddies. I even recognized one or two. But all the shots of Dawn she's alone."

"Mood shots," Cundo said. "I take them when I see her in different moods."

"I'd look at her," Foley said, "and have the feeling she was looking out of the picture at me."

Cundo's voice on the line said, "Yes."

"I mean like she could actually see me."

"Yes, I know what you mean, she can see you looking at her."

"Even though she's looking from seven years ago."

"Almost eight. It's her gift, man, she knows you there. Listen, when I'm taking the pictures I look in her eyes and see like she's thinking something. Or even I look at a print of her, the same thing. This is when we come back from Vegas and I can't stop taking pictures of her. I hold one up and say, 'Baby, what are you thinking about in this picture?' I wait for her to make a face, say how can she remember that? No, Dawn say she wasn't thinking, she was feeling love for me. All these years by herself, man, she still waiting for me, still saying she loves me. You believe it?"

No, he didn't. Foley said, "You can't ask for more'n that. When'd you start taking pictures?"

"Remember, I tole you the guy that shot me three times in the chest, barely missing my heart, took pictures? Negroes in church waving their hands in the air. A cemetery, people there in the rain. An old Jewish woman putting on her lipstick. Joe LaBrava, man, use to be in the Secret Service, quit and became famous taking pictures. I thought, Tha's all you have to do? Take some real-life shots like that, things you see every fucking day and you become famous? But all I've done so far is take pictures of Dawn."

"They're good," Foley said. "I like the painting of her too."

And knew as Cundo said, "What painting?" he'd made a mistake.

Foley said, "Oh, you haven't seen it?" The dark-haired Dawn bare naked had nothing to do with Cundo, eight years and three thousand miles away.

Now he wanted to know, "Who painted her?"

Foley said, "I don't know. But didn't you tell me one time she paints?"

"I don't know, maybe," Cundo said. "I don't remember. But listen, Jack? I like you to do something for me. Keep an eye on her till I get out. See does anybody come to visit her and let me know."

Foley said, "Isn't the Monk watching out for her? I thought he might come by here, but I haven't seen him."

"The Monk say she's fine, no problem," Cundo said, "what he always say to me, 'Yeah, Dawn is fine.' Sometimes he say, 'She wants me to tell you she misses you very much,' but I don't hear her saying that."

"They aren't her exact words," Foley said, "but it's what she meant."

"The Monk can't remember what she said? Why you making excuses for him? You don't know him."

"I don't want you to worry," Foley said, "get upset, with your release coming up."

"I can't help if I worry about her, what she's doing." Cundo raised his voice saying, "For Christ sake, all *right*," to someone watching him on the phone, and to

Foley, "Fucking guardia. He makes a sign like he's cutting his throat for me to get off the phone, line of guys waiting to use it."

"That's what I'm talking about," Foley said. "Stay calm, will you? Don't fuck up now you're ready to get out."

"I want to know Dawn is a saint," Cundo said, "not fucking some guy for painting her picture."

"You don't think it's a self-portrait."

"She don't fucking paint, Jack, her gift is to tell fortunes. I want to know she's a saint when I come home, I want you to see she's without sin, like a virgin. We road dogs, man, we do for each other no matter what."

It was a custom to pair off as road dogs inside, living among gangs with their own signs and tats; inmates who weren't with them were against them; gangbangers could make living inside a daily chore, watching not to look any gangsta in the eye. A five-foot homeboy, a new arrival, said to Foley in the yard, "What chew looking at, butt-fuck?" Foley said, "I'm looking at you, asshole," and nodded to the gangbangers watching. They took the kid away telling him not to fuck with Foley, he was the real thing, the star bank robber at Glades, respected, you could talk to him. While Cundo was the jive Cat Prince with money, lots of money he used for favors, Jack Foley watching his back.

"I see us more as social road dogs," Foley said. "We don't need to be that serious about it."

"How you see it don't matter," Cundo said. "Is how the population sees us. They know, even if you making a wrong move, do something stupid, they know I back you up. Con sees you come at him with a shank, he knows your road dog is right behind, also with a shank. Is how it is."

"When did I ever have a shank on me?"

"I'm telling you what is a road dog, tha's all. If I go to stick some guy bothering me, I know you right there to back my move."

"When did you ever stick anybody? You pay guys to take care of your business."

"I'm talking about the principle of it, of being road dogs. We road dogs as long as we together, here or outside."

Like being on call, Foley thought. Because Cundo had eased him out of doing thirty years with a check to Megan for thirty grand. What still bothered Foley as much as not having any money: why was Cundo giving him a free ride? Because Foley was the only gringo Cundo could talk to? Believe that, he could believe the little bugger's heart bleeds. He put money on you for the future. Watch over Dawn for now. It's when he's released he'll get down to the gritty. "Do a job for me, man, an easy one." He'll say, "Jus' this one, okay?" Then another one. Wait and see.

The only thing to do, get out from under him, out of this house that was a shrine to Dawn. Dawn everywhere.

Dawn in bed with the dark hair, his favorite.

He was thinking he should get in touch with Karen. Call the Miami's marshals' office, let her know he missed her. If she wanted him to do anything for her—like come back to Florida, rip her clothes off and throw her on a bed—he'd be happy to. When she came on the phone he'd say, "Is this my little zoo-zoo by any chance?" And she'd say—

The phone rang.

He was thinking, staring at the painting of Dawn in the giant bed, that lust could be part of love, or it just meant you were horny.

The phone rang again. Foley knew who it was without knowing why. He did, he picked up the phone and said, "Dawn? I was about to call you."

He heard her say, "Don't tell me you're psychic," sounding pleased in a quiet way. She said, "You're right, Jack, it's time we got together."

Eight

"I'll come over," Dawn said. "I haven't been across the bridge in weeks." She said, "Are all the pictures of me still up? Cundo made me swear I wouldn't touch them. You know I lived there almost a month but had to move. Everywhere I looked I saw myself and I never changed, the blonde with exotic eyes, so I moved to the pink house. It's terra-cotta, but Cundo says it's pink and he's too macho to live in a pink house." She said, "We could meet now if you want. It isn't too early, is it? I love to sip Jack Daniel's in the morning."

Foley said, "You're sure that's what I have?"

"And Mexican beer, but I like the sour mash."

"You must be psychic," Foley said, "or you've been going through my trash."

"Or I saw you shopping at Ralphs," Dawn said, "and I thought, Why that must be Jack Foley trying not to look furtive, a former inmate in the world again. I got that from your body language, Jack. What I learned about you took place your first night here, getting smashed on Puerto Rican rum till you went to sleep. I thought, Well, that's done. He's celebrated his release, spent a day hung over and now he'll call. I know you've been dying for us to meet, but had to settle in first. You're still uneasy being out in public, going to stores." She said, "Let's see if I can get you feeling like yourself again."

Foley said, "I always feel like myself."

"You think you do. I'll be over," Dawn said, "let's see, about twelve-thirty."

"You need an hour to comb your hair?"

"I want to bathe and look nice for you. This is a big day for us, Jack."

He watched her cross the footbridge over the canal, the dark-haired Dawn in a white sundress and pink heels, coming to visit in the early afternoon. He liked the way her hair came close to her eyes in a free fall to bare shoulders, this slim girl who could be a fashion model but told fortunes instead.

She took his hand and held on to it, both smiling, very pleased to meet each other. The sky gray but so what. Things were looking up for Foley, fresh out of stir. He couldn't stop grinning at this confident girl who lived by herself and posed in the nude. He said, "Why don't we go inside."

They went through to the kitchen, Dawn saying, "I want to see what you have in the fridge."

Foley got out the ice and made drinks, Jack Daniel's and a splash of water, while Dawn poked around in the refrigerator, used a spoon to taste his cold butter beans and onions, seemed to like it, found a wedge of Brie and spread some on a stalk of celery. She said, "I know where we should talk. Bring the bottle and a bowl of ice." Dawn running the show. Foley went along.

Up to the third floor, to the low table and red leather chairs in the alcove off the master bedroom, across from the painting of her by the bed. She said, "There's another one of me dressed, reading a book. Jimmy has it in his office."

"I like the one of you bare ass," Foley said. "I did happen to mention the painting to Cundo. He said, 'Wha' painting?'"

"You tell him I'm naked?"

"I only said I liked it."

"I haven't told him," Dawn said. "I wouldn't be his little saint if I let you see me naked, even in a painting."

"He wanted to know who did it."

"Little Jimmy," Dawn said. "Cundo has him watching over me. He calls Jimmy the Monk, because for twenty-seven years Cundo's believed Little Jimmy's gay. But the little fella himself has never been that sure. But which does he like better, pussy, or being one? Jimmy said he's beginning to lean toward pussy."

This girl who'd taken a bath and wanted to look nice for him talking about pussy in an offhand way that took Foley back to the yard. He said, "Cundo never called the Monk Little Jimmy."

"It's a name I gave him. He likes it."

"I told Cundo I thought you did the paintings."

It seemed to please her. "That's not a bad idea."

"He didn't go for it. He said, 'She don't fucking paint.'" Foley giving her his Cundo Rey. "'She only tell you your fortune.'"

"That's not bad either. Give me your hand," Dawn said. "Here, rest your arm on the table." She moved the tips of fingers over his fingers and his palm. She said, "You don't show it, but not having money is driving you nuts." She said, "You know what you should've been doing all this time? I mean instead of robbing banks?"

Throws it out—like telling Foley she knew all about him.

"You were a boy you wanted to go to sea."

"I thought of joining the navy."

"Now you wouldn't mind owning a deep-sea fishing boat. Operate out of Biloxi?"

"Costa Rica," Foley said. "How long have you been reading palms?"

"When you're a Sagittarian," Dawn said, "born with a Grand Trine in the center of your natal chart, you know you have a gift. You can call me Reverend Dawn, if you'd like. I'm an ordained minister of the Spiritualist Assembly of Waco, Texas, though I started out doing nails." She sipped her drink, still looking at him. "I went to beautician school, ran around acting crazy, did drugs, almost bit my nails off I was so fucked up. That was my Sagittarius rising with Mars on aspect. I got it together and now I'm a licensed psychic, clairvoyant, astrologer—what else—spirit medium. I interpret dreams and do past-life regressions. I can cite events in your personal life and tell you what they mean . . . your involvement with a woman, a federal officer, who was hot on your trail"—Dawn's eyes holding his—"you took to bed . . . Wait, and the next day she shot you?"

Foley said, "Cundo told you about that, uh?"

Dawn smiled now. "Yes, he did. What's her name, Karen Sisco? She sounds like fun."

His zoo-zoo, in his mind for only a moment, bumped out by Dawn Navarro playing with him, letting him know that right now she was more fun than Karen.

Foley said, "You ever use hypnosis?"

"Now and then. Would you like to be hypnotized?"

"It doesn't work on me."

"Will you let me try?"

"I know it won't work."

"Close your eyes, Jack, not too tight, and let your breath out slowly. That's it . . . I'll count down from three, all right? We'll take our time. Three, Jack. Your muscles are relaxing, your whole body is going limp. Two, you feel safe with me, you know you can say whatever you want." Dawn paused. "And one. Are we ready, Jack?" She reached for his hand on the table and pinched his skin.

"Jack?"

"What?"

"Did I hurt your hand?"

"No."

"You're willing to talk to me? Yes or no."

"Yes."

"You'll let me take you back to the prison, where you knew Cundo Rey? Yes or no."

"Yes."

"Is Cundo Rey a friend of yours? Yes or no."

"Yes."

"Do you trust him?"

Dawn waited.

"No."

Now she paused. "Would you say he's worth a lot of money, Jack? Yes or no."

"Yes."

"In properties," Dawn said, "and a partner in Little Jimmy's investment service. Did you know that?"

"No."

"Did you know Little Jimmy runs a sports book for him?"

"No."

"Do you know if Cundo has bank accounts?" Foley hesitated again and Dawn said, "Let's skip that one. Do you think he has money the IRS doesn't know about? Money he's never declared as income?"

Foley turned his head resting against soft red leather to open his eyes and look at Dawn. He said, "I think he's got a shitload of money that's never been close to being declared. What do you think?"

She smiled shaking her head, Foley grinning at her, Foley saying, "Are we getting to it now?"

Dawn said to her neighbor the bank robber in his clean white T-shirt, his hair parted and combed, "Well, aren't you the tricky motherfucker. I'll have to watch my step with you, won't I?"

"Reverend Dawn," Foley said, "you're asking me to conspire against my friend, aren't you?"

"I saw you coming," Dawn said. "I said to myself, This jailbird's too good to be true. But my God, you're the real thing, aren't you? You're into Cundo for over thirty thousand waiting for him to call it in, let you know it's payback time. With the vig it could more than double. You don't trust him, you don't respect him, but he's loaded, he's sitting on a fortune, and the way things are, you know you'd better get Cundo before he gets you."

Jesus, reading his mind.

"But it's all in Little Jimmy's name," Foley said.

"That's the next question. What keeps Little Jimmy from selling the homes and stealing away in the night?"

"You tell me," Foley said, "you're the psychic."

"I want to know what you think."

"Cundo saved Little Jimmy from getting cornholed eight or nine times a day."

"But that was twenty-seven years ago, in Cuba. Why do you suppose Little Jimmy's still loyal all these years?"

"I don't know if he is or not," Foley said, "but I'm pretty sure he's the key to the money."

"Sometimes he'll visit," Dawn said, "and sound like he's out of *La Cage aux Folles*, he loves to put it on. But when we talk about Cundo, Little Jimmy shuts down part of his mind, always careful of what he says."

"I imagine he likes you."

"He adores me."

"But doesn't trust you."

"He tells me what we'd do in bed."

"Yeah . . .?"

"In detail, trying to turn me on."

Dawn shrugged and took a sip of her drink. "It wasn't that outrageous. But the little guy will *not* say one fucking word about Cundo's money. I put him under hypnosis and asked if he was skimming from the investment business and the sports book. He said Cundo doesn't know enough about business to pay him what he's worth, so he skims to make up for it. He said he lifted a hundred and fifty thousand to buy himself a Bentley, used. I said, 'Why not a Rolls while you're at it.' He said, 'I am not one to exhibit myself.' But he is, he's a little show-off, in his Cuban heels maybe an inch taller than Cundo. I asked if he's ever thought of selling the houses and taking off with about seven million. He said no, never. I asked the key question, why he's dedicated his life to serving Cundo Rey. I said, 'Is it because you're in love with him?' He said, 'Yes, of course, always.' But I can't ask one question about Cundo and money. I say, 'I'm asking as his wife.' But he knows Cundo and I aren't actually married."

"You're not?" Foley said, surprise giving way to another feeling, glad to hear it. "He told me you exchanged vows."

"In the hotel room with rum and Coke. He said the vows we make to each other is what counts, not some guy in a cheap suit asking if we take each other forever and ever."

"How's it been having to wait eight years to score off the little guy?"

"How's it been taking free rides?" Dawn said. "The chick lawyer who didn't cost you a dime. While you find out all you can about him. I'm doing all right, Jack. I have clients, I do readings. Cundo said, 'Watch over my properties for—how you think about seven hundred a week?' I said, 'How you think about a thousand?' He said okay. I said, 'For each home?' The little guy said, 'Yes, of course.' He said it was what he meant."

"A hundred grand a year ain't bad," Foley said. "You manage to get by on it?"

"You're a little smarty, aren't you?" Dawn said. "It's part of your disarming charm. Yes, I can manage on two grand a week, and I bet the horses with Little Jimmy. He makes sure I win more than I lose."

"A psychic can't pick winners?"

"Isn't that curious?" Dawn said.

"We've been talking about Cundo's money," Foley said. "You haven't asked how the little fella's doing in stir. You don't worry about him?"

Dawn said, "Jack," in a lazy kind of voice, "how much time do we have, a couple of weeks?"

"He's out the end of next week."

"You want to know if I worry about him—doesn't he have bodyguards, little Latino guys with cute little mustaches?"

"He had me in stir," Foley said, "and guys he could always call on. I didn't see anybody mess with him. He said if they did, he'd have them burned alive."

"The inmates believed him?"

"He killed a Russian in Cuba, the *mozo* working at the hospital. Another one, a guy who came looking for him he called Uncle Miney." Foley paused. "There was one more. Yeah, the boatlift skipper, Cundo pushed him overboard. The kind of thing prisoners all knew about."

"He's killed four times?" Dawn said, not so much surprised as thoughtful.

"Reverend Dawn," Foley said, "you're smarter than the little Cuban, and I'm counting on you reading his mind. But—"

She said, "I don't know him as well as you do?"

"You don't think the way he does. He has a gift too, he makes crime pay, a lot. How to go down but stay on top. How to win friends and influence convicts."

"I know he pays for what he wants," Dawn said.

"With money Little Jimmy's making for him. Cundo Rey keeps his eyes open. He knows what's going on. Little Jimmy told you Cundo won't notice his skimming a hundred fifty grand for a car. You want to bet?"

"Yeah, but Cundo needs Little Jimmy," Dawn said.

"And Little Jimmy knows how Cundo thinks, so I'm not gonna worry about Little Jimmy. I'm gonna worry about you, Reverend Dawn."

"Jack, you're not funny."

"You've already looked through both houses for money stuck away and have come up empty."

She said, "I'm the psychic, okay? Why'd you hang out with him for two and a half years?"

"He told good stories."

"About himself."

"Always. They were still good."

"But you don't trust him." She took a sip of her drink and said, "Let's put little Cundo and Little Jimmy on hold for the time being, if it's all right with you, and give some thought to pleasing ourselves this lovely overcast afternoon. See how much we like each other."

Foley said, "Plumb the depths of our compatibility," grinning at her, having fun again.

"It must seem like an eternity," Dawn said, "since you've taken your clothes off with a woman. Watched her undress . . ."

He saw her eyes turn soft, dreamy, but now, the way she was staring at him, her eyes seemed out of focus and Foley would swear at that moment she was looking into his mind. Now she blinked and seemed, not confused, but less sure of herself.

She said, "It's only been five *days*?"

"You're close," Foley said. "Actually it's been four."

Now she'd have second thoughts. Who was he with, some hooker? But then realized, no, with her gift she'd know he was with his ex-wife the morning he left Florida, so they'd stay with the program, and they did, Dawn saying:

"I'm going to take my dress off."

Foley said, "And your undies?"

Dawn said, "I'm not wearing any."

So then all Foley had to do was pay attention and be tender, not rush into this and get carried away. It got him to grin as they looked each other over, the grin working all right here as they made it to the bed. Foley did not want to be as ready as he was and set his mind to picture the crowd at Venice Beach, the girls with long legs flying by on Rollerblades and it didn't help but didn't matter, Dawn came up like thunder, couldn't wait, Dawn the one dying to get it up to speed, and Foley revised his approach—put the tender moves away until they did it again, Foley believed after a cigarette and a few sips of Old No. 7 and that was pretty much what happened when they settled down to restore their lust. But by the time they were at it again, getting into what he thought would be slow love, sail for a while kissing and grinning at each other, but they found themselves stepping it up and this act of love turned feverish, as wild and perspiring as the first one, Dawn sounding like she was dying but putting up a good fight, Foley, Foley in there performing, feeling himself into it and they finished in a dead heat, Foley believing he was in love again.

He held her, kissed her hair, her ear, did all that, watched her breathe as she came back to earth, her lips parted, this innocent-looking girl with green eyes drawing him in as her little helper, knowing it was what he wanted before he did. She was psychic, clairvoyant . . . better than that, this girl was everything an ex-con like Jack Foley could pray for. Thank you, Jesus. A girl you had to subdue to reach where you were going. But once she opened her eyes there she was, she was aware, she was with it, back in her skin. He turned her on and they were closer now.

Intimate. She got out of bed and went in the bathroom, left the door open to sit on the toilet and smile at him.

"Did you have a good time?"

"My heart," Foley said, "soared like a hawk."

"You weren't bad yourself," Dawn said. "You surprised me."

She got back in bed with a cigarette to lie against the headboard now, Foley rubbing an ice cube over his chest, feeling male, satisfied. Dawn said, "Did he tell you about the bank Little Jimmy runs, with the numbered accounts?"

"Not much. It didn't sound like a bank."

"It is, Jack. It's a bank."

"This is only my second week outside, I'm still pure, clean, and you want to pull a bank job?"

There was a silence before she said, "Jack . . .?" and he turned his head to her.

"When Cundo was in prison he'd call and the first thing he'd say, he'd ask me if I was being a saint. Cundo believed saints never had sex. 'Are you being a saint for me?' 'Yes, I'm being a saint.' 'For me?' 'Yes, for you.' Finally I told him if he didn't stop asking if I was a fucking saint I'd disappear and he'd never see me again. And he did, he stopped saying it. Until last week, the day before you got here, he called and asked me again, after years of not asking, if I was being a saint. I said, 'All this time I've been alone?' I said, 'For more than seven years I've been waiting for you, and you ask me that all over again?'"

"Did you ask him," Foley said, "why he doesn't trust you?"

"That's not the question," Dawn said. "If he doesn't trust me, why did he invite you to come here?"

"Fresh out of the joint," Foley said.

Dawn nodded, looking at him.

"That's the question."

Nine

Lou Adams met the LAPD Gang Squad Detective at the Firehouse Bar on Rose Avenue. He knew Ron Deneweth from a police officer's funeral, the two sitting and talking after with a few beers. Lou still had Deneweth's card and called him once he'd decided to play this deal.

Deneweth said, "You know this place was actually a firehouse at one time?"

"Is that right?" Lou Adams said, waiting to look at the stack of rap sheets Deneweth was holding.

"Usually," Deneweth said, "you see some of those muscle freaks from Gold's Gym in here. They sit at the bar sipping Red Bull looking at themselves in the mirror, every so often popping a bicep."

Lou said, "You gonna let me see those sheets?"

"I don't know why you come to me," Deneweth said, "all the federal programs you have. S.T.E.P. Street Terrorism Enforcement and Prevention. You have C.L.E.A.R. Community Law Enforcement and Recovery. H.E.A.T. Heightened Enforcement and Targeting. You have S.A.G.E. Strategies Against Gun Violence. Shouldn't it be S.A.G.V.?"

"It should," Lou said, "but S-a-g-v isn't a word. You gonna let me look at the sheets?"

"You also have G.I.T.," Deneweth said, "Gang Impact Teams," handing the stack to Lou Adams. "The guy you want's on top. He's Gang Intervention, a very bright boy, leader of a program called Y.B.U. Young Boys United."

"Nice-looking boy," Lou said, studying the mug shot of Vincente Sandoval, also known as Vincent, Tico, El Niño: twenty-one years of age, five-ten, one-sixty, eyes brown, looking devilish in his do-rag, one earring, gang tattoos from his youth. The Hardcore Gang Division brought him up four times on suspicion of felony homicide, one conviction; did three years for first-degree manslaughter, still in his serious teens.

"In the L.A. area he's known as Tico," Deneweth said. "It's not on his sheet where he's from originally. I think Nicaragua, but I could be wrong. I'm thinking he has a green card or we'd of sent him back."

"What's he do as a gang intervention worker?"

"Nothing much. Tico has a bunch of teenagers, showing 'em how to be good boys, stay clear of V-13 and the Shoreline Crips and someday become grown-ups."

"Tico Sandoval," Lou Adams said. "What should I call the boy, Tico or Sandy?"

"**Sandy, you** know how many young men like yourself I looked at before naming you my second in command, my *segundo*? As many'll fit in a good-size holding cell. When I was told you go both ways I said, 'Whoa, you mean the boy's a fruitcake?' No, what they meant, you can pass as one hundred percent Latin doing a samba, or go African with a bone through your nose. I'm told you're even a speck Chinese, but I don't see it. What was your mother?"

"What *was* she?"

Sounding Hispanic.

"Where was she from?"

"Oh—my mama come from West Memphis, Arkansas."

See? Right before your eyes he becomes a colored guy. From spic to African-American nigger, Lou Adams believed, as the mood struck him.

"I'm told by Detective Ron Deneweth," Lou said, "gang intervention has turned you into a man of peace,

and I want to believe it. Ron says they have you looking at ways of bringing the Latins and the brothers
together, get 'em to work out their beefs. *Es verdad?*"

Tico said, "Is true, all right. I'm thinking of ways to
bring peace to the valley once again."

"Sandy," Lou said, "are you fuckin' with me?"

"Boss . . .?"

They were sitting on the sunporch of a yellow frame
house on Broadway near Oakwood Park in Venice,
where Tico was living with a good-looking black
woman who was supposed to be his *ah'nt,* the way he
said it.

Lou said, "You fuck with me, Sandy, I'll have
Immigration deport your skinny ass back to Central
America, drop you off home in Nicaragua. You savvy
'deport your ass'?"

"Yes, boss, of course."

Calm about it. A Spanish dude in his striped do-rag
and silver earring.

"Tell me," Lou said, "if you know a Jack Foley."

"I don't think so."

"He's only the most famous fucking bank robber
in America. Last week he was released from a Florida
prison and bought fake ID to get out here in a hurry."

"Can I ask why you looking for him?"

"He's gonna rob another bank."

"How do you know that, boss?"

"It's what he does, he robs banks. I went to the prison in Florida," Lou said. "I talk to inmates, I talk to hacks, administrative people—every one of 'em said, 'Jack Foley? Yeah, he hung out with Cundo Rey, they road-dog buddies.' So I'm thinking, Cundo's put him up. You know about this Cuban? He's still in the joint but suppose to have property out here. Buys homes and sells 'em, all he does is get rich."

"In Venice—*ya lo creo*."

"Speak English. You know him?"

"I hear of him only."

"Well, I checked with the county. They don't have him down as owning any. But then I find his name as a partner in an investment company. Rios and Rey, Incorporated, Financial Consultants. When'd Cundo learn to add a column of figures?"

Tico shook his head. "I can't help you, boss."

"This squirt's finishing up a homicide conviction in Florida while he's a businessman in California? Yeah, uh-huh. I spoke to a cute woman name of Tibby Rothman. You know her? Little bitty thing."

"I see her around, yes."

"She puts out the Venice newspaper, I understand, when she feels like it. I asked her did she know a James Rios. She said, 'You mean Little Jimmy the

bookkeeper?' and grinned at me like she'd said something funny." Now Lou asked his second in command,
"Sandy, you know this Little Jimmy person?"

Now Tico was grinning.

"Boss, everybody in Venice knows Little Jimmy.
He's what you call a character. *Sabe usted* character,
boss?"

This *federale* being a tough guy was a trip. *You fucking with me, Sandy?* The question on Tico's mind:
what was the guy doing here by himself? They send
him to watch a bank robber just got his release who
could sit on the beach all day watching girls, do whatever he wants? They send one guy only?

One guy can't do it. So he wants Tico, your young
Boy United, to watch the bank robber for him. The
man said, "And get some of those gangbangers, their
pants hanging off their ass, to help you." He said, "Four
times six is twenty-four." He did, he said that. "You
need four colored guys and four la Cucarachas, one of
each working surveillance at all times, six hours on, six
off. Can you handle it? You can't, I'll have your ass sent
back to"—what did he say, "Nicaragua"? The man not
knowing shit where Tico was from.

Tico's mama Shirlene—once she'd had enough of
West Memphis—found her way to Central America with

a light-skin Latino guy. Tico was born and she left the first guy for another light-skin guy, a musician famous for playing the marimba, and she began to sing with his band called Los Parados. Shirlene changed her name to Sierra and became famous down there doing Afro-Caribbean funk in San José clubs. Days she spent with Tico as he grew up, loving him, teaching him how to be black American on the beat, how to wear his hair long and a hat if he wanted with the do-rag, what kind of silver to wear, rings and an earring. Sierra spoke English to him at home, good English and street English, preparing him for his world. She said, "Baby, feel your cool self, who you are, somebody special." She told him every day, "There is no one else like you. Don't fuck up."

This Lou Adams had big hands and hard bones showing in his face. He was the kind of man believed he knew everything. Be talking, thumbs hooked in his belt, turn his head to spit, turn his head back and still be talking. Why's he want this bank robber? To make a name for himself? Catch this famous bandit Tico had never heard of? Why's he think the bank robber was staying at a house everybody knows belongs to Cundo Rey? The Lone Ranger says no, Little Jimmy Rios owns the house. Tico said, "Oh, is that right?"

"I looked up the records," Louis Adams said, "and saw the signature, James Rios."

What everyone who knew anything was suppose to believe. But if Little Jimmy belonged to Cundo Rey, going back to the time they left Cooba, wouldn't the homes also belong to Cundo? Why didn't the Lone Ranger know that? You own two high-price homes on a canal, the most expensive property in Venice, you had to be a millionaire, even if you were living in a prison cell in Florida.

Tico said to Louis Adams, "What are you paying us for this work?"

"You get to stay here," Lou Adams said. "I don't send your ass home."

"I don't do this work for you, you deport me?"

"I make a phone call, it's done."

"The guys I get for you, I tell them that?"

"They're illegals, aren't they?"

"I don't know. There would be a court hearing to find out, uh? I know of these situations, it could take weeks."

Lou said, "While you're being held in federal detention."

"I understand that," Tico said, "but while you holding us, who's watching the bank robber?"

Lou Adams said, "Sandy, are you fuckin' with me again? I'll get you sent home tomorrow."

Tico said, "You know my place of birth is Costa Rica? No, you didn't, did you? You know my mother was born in the state of Arkansas? I think you knew it and forgot. It makes me also a citizen of the United States. I have a passport."

Tico waited, giving the federal time to think of what he might say, the man trying hard to be a serious FBI man. Help him out.

"Still," Tico said, "I see what you need to do and I think, all right, I get the guys. We see the bank robber leave the house we know is owned by a criminal who isn't there, is in prison. The bank robber has left. Now, nobody is there, this place owned by a millionaire criminal."

Lou Adams said, "You gonna fuckin' act it out next? You want to know what you get out of it? Give your boys some T-shirts that say Y.B.U. across the front. You get to see your mama when she comes to visit. We won't detain her, have her x-rayed. 'Well, it looks like you're in a good shape. Except for those balloons in your tummy.'"

Lou turned to get in Tico's face.

"Don't fuck with me, boy."

Ten

"He'll be here the end of next week," Foley said, "unless he decides to lay over in South Beach and go crazy."

"He won't," Dawn said. "He'll be here the day he's released." She said, "I'll call Little Jimmy in the morning, have him come by so you can see what he's like. I would've called him today if you hadn't seduced me." She said, "I'm starting to sound like you, aren't I? That's a compliment. What was it you said, we were plumbing our compatibility? I have to say, Jack, you could be a master plumber."

They were in bed, lying close to each other in the dark, the night of their first day together, worn out but not able to sleep. He said, "What do you mean I could be?"

"That's not important now," Dawn said. "The main thing is we've found each other."

He'd accept that. Without looking at the odds, or thinking about what-ifs, Dawn was right. They'd met and it was done, they'd found each other.

She was lying on her side facing him, her arm under the pillow. He could hear her breathing and wanted to see her eyes. He reached for the lighter on the nightstand and flicked it on and saw her eyes in the glow, waiting.

"You don't have any doubts about this."

She said, "None. As soon as I saw you I knew we could make it happen."

"Walk away with a score."

"In time. Once we know what we're after."

"He gets out," Foley said, "we won't see much of each other. You'll be with him."

She said, "Sleeping with him—that's what you're thinking. There's nothing I can do about it, we bide our time."

"We could take off tomorrow," Foley said. "Put the top down, drive all the way through Mexico, Guatemala, Nicaragua, we don't stop till we're in Costa Rica."

"I wait eight years of my life," Dawn said, "to steal a Volkswagen." She touched his face, brushed the tips of her fingers over his mouth. "You call him the little fella, your prison buddy you know you can't trust. He tells me he's invested money in you and wants *me* to put you to work. So I'm thinking you could come on as the true love of a woman who's dead husband is giving her a hard time."

"How's he do it?"

"Makes appearances."

Foley stared at her.

"I do this all the time, have psychic house parties for rich old broads, never more than six or eight at a time, two bills to find out about yourself or your past life, your yearnings, reconnect with deceased loved ones. I hypnotize skinny ones who aren't too old to enlarge their breasts."

"You can do that?"

"Through visualization techniques. I have them write on a piece of notepaper something they want more than anything in the world. I take the notes folded, I don't peek at what they wrote. I look at the ladies one at a time. Suzanne wants to stop smoking. Another one wants to lose weight—those are easy. The best kind of all, Danialle wishes her dead husband would stop bothering her."

"How'd you guess that?"

"I didn't guess, I knew who she was, an actress before her husband died. He was a film producer. I bring you in as the ghost expert. She immediately falls for you and that solves her problem." Dawn said, "Hmmm, that's not bad."

Foley said, "I know how to handle ghosts?"

"You're good with spirits, but let's stay with Cundo. I want to tell you how you feel about him. You know he's a shifty guy, but there's something about him you like, his confidence, the way he struts. It's why you don't feel good about ripping him off—especially if he won't know about it. We disappear in the night. But you think it's sneaky and you've never been a sneak. You're not even sure he'll try to hustle you, get you into some kind of action. Am I right?"

"It sounds right," Foley said.

"Is robbing a bank much different?"

"It's face-to-face."

"With the teller. 'Sweetheart, give me all your big bills, please.' Isn't that why you're there? For money. You're not robbing the bank because it's out to fuck up your life. Money, that's the only motive you need."

"You want me to look at this," Foley said, "like it's a job, that's all."

"Exactly."

"I get him before he puts me to work?"

"Before he comes up with a scheme to use you. It's why you're here, Jack, his houseguest."

It wasn't yet clear to Foley how they'd work the job or how much they were after; he was counting on Dawn for the details. Getting his motive straightened out and what Dawn said about finding each other, that was enough for right now. The only other thing on Foley's mind:

"The one who's gonna fall in love with me—what was her name in the movies?"

"Danialle Tynan."

"Yeah? I've seen her. She wasn't bad."

In the morning Foley came off the roof with Cundo's binoculars, down to the kitchen where Dawn was putting bread in the toaster. She glanced at him. "You know who you're looking for?"

"Strangers," Foley said.

She said, "Aren't they *all* strangers?" Dawn wearing a navy T-shirt with BORN TO HOWL reversed across the front, the message the same color as her little white undies, Dawn's around-the-house costume, turning him on as she fixed breakfast.

"I was hoping," Foley said, "I might see a guy with a haircut wearing a Brooks Brothers suit and tie strolling along the canal. It would get my attention."

She said, "He can't be working alone. I haven't thought about it, but I'll turn my magic on it if you want."

"I try to think like Lou Adams," Foley said. "If he can't raise a posse of feds, who does he get to help him?"

"Bad guys," Dawn said.

"That's what I came to, offenders he can lean on. Felons, threaten to bust 'em for strolling without a destination."

Dawn said, looking to see if the bread was toasted enough, "We have all kinds of boys in the hood living in Venice. Go over to the Oakwood Recreation Center, you can buy dope on the basketball court. The police just had a big raid there the other day, took a bunch of boys in."

"That's where you get your grass?"

"I have it delivered."

"I saw a guy," Foley said, "a Latino I took to be a gangbanger, except he's wearing a purple scarf tied on his head, a do-rag, and I thought, Purple, that's a mix of gang colors, red for the Bloods, blue for the Crips, the guy showing he's not partial to either one. I saw him in the alley, he's talking to some black kids, teenagers, and he's Latino. You understand what I'm saying? He's jiving these kids, messing with them and they think he's funny, they're all laughing. I'm wondering what's going on? They're suppose to be bustin' caps at each other."

Dawn flipped up the toast, black, smoking, and threw it in the trash. She said, "He might be an intervention worker."

"What do they do?"

"Act like they're settling gang problems. They love the attention."

"This morning," Foley said, "I saw the same guy coming along the walk by the canal. He stopped to talk to the maid next door, in the glass house."

"It's my favorite," Dawn said. "The house is thirty feet wide and has a lap pool inside." She put two more slices of bread in the toaster. "You saw the Latin guy talking to the maid. Then later you went over and asked her who he was."

"I said I thought I knew him but wasn't sure. She said his name's Vincent, but here he's called Tico."

"Because he's from Costa Rica," Dawn said.

"You must've got a message from the spirit world. You hear a voice saying, 'Hey, Dawn? In case you didn't know it, guys in Costa Rica are called Tico and the women Tica. You might be able to use it when you're being psychic.'"

She said, "You know, I've never been to Costa Rica? I must have read about the Ticos and Ticas and stored it away. My poor head is crammed full of stuff, Jack, normal and paranormal all bunched together. I have to stop and think sometimes, where in the world did that come from?" She turned to the toaster saying, "So now you'll be watching for Tico from Costa Rica."

"If I see him again," Foley said, "I'll have a word with him."

He watched her flip up the toast, not quite as burnt as the first two, and look past her shoulder at him.

"You like your toast a little dark?"

Foley said, "Thanks, I'll make my own."

He was on the roof when the Bentley arrived, Foley wanting to have a look at Little Jimmy Rios before meeting him face-to-face. He watched the car pull up behind the garage. Watched a guy he took to be the bodyguard, a slim Latino in sunglasses, come out of the car and look around before opening Little Jimmy's door. Finally, there he was coming past the rear of the gunmetal gray Bentley.

Only it wasn't the Little Jimmy Foley was expecting. In the color shots from the past that Dawn showed him, Little Jimmy was Al Pacino playing Tony Montana in *Scarface*. Little Jimmy in a white suit, shirt collar spread open, dark hair like Tony's down on his forehead. Today's Little Jimmy was into another style, a dark suit cut slim and buttoned up, the shirt collar high and stiff, not anything like Tony's, the pants narrow all the way down to a pair of polished crocodile loafers with Cuban heels.

Foley had on a T-shirt, a pair of new Levi's that felt snug on him, and a pair of plain white Reeboks Adele had sent him more than a year ago. He reached the patio as Little Jimmy appeared, coming out of the walk that ran along the side of the house, Little Jimmy alone, the bodyguard left behind. Dawn was ready. She kissed Little Jimmy on the mouth and let her eyes melt on him before turning to Foley.

"Jack, this is my pal Little Jimmy, sometimes known as the Monk. Isn't he cute? Dyes his hair, but who doesn't. And this is Jack Foley, America's foremost bank robber, retired, who swears he'll never rob another one."

Where'd she get that? In Foley's mind he was through with banks, but had never sworn to it. He stepped toward Jimmy Rios, the little dude posing now, hands turned around on his hips, fingers behind him, his shoulders slumped in a casual way, nothing to prove. Foley decided to start off liking him. Why not?

He said, "Jimmy, Dawn showed me a picture of you, it was when you were still in Florida, and I said, 'Jesus Christ, it's Tony Montana.'" He watched Little Jimmy shake his head, tired of hearing it, but with a grin, so it

ROAD DOGS • 113

was okay. He touched his hair, thick and black, parted and combed across his forehead and fixed with a tortoiseshell barrette behind his ear. Weird, but it didn't look bad on him. Foley said, "I imagine you got tired of being taken for Tony."

"You right. Listen," Jimmy said, "back then every guy I know thought he was Tony Montana. Even ones don't look like him want to sound like him. Tony says, 'All I got in this world are my balls and my word. I don't break them for nobody, choo understand?'"

Foley said, "You're him, man, you're Tony," and said, "'Choo know I buried those cock-a-roaches.' How many times you see the picture?"

"I use to say more than twenty times. Maybe I did, I don't know, till we become tired of it. I quit when I ask myself, you serious? Why you want to sound like that punk? He's stupid, don't even know why he fucked up."

Dawn said she'd be pouring margaritas in the kitchen and left them. Little Jimmy watched her go in the house before turning to Foley.

"Talk to me about Cundo, how he's doing."

"He's the same. You'll see him the end of next week."

"Yes? How is his health?"

"I've never heard him complain."

"What is he say about me? I been a good boy?"

"He's proud of you," Foley said, "that's why he looks out for you. You're his boy."

"That's what you think? I'm his *boy*?"

"I didn't say it, he did. Cundo said he let you take over the businesses and you're doing a terrific job."

"He looks out for me—he tole you that? He say he let me run the business? Like he knows any fucking thing about it?"

"If you're running the show," Foley said, "I hope he's paying you enough."

"You know how much he let me have, to live on?"

"No, I don't. But he probably knows you're skimming on him. If he hasn't said anything it must be he expects you're taking a certain cut, so it's okay. I know he respects you," Foley said. "He made sure I understood you're a hundred percent loyal and always do what you're told."

"Listen, the only thing he tole me," Little Jimmy said, "outside of pay his bills, I have to take a blood oath, man, I will never leave him or cheat him or steal his money."

"What kind of blood oath?"

"We make a cut in our hands, here, and press them together. Cundo say now we one, we family, I have to stay loyal to him always."

ROAD DOGS · 115

"What if you don't?"

"He says something will happen to me. I could be run over by a truck."

Or shot in the head, Foley thought, taking Little Jimmy through the house to the kitchen where Dawn was pouring martinis.

"My mind was changed for me," she said. "No tequila, no margaritas. So I made a pitcher of silver bullets, Little Jimmy's favorite cocktail, *and* for my new friend, Jack Foley, my first bank robber."

Little Jimmy said, "You mean your new lover, don't you? He hasn't done it to you by now he's mine," and raised his glass to Foley. *"Salud."*

Foley raised his. He watched Little Jimmy take a sip, smack his lips, slide the rest of the martini down and lower the glass, looking at Foley again.

"Your time with Cundo, you always live together?"

"We were in different housing," Foley said, "but we saw each other just about every day. Took walks around the yard."

"He needed someone and you were there."

"The only time I patted him on the ass," Foley said, "was to get him to jog, run around the yard. He said, 'For what? I weigh one hundred twenty-eight pounds all my fucking life.' " Foley said, "I want you to know Cundo and I were friends inside—"

"And you owe him thirty grand, he tole me you don't have to pay it back."

"More than thirty," Foley said. "But I won't ever tell him how you feel. You know why? I don't blame you."

"Yeah, he tole me to pay your lawyer. You know what else? Twenty-eight hundred to the hacks for favors. His five years at Starke I paid out almost ten grand for gifts. Two hundred dollars to a tailor at Glades. You believe it?"

"That's how it is," Foley said, "you're in the life and you don't pay up front for what you want? You don't get it. Cundo makes money inside selling juice and taking bets on the ball games. He makes it outside watching the real estate market, buying and selling homes," and thought Little Jimmy was having a stroke.

"You believe is his idea, a fucking go-go dancer? You think he knows anything of business, of real estate, different investment opportunities? No, with him is the sports book, the old guys working the phones. Is like he's back in Miami. I tell him on the phone how we doing. I say why don't we cut out being bookies? Stop trying to compete with Vegas and the online casinos, man. I tell him I think we should buy foreign stocks and watch the euro. I say, 'You like that idea?' You know what he say to me, very serious? 'You ever see a snake eat a bat?'"

"He sold blow to movie stars," Foley said. "Give him that."

"You know why they never took him to trial?"

"They didn't want to burn their snitch."

"Tha's what he tole you? No, they not gonna waste their time if all they getting is me. I'm the one making deliveries. I'm in the kitchen rolling joints while he's entertaining movie stars. Choo know something? Listen, they could have put me away, but who the fuck am I? Waste a good snitch on me? They don't have enough to convict Cundo, so they send him to Florida where he can do life or be electrocuted, what they were thinking."

"But he does seven and a half," Foley said, "and he's out next week."

He watched Little Jimmy shake his head.

"Who you think found the girl lawyer? For a flat fifty-k win or lose?"

"Megan Norris," Foley said.

"Tha's the one. Megan, she offers what look like a cool deal, no trial. But I think it was to make sure he does time. She only pretend to like him."

"Hey, I had her too," Foley said. "She gets up in the morning she's out to win." He turned to Dawn and told her about Jimmy's blood oath to stay loyal to Cundo. "I asked him, 'What if you get tired of playing along? You decide to clean out the accounts and take off?' "

Dawn said, "He's afraid Cundo will come after him."

"I'm not afraid he will," Little Jimmy said, "I *know* he will. He tole me."

Foley said, "What do you think he'd do?"

"Kill me. What else you think?"

"Jimmy's sure of it," Dawn said.

"He already kill six guys in his life," Jimmy said. "Wha's another one?"

"Six?" Foley said. "I thought he was only up to four."

"He was at Starke," Jimmy said, "he had two cons done for him. Set afire in their cells, burnt alive, man, they can't do nothing but scream."

"He told you that?"

"Who do you think paid the guys did it? Listen, everything he tole you he did? Was never him, was me."

"When he comes home," Foley said, "set him straight. You're doing all the work—tell him you want a raise."

"I'll talk to him," Dawn said to Jimmy. "If you feel you should be rewarded. You can't *tell* Cundo anything, you put it out there and it becomes his idea."

"He can read a bank statement," Little Jimmy said. "All he wants to know is how much money he's got."

Foley said, "You don't want to start out with the idea he's dumb—" and stopped, not sure if Dawn heard him:

Dawn with Jimmy now, her hand on his arm, Dawn saying, "Jimmy," in her quiet way, "you know Cundo loves you. It's why he expects you to be loyal to him. Think of how long you've been together, as close as brothers."

It stopped Foley. Where was she going with this?

"What I see him doing, Jimmy," Dawn said, "he's giving you the chance to be important in his life, to stay with him no matter what. I think you do owe him that."

Foley said, "You don't think Cundo owes Jimmy?"

Dawn stunned him with a look.

"Didn't I say I'd speak to Cundo? Maybe you weren't listening, Jack."

Man—a quiet, killer tone of voice.

"Why don't you just get him a raise," Foley said, "so he doesn't have to skim? I bet Jimmy knows Cundo better than we ever will, even reading minds."

They'd get into it good once Jimmy left, Foley sure of it.

They killed the pitcher of martinis and he took Jimmy out to the alley. The bodyguard didn't seem surprised to see him weaving, grinning as they put him in the Bentley. Foley asked the bodyguard how he was called.

The guy said, "Zorro."

He was slim, as old as Cundo.

Foley said, "Where's your sword?"

"I'm a different Zorro."

"Is that right?" Foley said. He saw the name came from this guy's narrow face with the look of a fox, the guy standing with his suit coat open, patient. Foley said, "I like Jimmy—I hope you're taking good care of him."

"Yes, of course," Zorro said.

"What do you pack, a Glock?"

"Sometime. Most time a Colt Python."

"That's a big gun."

"It gets respect."

"Jimmy puts you in situations?"

"Mr. Rios is careful, always. He knows to be responsible."

"He gets ripped?"

"I take care of him. He don't do it often, except he's with Dawn, the *bruja*."

"You don't like her."

Zorro shrugged.

"But you respect Jimmy?"

"As long as he don't get sweet on me."

"I don't want anything to happen to him," Foley said. "He's crossing the street and gets run over."

"It won't happen," Zorro said. He took a cigarette from his shirt pocket. "So, you the bank robber, uh?"

Foley returned to the house with a glow-on and a bad feeling about Dawn. He'd ask her in a nice way why she turned soft on Jimmy and listen to her tone of voice: see if it was the one Adele and maybe all women used when they were looking down at you.

Dawn's advantage was her mystical gift she could spring on you, as a psychic and a medium too. She'd convince you she knew things about you from the past and could make up things in your future if she wanted. Put ghosts in your house if you didn't have any and charge you ten grand to get rid of them. Reverend Dawn scamming rich ladies. No, she'd tell you she was entertaining them. They felt the best they'd ever felt in their lives and would insist on paying her.

But disagree with her one time, she stings you without raising her voice.

Maybe you weren't listening, Jack.

What happened to *We've found each other, Jack?*

She was still in the kitchen, turning from the sink as he came in. Foley thinking that if she happened to use that other tone they had, like they're trying to be patient while explaining what she was doing with Little Jimmy—.

She said, "Do you still love me, Jack?"

He didn't see it coming. It stopped him and cleared his mind of accusations. He said, "I didn't understand what you were up to."

"I'm sorry, Jack. You know what I was afraid of? I thought, What if we got Jimmy too worked up, telling him he's the good guy and stupid Cundo doesn't know what he's doing. Jimmy could decide all of a sudden to clean out the accounts—you even suggested it—and make a run for it. If he did, where would that leave us?"

Foley said, "You're selling Cundo short."

"You're right," Dawn said, "he isn't stupid about pulling jobs. You mind my using that expression? I love it. We're gonna pull a job." She smiled but said right away, serious now, "Don't get me wrong, I'm not in this for thrills and chills, a new kind of adventure in my life." She said, "I've been thinking about this for a long long time," and smiled again. "Are you with me, Jack?"

Foley didn't answer. He'd been thinking she was with *him*.

"We started talking," Dawn said, "I couldn't believe it. You're the perfect guy for this, the dedicated pro."

It sounded better, but dedicated to what, going to jail?

"I hope you understand I see you in charge," Dawn said. "Whatever you say goes."

"Since you've never pulled a job?"

"Jack, don't make fun of me, all right?"

"I will if you stop reading my mind." Now Foley smiled, back in the game, feeling better about his partner. He said, "Jimmy's not ready yet, he has to work up his nerve. He skims and nothing happens, he thinks it's okay. But to go for broke, grab whatever he can put his hands on, now Little Jimmy's an outlaw, right up there with John Dillinger. He'll think about it until he sees there's no getting around it, he's gonna need help."

Dawn said, "You think so?"

"If he doesn't see it," Foley said, "I'll point it out to him."

Eleven

Foley came down from the roof, the glasses hanging from his neck, saw Dawn still in bed as the phone rang and saw her eyes open. Foley picked up the phone from the nightstand looking down at her eyes watching him now. He said hello and said yes, he'd accept the charge, waited and said, "Cundo, how you doing? You all right?" He listened and said, "Today? No, I haven't seen her . . . No, not since she came over and introduced herself," Foley staring at Dawn, telling Cundo, "No, we haven't switched yet, she wasn't ready to move, still getting her stuff together. I called her yesterday, see how she's doing. She said fine, she was painting." Foley listened and said, "How do I know, I'm telling you what she told me. She did the painting in the room here," Foley watching Dawn making a face now,

Me? "Yeah, I guess. I didn't ask her." He listened and said, "You mean in the painting? She has on a bathing suit, a two-piece." Listening now he looked away from her as he said, "I imagine she went to the store, maybe she needs eggs, I don't know." Foley listened and said, "How would I know? I said maybe . . . What I should've said . . . Cundo, listen to me. What I meant to say, if she isn't home, she probably went to the store. Isn't that what you'd think? Wait and try her again." He looked down at Dawn giving him a soft look, touching her lips with the tip of her tongue. "No, I only saw her the one time . . . yeah, right, and spoke to her on the phone." He listened and said, "I'm makin' it. I take walks, I eat out mostly." He watched Dawn slip the sheet down to uncover her left breast and mouth the words *Who am I?* Foley saying to Cundo, "I knew you were gonna ask me that. I can't think of the name of the place . . . No, but it's on Abbot Kinney. Listen, Cundo, why don't you call her in a while, give her time to do her shopping." Foley listened and said, "Just a second," and pressed the phone against his side so he could tell Dawn, "Go home, quick. He's gonna call you when he hangs up."

"You told him to wait, didn't you?"

"He called here first, didn't get an answer and tried you at the other house, almost an hour ago," Foley watching her throw off the sheet and run naked out of the bedroom. He walked to the front casement windows and waited to see how she would come out. He raised the phone, said, "Cundo? Gimme a minute, my man," and pressed the phone to his side.

She wasn't naked but close to it, Dawn streaking out of the house in his sixty-nine-dollar drip-dry sport coat hanging limp on her but looking good the way her bare legs moved in the sunlight, Dawn running down the walk lined with shrubs and plants, palm trees, all the way to the footbridge that humped over the canal. She stopped and was talking to somebody Foley couldn't make out, plants and trees hiding him, a guy. Foley raised the glasses hanging against his chest, and saw Dawn step up on the bridge and glance back as she started across. Now the guy stepped up on the bridge and stood watching her.

Tico, wearing his lavender do-rag.

Foley let the field glasses hang and raised the phone.

"Cundo, there's somebody out by the gate. I can see him but don't know who it is, he rang the bell . . . I don't know. That's what I want to find out." He saw Dawn on the other side of the canal now, coming back in this direction, and he raised the glasses to see her running toward Cundo's pink home, Dawn letting the front of his sixty-nine-dollar drip-dry sport coat flap open, barefoot, Foley thinking, *She runs like a girl.* He said to Cundo, "Give the hack ten and call me after-while, you still want to talk. I'll be here . . . I know, it can add up. You lucky you're rich. Listen, Cundo? I'm gonna hang up. I got to take a leak right now, okay? I'll see you when you get here. We'll have a homecoming party for you, I'll get Dawn to make a cake . . . Cundo, I'm kidding, we'll have margaritas in your honor, okay? I'll talk to you later," Foley said, Jesus, and pressed the phone off.

He saw Tico coming off the bridge to the walk, coming this way.

It was weird, seeing Dawn in his mind running like a girl:

While he flew down the outside stairs to the patio and through the gate to the walk:

And saw Karen Sisco now, in the bar on top the hotel in Detroit. Saw her alone at the table. Saw her in the elevator looking up at the descending numbers flashing on, Karen saying, "Hurry up, will you? I'm about to wet my pants." And saw her run down the hall to the room, Foley saying as he reached her, "You run like a guy," and watched her pull the card from the slot in the door and turn her head to him saying, "Wait till you see what I do as a girl."

It was the first time he'd thought of Karen since Dawn walked in the house.

Foley had maybe ten seconds before Tico would reach him. He turned to the gate, his back to the canal, timed it and came around as Tico started past him, gave the homey in the lavender headdress a shoulder that sent him through the hedge and down the bank, arms reaching out for Foley, to land in the canal on his back, thrashed around getting his feet under him and rose to stand in water that barely came to his waist.

Foley stepped through the low hedge to watch Tico pull off his do-rag, wring it out and wipe his face with it, looking up at Foley.

"I'd like to ask you about Costa Rica," Foley said, "all right? I'm interested in the job market—I should say I'm more curious than interested. Who wants to work if you don't have to. I want to find out how much property costs if you want to build, and I've got some geography questions. Do you worry about volcanoes erupting? I understand you have an active volcano that attracts tourists? I'd also like to know, hear it from a native, which beaches are the most popular. I'd guess the Pacific side. It looks like there's more activity along there."

Tico, standing in the water, said, "You think I come from there?"

Foley said, "You're a Tico, aren't you? I understand there can be a problem you buy land, go to build a house on it, a squatter's living there with his family, growing corn."

"A *precaista*," Tico said, "what they call them. You find one on your land you get a lawyer. But tha's in the country, the one squatting is always a farmer." He said, "There lot of gringos living in Costa Rica, man. Live on a beach, live up in the mountains if you want. You like to go there?"

"I'm thinking about it. Move there when I retire."

"When you stop robbing banks?"

This kid letting Foley know he was cool.

Foley said, "How much time have you done?"

"Three years, all of it."

"Got busted for being a tough kid?"

"For a homicide they didn't care about reduced to manslaughter. I didn't care for it either, the 'slaughter' part. I didn't cut the man up, I shot him in the head."

"After you robbed him?"

"The man dissed me."

"Listen," Foley said, "now that we know each other, why don't you come up? We'll have a drink and talk about Lou Adams."

Tico looked at the growth covering the bank to see where he would step. He raised his hand for Foley to help him. Foley told him he could make it on his own.

"Tell me why you push me in?"

"I knew you'd ask me that," Foley said. "I don't have a good reason, but felt I should, you working for that tin horn. I'm talking about Lou Adams."

"Is all right," Tico said, "I see what you mean."

Foley told himself, You guessed right, but you know you can't trust this dude, no matter how he comes off. He's a bullshitter. Sit him down in his wet shirt stuck to him—maybe get him a towel. No, you don't get him anything. Foley did step to the edge and stick his hand out for the guy to take, asking what he wanted to drink.

Tico said he didn't care.

He wanted to see what the bank robber would offer him, certain it would be American beer. No, he put a square bottle of whiskey on the patio table, Jack Daniel's and a dish of ice cubes, the bank robber saying they'd have some Old Number Seven if Tico didn't think it was too early in the day. Tico didn't know what he was talking about, then he saw OLD NO. 7 on the label. He watched the bank robber pour drinks in low glasses saying, "Tell me about Lou Adams. Is he crazy?"

Tico said, "A little, yes." He took a drink of the sour mash and then another one and watched the bank robber reach over with the bottle to refill the glass.

"He's betting I rob a bank in thirty days of getting out. My ex-wife told me. I asked her if she bet him. You know what she said, 'I couldn't.' I said, 'I thought you loved me.' You know Cundo Rey, the guy owns this house?"

"I hear of him. He still inside, uh?"

"Till next week. He says I'm gonna rob another bank since it's the only thing I know how to do."

Tico believed he could talk to this bank robber. "Lou Adams said he catches you in the next thirty days he retires."

"You see him, tell him I'll take the bet. Thirty days from right now, a hundred bucks. He wants to talk about it he can come see me."

Foley took a drink and lighted a cigarette. Tico's pack, wet through, was on the table. Foley pushed his pack toward him. Tico picked it up. Now he was reading the label to Foley. "Virginia Slims, Light, Menthol? This what you smoke?"

"What's wrong with Slims?" Foley said.

"I think is funny is all."

"They're Dawn's. I noticed you talking to her on the bridge. You know where she was going?"

"To her house, wearing some guy's coat was too big for her," Tico said, watching Foley to see what he'd say.

"You know her before Lou Adams got hold of you?"

"I know her maybe a month. I heard of her and we met one time she's walking by the Venice Pier. Yes, I see her, we talk."

"She tell your fortune?"

"She hold my hand and tell me things about myself, what I like to do. Who I use to be . . ."

Foley said, "What if I get in the car, I don't go to that bank over on the circle, I drive off."

Tico said, "Yes . . .?" surprised the bank robber didn't want to know more about Dawn Navarro. "I see you get in the car—you must mean the VW—I call Lou Adams."

"What if nobody sees me?"

"We all over the place, my Young Boys United, like Venice Boulevard and Dell Avenue, where you come out from the canals if you driving. What I like to know," Tico said, "why is he want you so bad?"

"He'll tell you," Foley said, "it's his job to bring me in. But this has to cost him, you and your little helpers? He can't be paying you on what he makes."

"I don't help him, I get deported."

"That's it?"

"You don't believe me?"

"He's giving you something besides free time," Foley said, "or you'd walk away. If Lou can't pay he's leaving a door open someplace. Maybe this house. But you can't bust in till he puts me away. It's some kind of deal like that? He wants me, he doesn't give a shit what you want."

"You think you know me," Tico said, "what I'm willing to do?"

"For money?" Foley said. "I've only met a thousand guys like you in stir. All you want to know is where's the hustle and what's the take."

"You saying Lou Adams can't pay me," Tico said, "so he lets me, what, come in here and loot this place when he's done with you?" Tico took a drink, having a good time with the bank robber, no problem. He said, "What about your boss, Cundo Rey, you mention. What kind of deal you have with him?"

"You think I work for him?"

"Lou Adams say Cundo pays your way, pays for everything, even your lawyer a lot of money. So he say you in Cundo Rey's debt, you have to do what he tells you."

Foley said, "You believe it?"

Tico said, "I think a guy who robs two hundred banks don't need to work for nobody he don't want to. Can you tell me how many you rob?"

"A hundred and twenty-seven," Foley said.

"Some more than once?"

"A few. One of them a bank in L.A., I didn't realize I'd been there before till I was at the window and I recognized the teller, this good-looking black girl, her name in a thing on the counter. I could tell she knew who I was. I said, 'Monique, I only want change for a twenty, all right?'"

"Tha's what you said?"

"In a soft voice. 'Monique . . .?'"

"She say anything?"

"No, she starts laying it out, hundreds, fifties, all in bank straps, not looking at me, watching what she's doing. I'm thinking she either didn't understand what I said, or she pressed the alarm and she's showing the money to keep me there."

"You took it?"

"I felt I had to. The bank straps made it easy to pick up and slip in my pockets, my shirt. I said, 'Thank you, Monique, for the change.'"

"She think that was funny?"

"She didn't look up. I patted her hand."

"Give her a thrill."

"I got to the front entrance and looked back. Now she's watching me. She looked calm, didn't scream or go nuts. For a moment there, you know what I thought she might do? Wave. But she didn't. I got out of there with fifty-two-fifty. Thank you, Monique. But did I steal it, or was it a gift? Something I'll never know."

"Man, tha's cool. So is robbing one hundred and twenty-seven banks," Tico said. "I bow to you. You know how many banks I rob in my entire life so far? Three, tha's all."

"Do any more," Foley said, "it begins to get tiresome."

"Yes, you get tired doing it?"

"Bored. But you still keep your eyes open."

Now he was talking about Costa Rica, saying, "You know how many Americans would move there tomorrow if they could? At least a million. What do you do, you leave the promised land and come here."

"San José is no L.A., man. You leave when you can."

"You doing all right?"

"Now and then. You know how it is."

"I'll trade you," Foley said. "I've been reading up on Costa Rica. They don't have revolutions anymore, they don't even have an army. It's the Switzerland of Central America."

"Yes, is nice," Tico said, "if you have money. You make enough to live high there, sure, have a big home with servants waiting on you. You going there, uh, soon as you become rich?"

It got the bank robber smiling a little, smoking his Light Menthol Virginia Slim.

"But if you not robbing banks no more, you think is so boring, where you get the money?"

He watched the bank robber shrug, watched him pick up his glass and take a drink.

"You're having a good time poking around," Foley said, "trying to find out what I'm up to, aren't you?"

"I enjoy to talk to you," Tico said, "one bank robber to another, uh?" and waited for Jack Foley to see he was being funny.

He did, but smiled only a moment.

"We're now and then in the same life," Foley said. "That's all I can tell you."

"Tha's right, we go to prison, we come out. Okay, now what do we do? Check around to see what looks good, what kind of hustle we can work. Maybe something your friend Cundo Rey has in his mind."

"I just got here," Foley said, "and I've known you what, a half hour?"

Tico said, "Yes . . .?"

"That's not long enough," Foley said, "for me to be telling you my business. All I know about you so far, Tico, you're a bullshitter. You do it pretty well, but you're still a bullshitter. You've never robbed a bank in your life, have you?"

"Man, I want to," Tico said, looking earnest, his eyes innocent. "Don't that count for something?"

"Not to me," Foley said. "Talking the talk doesn't inspire any confidence, nothing I hear I can count on. But," Foley said, "it sounds like you're a pretty good friend of Dawn Navarro's."

"I can say we very good friends."

"I hear Dawn saying nice things about you," Foley said, "that makes you worth talking to."

Foley nodded toward the canal.

Tico looked that way and saw her on the other side, Dawn walking past the line of low hedges toward the footbridge, Dawn wearing a shirt and jeans now, the limp coat over her arm. Tico said, "Oh, now you gonna check on me, uh? Ask her if we friends, if I was ever intimate with her? No, I wasn't."

Foley said, "Try to stay calm, Tico."

Twelve

They watched Dawn come through the gate saying, "You're starting early, aren't you? I have to have my coffee first."

Foley said, "Did he call you?"

"I've been talking to him all this time, telling him where I've been."

"He was worried about you."

"Now I have to find a straw beach hat, a big one, and stop by Ralphs, pick up whatever I told him I had to get."

"He ask you if you're being a saint?"

"Not today. Let me get a cup," Dawn said. "I'm regressing Tico, finding out who he was in a much earlier life. My spirit guide put me in touch with a spirit"— Dawn looking at Tico now—"who knew you sixteen hundred years ago, if you can imagine that. I'll be right back."

"You hear her?" Tico said. "Is no bullshit. Dawn is been trying to find out who I was in another life, she say now was sixteen hundred years ago, man."

"How does she know where to look?"

"She has her spirit guide help her. Didn't she ever look at your past life for you?"

"She couldn't find anything prior to '63," Foley said. "At first she thought I might've been Jack Kennedy— I've had a bad back off and on—but she couldn't tell if I was ever president of the United States."

"Yes, but maybe you were?"

"It's possible," Foley said.

"She say I was of the Maya race in Guatemala," Tico said. "I tole her I come from Costa Rica. She say is close enough. She didn't know what I was called, so she couldn't find out what I was doing there"—Tico looking anxious—"but now I believe she found out."

They waited, smoking Slims and sipping whiskey. Dawn returned with a cup of coffee and sat down with them at the patio table. She said, "Oh, would you like one of my Slims?" in her innocent way. Tico said he already had one. If he didn't know she was putting him on, he didn't know her, Foley thought. They still could've got naked together—or why bother to deny it? Now she was telling Tico, "It seems you appear in the early part of the Maya classic period, about the year 400. You're the son of a god-king, the one and only Fire Is Born. Really, that's his name, Fire Is Born. Your name, Tico, was Spear-thrower Jaguar. You were a famous warrior."

Tico said, "Spear-thrower Jaguar," nodding his head.

"Your girlfriend," Dawn said, "is taken up to the top of the temple to be sacrificed as a gift to the gods, who will freak when they see her, she's a beauty. But," Dawn said, "you can save her life if you're willing to take her place, have your heart cut out instead of hers."

Foley said, "What's the girl's name?"

The way Dawn hesitated he knew she was taking a few moments to think of one.

Foley said, "How about Spear-chucker's Honey?"

Dawn stared at him with a straight face getting her act back together. She said, "You know who the spirit is I was put in touch with? Spear-thrower Jaguar's girlfriend herself. Everyone on the other side calls her Heart, short for Heartless Virgin, because of, you know, what happened to her. She passed over and loves being a spirit guide. Tico, she said you turned chicken, even though the chance you'd be sacrificed was next to zero. You're the son of Fire Is Born, you're popular, brave, you're a good-looking guy, especially in your head-dress, with all the feathers and ornaments. Heart said the headdresses were quite heavy and resulted in neck

ailments. But you wouldn't risk it, you let Heart be sacrificed. Aren't you sorry, Tico, you didn't step up?"

"You telling me," Tico said, "she's my girlfriend but
she's still a virgin? How long am I going with her, a
day or two? I don't see I know her well enough to, you
know, offer my life."

"You're saying you wouldn't try to save her?"

"I don't even know her. Maybe if I see her again."

"According to Heart," Dawn said, "when you didn't
do the right thing, it got our Higher Power pissed
enough to make you, in your next several reincarna-
tions, bugs. That's why I had trouble locating you in a
previous existence."

Foley said, "Did she say what kind of bug he was?"

"No, she didn't," Dawn said, refusing to look at him.
"She did say Tico, when he passed over, would come
back as another insect unless he redeems himself."

"How's he do that?"

"The usual way." Dawn said to Tico now, "You have
to risk your life to save someone from certain death."

Tico said, "I do?"

"You'll know it when it happens," Dawn said. "It's
your only chance to get a better life from now on."

Tico said, "Man, I don't know."

"Go home and think about it," Dawn said. "Do you
want to be a bug all your lives?"

"Getting swatted," Foley said, "and stepped on?"

Tico looked confused saying he wasn't sure what to think about. Dawn told him the secret was to empty his mind, keep a channel open by trying *not* to think, and there was a good chance the spirit guide would contact him.

Foley said, "Maybe your old girlfriend, the Heartless Virgin."

After Tico had left Foley said, "If he wasn't aware of being a bug until you told him, what difference does it make if he was?"

"I got carried away," Dawn said.

"I thought you were setting him up."

"For what?"

"I don't know—to use him?"

"You knew I was making it up," Dawn said, "most of it," turning her eyes on him. "You want to take a shower?"

Once they were in there soaping each other up, Foley said, "Don't forget, you have to put a bathing suit on you in the painting."

Dawn said they should get Little Jimmy to do it. "He finished and took his paints with him."

Foley said or they could buy a tube of paint and dab some on her here, and here . . . and here. What color did she like?

Dawn said, "Mmmmm, black?" and slipped her clean shining arms around his neck. She kissed his mouth and said she wasn't sure about the color, he should ask Jimmy. She said, "You ready?" Then had to ask him, "Jack, why're you wearing shoes in the shower?"

They were lying across the bed now on their towels.

Dawn said, "I almost told you about Cundo, what he said on the phone, but decided not to ruin our shower. They're releasing him a week early. He'll be here Friday, the day after tomorrow."

Foley said, "Why didn't he tell me? I spoke to him—I did everything I could to get rid of him. I put him on hold to watch you come out of the house in my sixty-nine-dollar drip-dry sport coat. Why didn't he tell me he's getting out early?"

"You're a little ripped, aren't you?"

"I was."

"Jack, we've only got forty-eight hours to act crazy, maybe try something new, like I'm on top."

"There's a reason he didn't let me know."

"He wanted to tell me first," Dawn said. "He likes you, Jack, but doesn't go to bed with you. The way to look at it, the sooner he gets here, the sooner we pull the job and leave."

The job.

Foley closed his eyes.

The sooner we pull the job. After we find out what the job is and how we go about pulling it. We're not going in a bank. Not we. You. Keep it simple. Do you know where this is going? What you're getting into? Who's who? If you don't know that you don't know anything. *The sooner we pull the job.* Why isn't she biting her nails? What does she have going with Tico the spear-chucker? Why didn't Cundo tell you he's getting out early? Why wasn't he excited, wanting you to know about it, his old buddy? Why was it the other day, you and Dawn finding each other, talking about the job, you didn't see a problem? Didn't get down and look at what you'd have to do. It left Foley with the feeling, *What you see isn't what you think it is.*

He opened his eyes.

Dawn was lighting a cigarette.

"Are we picking him up at the airport?"

"He said a friend at Glades is arranging for a guy in L.A. to meet the flight and bring him here."

"He doesn't have a friend at Glades."

"Well, someone is saving us the trouble."

She placed her cigarette between his lips and watched him draw and let the smoke drift out of his mouth.

She said, "You want to rest a little more . . .?"

Thirteen

Foley called Little Jimmy about the painting that needed to be fixed before Cundo arrived, walked in the bedroom and saw Dawn on the wall bare naked. "It's where I've been sleeping," Foley said, "since I got here."

Little Jimmy said there was time. Didn't they have a week or so?

"He'll be here tomorrow," Foley said. "They're letting him out early."

It caused an alarm to go off in Jimmy, wanting to know, Jesus Christ, why nobody told him.

"What'll it take you," Foley said, "three minutes. That gives you a minute a dab. Or, you decide to paint a one-piece suit on her I think you'll have time."

Little Jimmy told Foley to fuck the bathing suit—why didn't somebody tell him Cundo, Christ, was almost here?

"I'd like to come over and see you," Foley said. "You can show me your office, what you do."

Ten years ago Cundo told Jimmy to buy the three-story building on Windward, a block from the beach, and fix it up. Before this the property had been a youth hostel. Jimmy had walls removed and rearranged and now his offices took up the second floor and his apartment was directly above: a big one he did with an art deco look, lots of color and round corners. There were also rooms on the third floor for Zorro, who lived here and was always close if Jimmy needed him. The street floor was occupied by Danny's Venice, a café with smart red-and-white-striped awnings in front, where Jimmy had his lunch every day.

Foley went up the stairs to find Little Jimmy waiting for him, Jimmy in his realm, his life here. He brought Foley into his office done in a pale gray for business, no distracting colors. Even the photographs on two of the walls were black-and-white shots of Venice Beach: tourists crowding the walk, street performers, the drummers' circle, homeboys hanging out, while the wall behind Jimmy's marble desk was bare, with nail holes showing.

"Dawn used to hang there," Foley said, "looking over your shoulder?"

Little Jimmy sat in his black velvet throne in shirt-sleeves, black stones in the French cuffs. He said, "She's gone from my life. I have nothing to do with her now he's coming. You understand? I see she's paid every month, tha's all. Take that painting of her and destroy it."

"He knows about it."

"You *tole* him?"

"I said she's wearing a swimsuit."

"Jesus Christ—man, I don't have no paint here. I have to get some, come by the house later."

"She wants to look modest," Foley said, "if that's possible."

Jimmy got up from his chair but didn't seem to know where he wanted to go, got to the end of his marble-slab desk, nothing on it, and stopped. "Cundo call me yesterday morning, I'm still in bed sleeping. He say, 'I hear your car was stole.' I ask him what he's talking about. It's in back, where Zorro keeps an eye on it. He say, 'Oh, is that right? Take a look.' I go down-stairs, my fucking car is gone. Stole while I'm sleeping, the Bentley, man. Zorro shakes his head no, he don't hear a sound. I talk to Cundo again. He say he can get the car back but it will cost me two hundred thousand. He say, 'From your account, not from Rios and Rey Investment Company or the sports book.' Or the account I pay guys out of for things he wants, like guards at the prison."

"Letting you know," Foley said, "your skimming days are over."

"I tole him I don't have no two hundred-k to give him. He say okay, then I don't get no more pay for a year."

"Giving you a break," Foley said, " 'cause he needs you."

"He say I do it again he has to get another book-keeper. Jesus Christ, like all I do is accounting for the real estate and the investing, the number accounts we keep. He don't know how to do any of that."

"I tried to tell you," Foley said, "Cundo isn't dumb. He can't add figures, but always knows what the balance is. How long you been skimming on him?"

"Now and then only, not much."

"This time you dipped too deep and somebody told on you."

Foley sat down and lighted a cigarette and Jimmy got an ashtray from a drawer in the marble desk.

"Was there a big *Z*," Foley said, "cut in the wall in back?"

"What're you talking about?"

"I wondered if it might've been Zorro boosted your car."

"You think is a joke—man, I could get whacked."

"I see two ways you can look at your situation," Foley said. "Cundo's fond of you, Jimmy, he's brought you along through good times and piss-poor ones, hasn't he?"

"He would get upset," Jimmy said, "and lose his temper—this was during the time of the drug business—and would let me use my way to soothe him and he would become calm. At Combinado del Este and when we first came to La Yuma, he would let me soothe his nerves."

"Well, now he's got Dawn," Foley said, "to do the soothing while you keep working your tail off for him, scared to death of his wrath. He gets the idea you're skimming on him again—"

"I promise him I won't."

"Or thinks you're fucking him some other way—"

"He'd have me whacked."

"He's too fond of you," Foley said. "He wouldn't kill you, Jimmy, he'd slam a car door on your fingers. The left one, so you can still work the calculator."

"Jesus Christ—"

"Or break your legs with a José Canseco bat. He won't admit it, but he knows he needs you. You can stick around and put up with his arrogance if you don't mind being his slave." Foley said, "Jimmy, there's another way to look at it. Make out a check to 'cash' from every account you can, and deposit the checks in a bank in Costa Rica. I'll give you the name of the bank in San José, the capital, and show you how to send the money by wire. Or, you could send it in care of my account and I'll hold it for you. I get down there I'm moving to a spot on the Pacific side I've picked out."

Jimmy said, "I know how to wire money."

"What account did you skim the Bentley out of?"

"One for guys Cundo tells me to pay. I transfer money to it from other accounts." Jimmy moved to his throne behind the desk but didn't sit down. "You said when we drinking, I become tired of how he treats me, I could clean out the accounts and take off. You remember?"

"What I meant," Foley said, "if you ever felt like taking what you have coming and make a run for it, I wouldn't blame you."

"How much money you thinking?"

"I won't tell you how I reached this figure," Foley said, having taken it out of the air, "but I'm thinking you can write checks for upward of two and a half million."

"You way off," Little Jimmy said. He closed his eyes for a few moments, opened them and said, "Out of four accounts I can draw six hundred-k. Maybe six and a half."

Foley said, "That's it? With all the ways you have of making money?"

"You ask me what I can write checks on."

"No savings accounts?"

"I'm counting one we have," Jimmy said. "Listen, I already been to prison. I won't do nothing is illegal and go back inside again."

"I would never ask you to," Foley said. "How about a way that's legal but might take some setting up?"

"Cundo finds out," Jimmy said, "he don't kill me, no. You said he break my legs with a baseball bat."

"A Louisville Slugger," Foley said. Shit. He stubbed out his cigarette and got up.

"You're gonna come by, fix the painting?"

"After work."

Foley looked at Jimmy, his hand on the high back of his chair. "You own the houses free and clear. He told me that more'n once, saying how much he trusts you."

"Now you want me to sell his fucking homes and they evict Cundo? Throw him out in the street?"

"It would be in the canal. No, you don't sell the houses," Foley said, "you finance 'em for loans, get a few mil to play with."

"You crazy," Jimmy said. He sat down in his chair, put his crocodile loafers on the desk, then brought his legs down and leaned on the desk to say to Foley going to the door:

"Where would I keep the money so he don't know? Do I make payments on the loans or what?"

Foley said, "You'll figure out how to do it," and walked out.

Fourteen

They swapped homes in the early afternoon, Foley moving his clothes slung in a blanket from the white house to the pink one, then went back and forth over the footbridge five times with Dawn's, a wardrobe of styles from buttoned-up to bimbo. He laid an armload of dressy dresses in plastic covers across the bed. Dawn came from the bathroom in her white-and-rose kimono hanging open.

"Is that it?"

"Everything."

"You know tonight will be our last time," Dawn said. "And you were just getting good."

"What time's he arrive tomorrow?"

Dawn looked at her watch. "About right now, on Northwest three-ten from Miami." She said, "Well, since we're not doing anything, you want to do it? Or wait till tonight." Dawn smiled. "Will you get mad if I tell you what you're thinking?"

"No, go ahead."

"You're wondering, Why not both?"

He was and he wasn't. He was thinking about Little Jimmy all dressed up in his semibare office, the black-and-white Venice photographs, nothing on his marble desk but a laptop with the lid closed. Jimmy sitting by himself thinking. He had to be thinking. How could he break free of Cundo if making the move scared him to death? The little guy needed encouragement, a pep talk.

At one point during his visit Foley said, "How can you deal in a lot of money, millions, and you don't have even a scratch pad on your desk?"

Jimmy said, "I have a kid in the next office with three screens. He gets real-time numbers from the stock exchanges, New York, Tokyo, the ones that interest me. He's got bar graphs, charts, spreadsheets . . . He's twenty years old. What do you want to know? Ask Gregory."

"Do you want to or not?" Dawn said and looked at her watch. "It's half past two. Come on, if we're going to do it"—Dawn clearing the bed of her clothes—"let's get going."

"We make it a quickie?"

"Whatever your desire permits, Jack."

Cundo arrived in a Dodge pickup at ten minutes of four, a day earlier than Foley was expecting him. The idea, walk in the house after eight years and find Dawn busy with her laundry or watering plants, maybe sitting down with a cup of tea, reading. Or, he could catch her fucking Jack Foley.

The guy driving the pickup, Mike Nesi—a big guy six-four, two-forty—believed in white supremacy but would act as Cundo's bodyguard for five bills a day. At the airport Cundo brought out five hundred-dollar bills, handed Nesi three of them and put two back in his pocket. "The rest you get I see you do your job."

Mike Nesi stared at the little Cuban. He said, "Long as you got it." The sleeves of Mike Nesi's black T-shirt were cut off to show his tattoos, a crucifix on one shoulder, Jesus bleeding down his bicep, a swastika covering the other. On the short trip from the airport to Venice, the truck's dual pipes rumbling when they slowed down, Nesi said, "That's my three-forty-five Hemi clearing its throat."

Cundo said, "I had a Trans Am sound like that. Black with black windows. You couldn't read signs for shit, but I love that ride. Had a mean growl in idle.

Gas it she howled and pressed you back in the fucking seat."

"When was this?" Nesi said. "In olden times?"

Cundo looked at Nesi, his shaved head, his beard shadow like dirt, the blue and red crucifix from his shoulder to his elbow.

"When I came from Cooba," Cundo said, "and began to make my fortune so I can hire guys like you to take me where I want to go . . ."

Nesi glanced at him. "I thought I was to watch some dink. Rough him up if you want me to."

"Keep him in one place so he don't move."

"This is the bank robber?"

"The one I jail with almost three years. Foley, he's a good guy. He don't like to mix it up, get his hands dirty, so you won't have no trouble with him."

"I've heard of Foley."

"Robbed as many as two hundred banks. He's a professional, he shaves every day, but not his head. He keeps himself clean, he would never in his life have a fucking sacrilegious tattoo on his body."

Mike Nesi looked over at him. "You don't want your eyes swole shut, watch how you talk to me."

"You want my respect," Cundo said to this ignorant piece of shit, "or five bills a day? I don't have to give you both."

"Man, first day out the door you come on frisky, don't you? By the time it wears off, you better've settled down."

"Do what I tell you we get along."

"While I'm watching Foley, the fuck are you doing?"

"You find out," Cundo said.

Foley was in the kitchen having a beer, barefoot in his Levi's, no shirt on.

Dawn was upstairs in the shower.

He tilted the bottle up, took a swig of Dos Equis, and there was Cundo crossing the bricked yard from the garage, Cundo looking at upstairs windows; the guy behind him, a redneck Nazi with big arms hanging free, was looking past Cundo at the open doorway. Foley stepped into it.

"What're you doing home? You're not supposed to be here till tomorrow . . ." Went through all that, Cundo reaching up to hug him, Foley looking at the Aryan Nazi Brotherhood guy staring at him.

"Where is my dream girl?"

Foley said, "Who, Dawn?" kidding with Cundo the way he used to. Foley said, "She must be upstairs." He said, "We didn't swap houses till today. She's probably putting her things away, straightening up . . ."

And thought of the painting.

Cundo was moving around him now, into the kitchen. Foley said, "Wait," and Cundo stopped and looked back at him.

"Is it all right you stay here while I go see my wife I haven't seen in eight fucking years and we talk later?" Cundo walked through the kitchen and down the hall to the stairway.

It was in Foley's mind not to make anything out of the painting. Admit he saw it, yeah, since he'd already told Cundo that on the phone. He told himself to forget about it and turned to the redneck.

"I'm Jack Foley."

Mike Nesi said, "I know who you are. I had a buddy was up at Lompoc the same time as you. He kept saying how he liked talking to you. I said, 'What about?' He said, 'Robbing banks, the hell you think?' He said you were pretty good shooting hoops. I said I bet he wouldn't swish any I was guarding him. I took up basketball the time I was at Huntsville, down in Texas."

"The guy at Lompoc," Foley said, "was that Johnny Evans?"

"The same," Mike Nesi said. "Uptown Johnny—or was he Downtown Johnny? Yeah, he grew his hair out and got work in the music world. His first job, playing tenor sax behind poetry readings at a bookstore. You ever see that?"

"I don't recall," Foley said, "but I doubt it. You know he wanted to start a rock band at Lompoc, but your Brotherhood hard-ons wouldn't let him. They'd only allow him to play if it was Nazi death metal."

"Yeah, he got out, grew his hair, he's playing with the Howling Diablos now in De-troit. I saw Kid Rock with the band one time, was before he gained international fame with 'Devil Without a Cause.' Now he's got another hit, 'Rock N Roll Jesus.' You heard it?"

"I doubt it."

"The Diablos are still playing those grunge joints in the Motor City. You listen to 'em kick out their fuckin' jams you want to be on reefer or E. Or that other one, Salvia. Chew it or smoke it, it rounds off your edges. 'Less you start laughing and can't stop. That's the only trouble with it I know of."

"What're you doing with the little Cuban?"

"Watching you."

"In case I what?"

"I don't know you have to do anything."

"He surprised us, a day early."

"He's known he's getting out today. He wanted to sneak up and surprise you. He did too, didn't he?"

He looked past Foley.

"Here he comes, bringing his wife along."

By the arm.

Dawn in her white-and-rose kimono, holding it together. Foley had turned in the doorway. He started toward them and Cundo, across the kitchen, held up his free hand to hold Foley there with his beer bottle, Cundo's other hand in a fold of sleeve gripping Dawn's arm, Cundo standing almost shoulder to shoulder with her, nothing in Dawn's eyes staring at Foley.

"You saw the painting," Foley said.

"*I* saw it, *you* saw it," Cundo said, "every time you went to bed. You tole me she's wearing a bathing suit."

"I didn't know what you'd think—"

"If you tole the truth? I would think you looking at my naked wife whenever you come in the room. I say to Dawn, 'You never tole me of this painting.' She say she want to surprise me. I say, 'Oh, but you leave it here to tempt my friend Jack Foley? Show him your pussy so he gets the idea?' She say, 'Oh, no, I just hung the painting in there today to surprise you.' Yes, but Jack Foley knows the painting very well, he's been sleeping by it."

Foley said, "I'm not gonna tell you I haven't admired it, as a painting."

"You think is good, uh? Very real-looking. What do you like best, Jack, the breasts or the pussy? No, tell me instead who painted her naked like this?"

"Little Jimmy," Dawn said, "so you don't have to worry."

Cundo took a half step away from Dawn to look at her. "You right, the Monk don't worry me. You show yourself to my friend, it don't worry me either. It disappoints me, you thinking if you show yourself you can make him love you." Cundo looking at Foley now, said, "I ask her is she being a saint for me. She say, 'Oh, yes, for you always.' But she hangs her naked picture next to the bed where my friend is sleeping."

"It wasn't like that," Foley said. "I never thought of it that way."

"I don't worry about you," Cundo said, "we good friends, Jack. I know you would cut off your dick with a butcher knife before you ever dishonor me, commit the adultery with my wife."

Foley stood rigid. He could feel Mike Nesi close behind breathing on him, the redneck Nazi saying, "You move, I'll put you down."

Foley said, "Cundo—"

"You going to tell me is my own fault," Cundo said. "I make her wait so long by herself, a good-looking guy comes along . . . Okay, I take some of the blame.

But she lie to me, Jack. I see she can't still be a saint when she makes a promise. Man, what am I suppose to do?" Cundo said, "Remember at Glades, Jack, there was a homeboy sold joints for me, machine-rolled, man, perfect, one joint for a pack of king-size cigarettes. Only instead of the cigarettes the homey is getting the dust knocked off his joint. I say to him, 'You getting a blow job, the fuck am I getting?' Here he is smoking my ganj he suppose to be selling. I tell him, 'Homes, you owe me some packs of smokes.' He say yeah, okay, don't worry about it. Oh, I don't have to worry? Thank you."

Cundo let go of Dawn. He turned to the kitchen table next to him and slipped a paring knife from the block of knives at the end of the table. He took hold of Dawn's arm again, the knife in his right hand now.

"Why would I worry about it? I pay one of the dum-dums to see the homey in the yard. 'Hey, how you doing?' Puts his hand on the homey's shoulder like this"—Cundo laying his hand on Dawn's shoulder—"and came around to shank him in the gut like this," Cundo said, coming around with the knife in his right fist and plowed the fist hard into Dawn's belly, Dawn collapsing to her knees hugging herself, her forehead pressed against the tiled floor.

Cundo raised the paring knife, telling Foley, "The homey got what was coming to him. He lives, no problem, but wasn't so smart after this." Cundo tossed the knife in the air, underhand, and turned to Dawn as the knife made a single loop and came down to stick straight up in the kitchen table.

"You see blood on the knife? Of course not. I struck her, yes, as a man has a right to strike his wife she needs to be punished. All right, and I forgive her for what she did. So now we can show the love we have for each other and never speak of this again." He said to Foley, "You wish us a happy life?"

Foley didn't know what he wished him or what to say, Jesus, feeling like a dummy standing there facing the guy. Cundo didn't seem to care if he said anything or not. He had Dawn on her feet, his arm around her, going down the hall now holding her against him and not looking back.

Mike Nesi said, " 'The only thing different between sinners and saints'—you know that one?"

Foley said, "Ole Possum," without having to think.

" 'One is forgiven,' " Nesi said, " 'and the other one ain't.' But it didn't sound to me like she was trying to get you to fuck her. I saw you're already at her— why you couldn't yell nothing at Cundo. What're you suppose to tell him, 'Yeah, shit, I was fuckin' your

wife but I didn't mean to?' I never saw this painting
that got him worked up. He was already worked up
coming here, before he ever saw it. Like he knew you
was fuckin' her, not needing any picture. He had in
mind what he'd do and was talking tough to me, this
little banty fella working himself up to it. I said to
him, 'I'm watching Jack Foley, what're you doing?' He
goes, 'You find out,' with his spic way of talking. I bet
he already knew he was gonna put on a show, get us
thinking he stabbed her, we're going 'Oh, no,' but only
punched her."

"That was for me," Foley said. "Hits her and waits
to see what I'll do about it."

"You went for him, I'd have you on the floor, my
foot on your neck. I don't know if I'm through here or
not. I think it depends on what you're gonna do. You
need a ride I can drop you someplace. You're staying,
I think he'll want me around." Nesi said, "You got a
basketball? We could shoot some hoops."

"I'm not leaving her here," Foley said.

"So take her with you. She wants to stay—I don't
know why but she might—kiss her good-bye when
Cundo ain't looking."

This guy was the only skinhead Foley had ever
known doing time who came close to having a sense of
humor.

"I don't see she's your problem," Nesi said. "Cundo's the one keeping you from fuckin' her, if that's your pleasure. I don't care for the man myself. You heard him refer to the one shanked the homey as a dum-dum? He's talking about a guy in the Brotherhood. You want, I can pop Cundo for you. It'll cost you, but I'll make you a deal."

Fifteen

He took her up to the bedroom and they made love and then again in the late afternoon. The first time Cundo got her on the bed was like the first time in her life, in the backseat of the boy's dad's Buick, the boy breathing hard in her ear for a minute and it was over. She couldn't think of his name, this boy with a reputation for being hot, but remembered saying to him, "That's it? All there is?"

When Cundo was on her again, holding himself up on his arms, he said, "I keep my weight off your poor little tummy." Dawn believed her poor little tummy had nothing to do with his hovering over her; Cundo's game now was to stare at her face to see what she was feeling.

"Baby girl, are those tears I see?"

You bet they were. Dawn could get her eyes to shine with tears in twelve seconds or less, offering a sad little smile that worked with tears, sorrow showing signs of hope. In a few moments she would be timing her breathless gasps and cute grunts to the little killer's thrusts, hoping he wouldn't cause her to break wind and disturb the performance. She loved the idea of clearing the decks with the first one and let the little guy rest before throwing himself into the next one. What she hoped to give him would be the most unforgettable fuck of his life and what happened earlier today would be shoved to the back of his memory.

Actually the little go-goer wasn't bad; he was hung for a little guy and had some nice moves. She believed she could help him ease out of his male dominator role and think of them as a couple of kids having fun in bed.

If he had Foley's looks, if he was *anything* like Foley, she could sit still, forget about the job. She remembered telling Foley she'd get him feeling like himself again, and he said he always felt like himself. It could be true. He didn't play any obvious roles, he stuck to the part he was playing and it seemed to be who he was. She knew from the moment she saw him he was the guy, and was still here, ready for action. But he didn't have his heart in the job, separating Cundo from a few million bucks.

The little guy wasn't bad-looking, he had a way about him, relaxed but very sure of himself. She liked his strut, the way he moved. She did wish he was taller; she could not see herself in flats the rest of her life. She thought Foley would at least yell at Cundo, show some fucking emotion, for God's sake, his lover being treated like a whore. He did try to say something and Cundo cut him off. She was surprised the way Cundo played the condemnation scene fairly straight, knowing what he was going to say, certain she must have fucked *somebody* in the past eight years. Couldn't believe his eyes when he saw the painting. It gave him a direct shot at Foley, sleeping in the same room with the little guy's naked wife on the wall.

But then what Cundo did, he made a guy thing out of it with the prison-buddy bullshit, knowing his pal would cut off his weenie before giving in to temptation, Foley standing there with a dumb look on his facing thinking, I *would*?

These boys were a handful. She hoped her bruised tummy would turn vivid colors; she'd walk around naked so the little killer could see what he did. But she would never say a word about his punching her. Never complain, never explain. Words of wisdom from Henry Ford II.

Now they were in bed naked, propped up with pillows, Cundo, a Cuban cigar clamped in his jaw to foul his breath, Cundo swirling a snifter of cognac, Dawn, snuggled close to him, sipping a tall bourbon Collins, thirsty after the workout.

She said, "Hon, if you're not careful you're going to spill cognac all over Ricky."

It was Ricky limp, Ricardo when it had grown to its playing size. Cundo loved it that she gave his pecker a name. He said something, talking with his mouth full of cigar, maybe in English, maybe not. Dawn said, "If it burns I'll have to make it better, won't I?" He seemed in a good mood, pleased with his performance. She took a sip of her drink, put the glass on the side table and lighted a Slim.

"I want you to know," Dawn said, "I completely forgot the painting was here."

Cundo puffed on his panatela looking straight ahead. He said, "Yes . . . ?"

"Sweetheart, I've been living in the other house. The only time I came up to this room was to hang that painting. I didn't expect what's his name, Foley, coming and . . . I forgot it was here. Jimmy wanted to take his work to the beach and sell it, he said for a lot of money. I said, "Are you out of your fucking mind? This is for my darling. I said it's why you did the painting, don't you remember? I told Jimmy I wanted to surprise you. Then what's his name, Foley, almost gave it away, telling you about it. He wanted to have Jimmy paint a bathing suit on me."

"What did he say when he saw you naked?"

"Foley? The first thing he said was, 'Is that you?' I said of course not. But I could tell he didn't believe me. He said, 'I thought that might be my neighbor in the bed.' I wanted to take the painting down, store it away until you came home. Foley said I might as well leave it, it'll only be a few more days. He said, 'Even if it isn't you, I know Cundo will love it.'"

Cundo turned his head to Dawn, the cigar pointing at her now. "He said that, Jack Foley?"

"He knew it was for you—who else? I mean even before I told him. I did *not* leave it here to turn him on, I swear. He's your friend," Dawn said, "he'd never do anything to hurt you."

"Make me look foolish," Cundo said. "Well, I already forgive you. I like your dark hair too, the natural shade for Navarro, yes? You not some blonde. What else you want?"

"*You,*" Dawn said. "I want you to love me and trust me." She thought of saying if he didn't believe her and kicked her out—well, there'd be nothing left for her to do but swim out in the ocean as far as she could, and not come back. Except the little bugger might say, "Oh, you want to go swimming?" And she'd have to melt all over him with love. It was work.

He was swirling his cognac again, tilting the glass over his sucked-in loins. Dawn said with her sly smile, "You're trying to spill some on little Ricky, aren't you? I hope it doesn't burn."

"It does," Cundo said, "you can make it better, uh?"

Dawn stubbed her Slim in the ashtray and turned to Cundo again with her sly smile.

"I can," Dawn said, her lines committed to memory, "but we'll be telling little Ricky so long, see you later, buddy."

She had Cundo grinning at her, eating it up.

"Then wha' happens?"

Dawn said, "You don't know?" her eyes open wide to show surprise. Times like these she felt like an idiot, but managed to keep her chin up.

"I like you to tell me," Cundo said.

"Well, *then*, before we know it," Dawn said, getting ready to go to work, "we'll be saying hi to your one-eyed buddy Ricardo."

"You kill me," Cundo said.

If it were only that easy. Jesus, keeping the little guy entertained while dying to know what Foley was up to.

Foley was in Cundo's house across the canal, the pink one. He wasn't familiar with the layout, the rooms, he hadn't poked around yet or been upstairs. He had Mike Nesi on his back, the baldheaded hard-on sitting in the living room with him, not a bad-looking room, brown walls and the chairs and sofa in soft colors, Foley in a big pale yellow chair across from Mike Nesi on the sofa, drinking beer from a clear bottle, the glass-top coffee table between them, Foley listening to Mike Nesi telling him it was a good life if you didn't weaken and start taking shit from people trying to tell you what to do, was his drift. He was on his fourth beer.

Foley had had a couple of shots of Jack Daniel's. There would be a silence. Foley couldn't think of anything to say to this dumbbell, but could listen to him and at the same time wonder what he was doing here and how long he'd stay and if he owed—not owed, if he should think of Dawn if he got ready to do something different. Find out where he was in his life. If he was still any good.

He liked where he was ten years ago, before the two falls. But then thought, No, you don't go back, you go straight ahead. He was still the same person. Age had nothing to do with it; he was fine. And Cundo was Cundo. But it was different now. He should wait for Dawn, talk to her.

Mike Nesi had his feet resting on the oval edge of the coffee table. Foley saw he was wearing work boots with metal toes, before he said, "Mike, would you take your feet off the table?" He almost said "please" but changed his mind in time.

Mike Nesi said, "The fuck you care, it ain't yours."

"It belongs to the guy who's paying you."

See if that moved him.

"Cundo don't care where I put my feet."

"Yeah, but I do," Foley said. "I'd like you to take your feet off the table." Then waited as Nesi took a swig of his beer and Foley said, "What're you wearing the shitkickers for?" knowing they were a skinhead weapon.

Nesi said, "My feet feel at home in 'em."

"Would you mind taking them off the table?"

"I don't, what're you gonna do, hit me with something?" He looked around. "There's a brass candleholder over there. Let's see if you can get to it."

"Why would you and I," Foley said, "want to have a fistfight?"

"Hell, knives, baseball bats, you name it."

"I'm asking why," Foley said. "I'm not gonna get in an argument with you, it would be the same as banging my head against the wall. You and I hold different views of life's fundamental truths. I don't want to argue or fight with you. I still want you to get your feet off the fucking coffee table."

"I don't know where your head's at," Mike Nesi said, "but soon as you stand up I'm gonna knock you on your ass and show you what my shitkickers are for."

"Or," Foley said, "we could go down to the beach and shoot some hoops. Even play for money."

They drove to the courts in Mike Nesi's pickup, the skinhead saying it was getting dark till they came to the beach and saw the wash of light out on the edge of the Pacific Ocean. Foley, his basketball resting in his lap, said no, there was plenty of time. He said, "How about taking the ball out at midcourt and show what you've got, shoot a jumper or drive to the basket." He said, "Not having a ref doesn't mean you're gonna foul me every chance you get, does it?" Foley showing Mike Nesi a grin, maybe kidding, maybe not.

Mike Nesi said, "You mean they's rules? Like I can't hang on to your shirt or stomp on your tennis shoes I get the chance? As I understand the way the game is played, you want to put the ball through the hoop and I want to stop you from scoring, right? That's the game of basketball. But if they's no ref, we don't have to worry about rules, do we? We put up a hunnert each and play to twenty-one. How's that sound? First one to score that many points takes the pot." Foley asked if he'd ever played with black guys. Mike Nesi said it wasn't ever done in his recollection. "The niggers play their show-off, shoot-from-anywhere game, while us white folks like to take the ball directly to the basket."

They got on a court and warmed up shooting jump shots, Foley swishing half of his from outside the circle, Mike Nesi dribbling in with a heavy hand, pounding the ball on the concrete before pulling up to take a shot. They flipped a coin. Foley took the ball out and swished a three-pointer, Mike Nesi's hands in his face.

Mike Nesi took it out, fired his ponderous jumper and missed.

Foley took it out, head-faked Nesi on his way to the basket and got caught from behind, Nesi hanging on to his back pocket and Foley lost the ball.

Nesi took it out. Foley saw him getting set to drive and gave the big skinhead room coming straight at him, Foley staying close and stuck himself to Nesi going up to stuff the ball, Foley reaching to swat it off the backboard and got hold of Nesi's wrist, held on and brought it down on the metal rim of the basket, Nesi screaming in pain as they fell with Foley on top, Nesi hitting the concrete floor on his shoulder, his arm under his body. It brought out another awful scream of pain.

He lay on the concrete now looking up at Foley.

"You broke my fuckin' arm."

"I didn't break your fuckin' arm," Foley said, "you broke it."

"And broke my fuckin' collarbone."

"I think you separated your fuckin' shoulder," Foley said. "Gimme your arm, I'll yank on it, see if we can put it back in place."

"Don't touch me," Nesi the Nazi said, holding up his broken arm, nasty-looking, to keep Foley away from him.

He was inhaling now and letting his breath out trying to settle down, his compound-fractured left arm resting on his stomach, Mike Nesi trying not to move his fucking shoulder that must hurt like a son of a bitch.

He said to Foley, "Jesus, who you been playing basketball with?"

"You said no ref, no rules," Foley said. "That's what we were playing."

He felt better than he had in a while. He felt a lot better, acting in a familiar way now, his old self once again. Or maybe a new version of the old self looking at where he was.

He said to Mike Nesi, "What do you want me to do with you?"

Sixteen

Later in the evening Foley sat with Cundo in the front room of his white home, alone with him finally, photos of Dawn in lamplight watching him from three walls. Cundo had hugged him saying, "We made it, we got out with our lives, the way we want to be, to do what pleases us." They raised their glasses of table-red from Australia Foley had bought at Ralphs and Cundo said, "What's that bad boy Mike Nesi doing?"

"I had to take him to UCLA Medical," Foley said, "in Santa Monica. We were fooling around shooting hoops and he injured himself."

Cundo grinned. "You faked him out and he twist his ankle trying to catch you. I can see it."

Foley said, "Actually he's out of action for a while, couple of months."

Cundo wasn't grinning now. He said, "You decide I don't need him, uh?"

"Not anymore," Foley said. "I'll give you the parking ticket for his truck, at the hospital. I told them you were his employer and would take care of the bill. I asked if the white-power brotherhood had group insurance and he said he didn't think so."

Now Cundo was grinning again. "You still a smart-ass. You stop talking for a time looking at the thirty years, but now you back to life with the smart-ass things you say, but very quiet. I already tole you that. Miss Megan brought you back from the living dead. Listen, I hire the dum-dum because I don't know what you going to do."

"You knew you were gonna hit her. The painting had nothing to do with it. You came home to put on a show, hit Dawn in the gut and forgive her—what a sweet guy—but forgive her for what?"

"See, you don't want to start talking about that," Cundo said. "Tha's why I forgive her and is done. No more talking about it, okay? Ever again. Or thinking about it. Thinking too much can fuck you up."

"How's Dawn, she all right?"

"In good spirit now, very entertaining, yes, showing her love for me. Everything," Cundo said, "is now as it should be. Am I right? Tell me how you think about it."

"I'd like to know what you're gonna do with the white-power freak, Nesi."

"Can he drive?"

"I don't know. If both his arms are in casts it might be hard."

"Man, what did you do to him?" Cundo said, but didn't seem to care. "I'm not going to worry about him. I'll fire him, let him pay the fucking hospital. Listen, Dawn has an idea, how you can be in one of her skits."

"That's what she calls them?"

"Her shakedowns. Get a woman's dead husband's ghost to leave her alone, kick him out of the house and charge a lot of money for it."

"She mentioned it to me."

"I was going to be the ghost expert, but Dawn say you be better at it. Good-looking guy, the woman falls for you, she's happy again and pays whatever Dawn says."

"After that, I don't see her again?"

"The woman? No, is done, is over."

"She's back where she started."

"Yes, you broke her fucking heart."

"How old is she?"

"I don't know, I think she's middle age. Listen, you can't pull off this kind of grif', man, and feel sorry for the woman. This one I know has all kind of money to make her happy."

"But you say I break her heart."

"It can happen, yes, but she can find another guy. Her money, she attracts guys like flies."

"You ever work this with Dawn?"

"Man, where was I until today? We only talk about it. The woman was Cuban, Puerto Rican, sure, I could be the guy knows about ghosts, throw in some Santería shit. This one Dawn say is tall. I forgot her name, very rich woman."

"I don't care much for the idea," Foley said. "I get her to like me and walk out on her?"

"You don't know," Cundo said, "she gonna fall for you or not. Maybe she's glad you don't come back."

"After I spent time being nice to her?"

"Man, you got some opinion of yourself. You believe the only thing can happen, you going to break her heart?"

Foley kept quiet this time, but shrugged.

"Your wife divorce you, didn't she?"

"Yeah, but she's still, you know, fond of me."

"Man, what you need is a woman to leave you flat. Be good for you."

"You ever have one walk out on you?"

"One time, yes," Cundo said, "when I was fifteen years old. But I think it was her old man made her stop seeing me."

"Her father," Foley said.

"No, man, her husband."

"Now I'm your straight man," Foley said.

"When you want to be," Cundo said. "You listen to what I'm saying, and then you tell me something I have to think about. Is why I like you, you keep me thinking. My friend, is my pleasure to be with you again. You always make me feel good."

Cundo nodded his head.

Foley nodded his, thinking, Shit.

Thinking, You got to get out of here.

He took the VW to Ralphs to buy provisions for a few days, a bottle of Jack Daniel's and a case of beer. A fifth would last him three days, almost. He'd need another one or two if he had company, if he ever saw Dawn or Cundo, or if Tico happened to stop by. Or Lou Adams—have a talk with him, if he had to go out and find him. Tell Adams he'd be leaving soon and not say where he was going, since he had no idea. Or maybe tell him he was going back to Florida.

What Foley did, he picked up three fifths of Jack Daniel's he'd bring out for company. How about a glass of Old No. 7? He felt at home with it.

The third day of his return to the world Cundo crossed the footbridge and sat down with Foley for a drink and to give him Dawn's notes on observing and dealing with ghosts. "So you can become the expert."

"You believe in them?" Foley said.

"You die," Cundo said, "your body is no more but your spirit is still alive, is alive forever. Okay, it heads off to the light, the one I saw when that fucking Joe LaBrava shot me three times. Or the spirit stays for a while or comes back to tell you something or fuck with you. You learn a ghost has no power over you unless you give it an advantage, show you're afraid of it."

Foley said, "You aren't spooked by the idea of ghosts in your house, even if there aren't?"

"Read this, you'll know more than I do."

"But you believe in ghosts?"

"You look for them you find them."

"How?"

"Read what Dawn says, you want to sound like you know what you talking about. Listen," Cundo said, "the white-power asshole went home—lives somewhere on the Westside, but say to tell you he's coming back to teach you a lesson, when he gets his cast off."

"Just one?"

"For the fracture of his arm. The other arm is tape to his body so he don't move his shoulder. He say his hand sticks out the front of his shirt, so he can hold a piece when he comes to see you."

"I'll be gone by then."

"What are you talking about?" Cundo sitting up straight and frowning, telling Foley, "You got a cool place to live, all those rooms with high ceilings done up the way Dawn wants them that don't cost you nothing. Man, we out of prison, now we have a good time. Make some money you feel better."

"I don't think this grift idea, shaking down some old lady, is the kind of work I want to do."

"You want to stick up a bank?"

"I haven't had a good feeling about it lately," Foley said, "like I'd jinxed myself and wouldn't be good at it anymore. But I got over it. I could do a bank this afternoon and take five grand, but I wouldn't get the same kick I used to. I want to do something I can throw myself into."

"Some kind of robbery."

"No, it can be legal."

"I give you a gun," Cundo said. "Zorro holds mine for me. Do a bank with a gun, uh, what do you think? It would give you a different feel. But you don't want to be caught with a gun, anybody has done serious time. Tha's why this grif' could be what you looking for. Take this hex woman for fifty-k, you and Dawn split it down the middle. You think you break the woman's heart? Listen, you show her she can be happy again taking a stud like you to bed. You turn it on, man, put on a good skit and make twenty-five-k, or more than that, easy."

Dawn, a new Dawn, came to visit this morning of Cundo's fourth day home, Dawn in tan warm-ups and tennis shoes and stood in his doorway smiling.

"I'm dying to know if you feel you have enough of a handle on ghosts to play the expert," the new Dawn turning to glance across the canal. "I know what you're going to ask. Why are ghosts always portrayed as spooky when in fact the attitudes they affect are the same ones they had when they were embodied? And with much the same personalities. Unless of course you show evidence of being afraid. That gives them an enormous advantage and they may try to spook you out, even if it's just for fun." She smiled again.

Foley said, "No hugs and kisses?"

Dawn didn't move. She said, "Jack," and took a quick glance across the canal as he brought her by the arm into the house and closed the door and now he was holding her and for a few moments they were at each other mouth to mouth like a couple of kids until she got her hands against his chest and Foley let go of her.

"We're alone. He can't see us, even if he's watching the house."

"You know what will happen"—Dawn shaking her head—"we start taking chances. Once we think we can get away with it we get caught." She said, "You read my notes?"

"Every word."

"How can you tell a ghost is in the house?"

"You're gonna quiz me?"

"I want to see how much you know."

"Well, as soon as I walk in the door," Foley said, "and a spirit is in the house, I'll feel its presence. I don't have to be told about things being moved around, books on the shelf upside down, or a familiar scent in the air, a fragrance, I'll know if a ghost is in the room. Or more than one."

"That's not bad. You've been practicing."

"I've been practicing the art of detection for close to twenty years, since I was first certified as an Advanced Paranormal Investigator."

"No, you've been practicing your esoteric art for twenty years. Pour me a drink, one shot of bourbon, that's all. I don't want to lose my inhibitions."

"I didn't know you had any."

"You're sweet. Just don't make up anything when you're talking to her. It might be different from what I've left with her. I told her yesterday I'd be talking to a paranormal investigator who specializes in ghost appearance. I'm hoping," Dawn said, "you'll feel expert enough to see her in a day or two."

He watched her, the new Dawn back in business, trying to sound like herself.

"Did he hurt you?"

"My tummy's bruised. It's purple."

He touched her face. "Can I see it?"

"Jack, I don't want to start, okay?"

He saw nothing in her eyes that told him how she felt and let his hand fall to her shoulder, feeling her arm inside the cotton jacket before his hand slipped off.

"I'm ready as I'll ever be," Foley said. "Danialle Tynan—she's still making movies?"

"She's only made a few. Left the screen to become Mrs. Danialle Karmanos, wife of Hollywood producer Peter Karmanos. Last year he made her only hit, *Born Again*, about the stripper who's struck by lightning and becomes a faith healer with a televised tent show. Lays her hands on the infirm, lifts her eyes to heaven, cries out, 'Lord, heal this poor child from stuttering.' The little girl looks up at Danialle and says, 'P-p-p-praise Jesus,' and the audience goes wild."

"I missed that one," Foley said. "What happens?"

"I didn't see it either," Dawn said. "I'll get us a DVD. She and Peter were married only a few years when he had a heart attack and died on the set of the sequel they were making, *Born Again and Again*. It left Danny a widow at thirty-five with a ton of money."

"That's all she is?" Foley said. "I thought she was older."

"She's starting to let herself go. She's depressed, looking for love in the prime of life and can't find it."

"Come on—she's loaded and doesn't have a boy-friend?"

"She can have all the guys she wants. That gypsy fraud told her Peter Karmanos has put a hex on her from the other side, and Danny believes it. What she can't find is true love. Whatever that is."

Foley said, "You told her she has ghosts in her house and she believes that too?"

"I added the ghosts to make it more interesting. Then when you came on the scene I thought, You're not only the ghost expert, you could turn out to be the true love."

"She's only thirty-five?"

"When Peter died, eight months ago. Since then she's been feeling sorry for herself. She sits alone in dim rooms waiting for a sound or for something to move. A rocking chair starts to rock. A door slams closed."

"She sees weird things going on?"

"Or imagines she does. Otherwise, she's intelligent, she's aware."

"You're saying there might be ghosts in her house?"

"That's what we're going to find out. Either way," Dawn said, "whether we discover ghosts or not, you'll make a show of getting rid of them."

Foley said, "You're up on all this ritual stuff—why don't you do it, and send her a bill?"

"Because the big part of this is the true-love thing. That's you, Jack. All you have to do is get her to fall in love with you and we're good for a hundred grand."

"Cundo said maybe fifty."

"He doesn't know Danialle. I'm counting on love at first sight, the way it happened to me."

"You were horny."

"Well, she should be too. I'm seriously thinking now," Dawn said, "if she sees you the same way I did, my dream come true, asking two hundred grand wouldn't be outrageous. I think you'll like her, if you can get her to show some life. You'll love the house, it's in Beverly Hills."

"We split the two hundred?"

"I think anything over fifty, we'll have to give Cundo a cut." She said after a moment, "Unless we don't tell him. You'll need to dress up a little, and you have to be serious, very conservative, if you want to pass for an actual ghost hunter. Okay? And don't forget the smudge pot. We'll visit Danialle this evening."

A few minutes before noon Dawn set out on her exercise schedule, walking and running four days a week: walking till she saw a jogger approaching and she'd start running, lengthen her strides and nod as they passed, The Pretenders blasting in her headphones, Dawn wailing along with "Back on the Chain Gang."

Today she followed Ocean Front Walk up to Breeze, turned from the ocean and followed streets inland till she came to Broadway, and Tico's aunt's yellow frame bungalow at the north end of Oakwood Park: about two miles and a quarter she could do in thirty minutes, arrive sweaty for Tico.

He'd told Dawn his ah'nty's house, worth less than a hundred thousand anywhere else in America, would sell now for three-quarters of a mil in Venice, at least, his aunt smoking eighteen dollars' worth of cigarettes a day, six bills a pack. One day he stole two cases of Newports out of a truck and gave them to Tilly, Tico hoping before she'd inhaled the last one she'd be dead. He'd sell the house and get the fuck out of Venice for good.

The door opened. Dawn said, "Tilly's out?"

"For two hours. I gave her fifty dollars and pointed her to the bus stop, get her to Hollywood Park." Tico said to Dawn, "Lady, who you want me to be for today, Mr. Jigaboo or La Cucaracha, what Lou Adams calls Latinos. I'm already into being a jig for my ah'nty," Tico grinning at Dawn. "You nice and slippery-looking the way you sweaty, but you smell fine."

Dawn took off her warm-up top. Tico handed her a bath towel and watched her naked from the waist up drying herself, Tico saying, "You ain't drying the rest? Gonna leave the nether region gamey?"

Dawn said, "I'd like a tall glass of ice water."

By the time he was back from the kitchen with it, Dawn's running pants were on the floor and she was drying her lower half. She drank the glass of water and said, "One more, please."

She sipped this one sitting down, Tico watching her, admiring her pure white skin he was waiting to get at. He said, "We got a hour and twenty minutes left on the clock, time slipping away on us."

Dawn said, "You know what you haven't told me about, the times you were arrested for homicide."

"Three out of four," Tico said. "I told you about the one I was convicted on. The other two were like that. You join a gang, you got to pop somebody to show who you are. There was a war and I shot another dude."

"Black or Hispanic?"

"Latin. I was riding with the colored folks at the time. We all got hauled in but nothing came of it and they let us go."

"What was the one you got away with?"

"I musta told you. Was the dude work at Saks Fifth Avenue, wouldn't sell me a suit I wanted. Was a dark gray pinstripe I coveted, age sixteen years old, I had to have it."

"Why wouldn't he sell it to you?"

"I'm a skinny nigga kid. How could I have enough money? The suit went for six bills."

"Really."

"I went home and come back with a piece, drove all the way to Beverly Hills, the Saks on Wilshire. I say to the dude, 'You gonna let me have the suit?' No, he's about to call security on me I don't leave. I say to him, 'See, what I got?' Show him the Walther PPK three-eighty, beautiful piece."

Dawn said, "Oh," sounding surprised. "The same gun you gave me to hold?"

"How many you think I got? I told the Saks dude to put the suit in a hanger bag. He got one and now I'm twisting a suppressor on the barrel. Cost me six hundred with the piece, as much as the suit. The dude is all eyes watching me fix the silencer on this cool pistol. The dude say, 'Don't you want the tailor to fit the suit on you?' I say, 'No, thank you, I have my ah'nt fit it to my size.' I shot the Saks dude in the head and walked out."

"No one saw you?"

"Wasn't nobody there but me and him."

"You were lucky," Dawn said.

"You don't think I was cool, I'm sixteen fucking years of age?"

Dawn came out of the chair raising her arms to slip them around Tico Sandoval's neck, telling him he was the coolest dude she'd ever known in her entire life.

"Cooler than the bank robber?"

Dawn said, "What bank robber?"

Seventeen

What does a certified Advanced Paranormal Investigator say to a woman who's had a hex put on her and is visited by ghosts? Once Dawn introduced him Foley said to Mrs. Karmanos:

"You remember Gene Wilder in *Young Frankenstein*? He's admiring the door to the castle and says, 'Look at those knockers!' And Teri Garr says, 'Thank you, Doctor.'"

Danialle seemed to smile, though he wasn't sure. She looked stoned, or hungover. "You have the same kind of knocker," Foley said, "on your front door, that ring of metal."

Dawn had said on their way here—in the new Saab Cundo had leased for her—Danny Karmanos wasn't on drugs or drinking to excess, she simply acted drained, devoid of hope. Though she'd become quite disturbed, Dawn said, when asked about ghosts manifesting themselves—especially her husband's spirit, and what Danny said Peter was telling her to do.

They stood in the front hall, Danialle wearing a black cashmere sweater, loose on her, and jeans, her feet in silver low-heeled shoes with laces, her blond-streaked hair not combed or brushed today, or perhaps lately, layers of rich-girl hair that a former movie star would wear whatever way she wanted. She might be depressed, but still looked good to Foley. She brought them into the living room, where lamps turned low showed comfortable pieces in tans and reds, more colors in the pillows scattered over the chairs and sofa.

Following Danialle, Foley said, "Remember Marty Feldman in the movie, with the bulging eyes? They come off the train and he tells them, 'Walk this way,' and Gene and Teri Garr try to walk the way Marty does, like they have curvature of the spine and drag one of their feet."

Dawn gave him a look that said, *What are you doing?*

Danialle turned to him with a smile he was sure of this time, beginning to show signs of coming alive.

He said, "Mrs. Karmanos, tell me, are you afraid?"

"Of course I am."

"Of what?"

She didn't answer but looked at Dawn.

"It's Peter's spirit," Dawn said, "who's disturbing Danny. I can't help but feel sorry for him"—Dawn turning to Danialle now—"once I understand what he's going through. You were the love of his life, he doesn't want you falling for someone else. But, his behavior is unacceptable." She said to Foley, "I hope you'll have a talk with him."

"Once we locate him." He said, "Dawn, why don't you look around, see what the signs are and I'll come and make him come out. But first I want to talk to Mrs. Karmanos."

"Doctor, I have all the information we need."

"Very telling. But I have to look at this from my vantage, if you want my opinion. I'll talk to Mrs. Karmanos while you check on the signs. I'm already thinking the house is probably in need of a good spiritual cleansing. Afterwhile I'll get the smudge pot out of the car. Unless you'll have time to get it. Dawn, I'm hoping Mrs. Karmanos can tell me whether or not we're looking at hypnogogia here, and I want to be absolutely sure about it."

It stopped Dawn, as if she wasn't sure what to say, but told him all right, go ahead.

He said to her leaving them, "I appreciate it." And to Danialle, "Where does he make himself known?"

"All over."

"Wherever you are in the house?"

"Yes, he shows up."

"He's always with you?"

"No, not always."

"You see him in dreams?"

"Almost every night. He comes—it's like a dream but it's different."

"He's rough with you?"

"He'll yell at me, something he never did when he was alive. When I think he might appear I try to stay awake."

"You don't go to bed?"

"Finally I have to."

"There's a drug called brown-brown," Foley said, "from Africa, a mixture of cocaine and gunpowder. You turn numb and stay awake for days."

"Can you get me some?"

"I wouldn't prescribe it for anyone," Dr. Foley said. "Your disturbed state made me think of it, that's all."

Danialle brought him to the master bedroom on the second floor where, she said, Peter made his most threatening appearances. Foley could see her hiding in the ultra-king-size bed while the ghost of her husband groped beneath the covers for her—this nifty-looking young widow desperate to be free and find love. What's the problem? It was everywhere, fooling-around love to going-the-distance love. She could have any kind she wanted if Peter ever got off her back. Even true love, someone with an open mind who wasn't weighed down with rules or serious flaws, like Adele saying, "I don't want to talk about it anymore," when she knew she was losing an argument. Maybe Adele's flaw wasn't that serious: they'd only quit speaking for five minutes. The bed wasn't made, a shorty nightgown lying on the quilt pulled up to the pillows, an impression in the one where she'd slept, or lain awake. He could imagine her in the nightgown, her bare thighs out of the jeans slender—not as hefty as Adele's, though Adele's thighs weren't bad, once you got used to them. Danialle brought him to a table that had a game board inlaid in the surface, with chess pieces in position.

"You play?"

"We did now and then. Peter was a master. I didn't care much for it."

"And that's his rocking chair?"

It was the kind of rocker he had seen pictures of President Kennedy sitting in, resting his bad back.

"The infamous rocker," Danialle said, "Peter's seat of judgment."

Foley said, after a moment, "Is it starting to move?"

It was, barely at first—Foley staring at the empty natural-wood chair—but gradually gaining momentum to rock back and forth at a leisurely pace.

"How do you do that?"

"You think I'm making it rock? It's Peter, letting us know he's here. It means he'll show up tonight and get on me about my irreverent conduct."

Foley didn't know what to think about a rocker that rocked on its own or was put in motion by a ghost. It didn't seem to bother Danialle. Wasn't there a guy who caused spoons to bend? It wasn't the kind of thing Foley ever thought about looking into, though he'd ask Dawn about this one. By now, Danialle must be used to weird shit going on.

"The reason a departed spirit remains earthbound," Foley said, "usually means he's lonesome and wants you to know he's still around. Or, there might be something he wants to tell you."

"You know what Peter's message is? Behave yourself. Quit acting like a tramp. I haven't had what you'd call a serious date since Peter passed away—and he calls me a tramp."

"Accuses you of fooling around?"

"The point he makes over and over, his message from the other side? Forget about finding another guy, I belong to *him*. He's defiant about it."

"You said he appears in a dream?"

"It's more real than a dream. I have the feeling I might still be awake."

"Can you move?"

"Barely."

"You feel something holding you down."

"Yes, and I start to panic."

"You're experiencing hypnogogia," Foley said, hearing himself actually using the word he'd picked out of Dawn's notes. "You don't know whether you're dreaming or it's actually happening. You feel you're possessed by the spirit of your dead husband"—Foley looking her in the eye, showing he was serious—"and there is not a darn thing you can do about it."

"That's it exactly," Danialle said. "Can you make him stop? Tell him to please leave me alone?"

"Do you talk to him?" Foley looked at the chair, still rocking but maybe a bit slower. "I mean if you know he's there."

"I've told him I'm sorry. I leave the room and he follows me. I can't find a way to tell him how I feel. He knows I'm not fooling around. I'm not in a rush, but I'd like to get my life going again. Is that wrong?"

"No, of course not," Foley said, with what he thought of as a sad smile, a wise sad smile, "not as long as you remain in a natural state of being yourself, obeying your instincts that are second nature to you. Use what you feel as well as what reason tells you and you'll stay on the right path."

That wasn't bad, words he pulled out of the air that sounded like Dawn running her psychic spiel.

"But I'm scared," Danialle said. "I've never thought about the afterlife before and now I feel like I'm in it. Miss Navarro, Dawn, must've told you, she's afraid that the state Peter is in now, he's become an incubus, an evil spirit."

And the female evil spirit—Foley getting them straight in his mind—was a succubus?

"What you see as Peter's evil intentions," Dr. Foley said, "seem perfectly reasonable to him. Why? Because your husband, Mrs. Karmanos, is still deeply in love with you. Tell me, has he ever, while you're sleeping, got on top of you?"

"You mean to have sex?" She said, "No, he's never done that," sounding somewhat wistful. "When I can't move it's like I'm paralyzed, feeling the weight of his words, Peter admonishing me to quit thinking about getting married again. I tell him I'm *not*. I don't think about it with any, you know, purpose. But he doesn't believe me. It's why I feel the force of this hex he's put on me. Call it whatever you want, it's a curse."

The curse of the gypsy woman.

"You spoke to Madam Rosa," Foley said, "about Peter, and she told you he's responsible for the hex. Why do you believe her?"

"Because it's real, it's happening to me and it's driving me fucking nuts." She said, "I'm sorry, Doctor, I never use that word. I certainly don't as a rule. Doctor, I'm so distraught I feel helpless. I don't know what to do about it."

"Was he driving you fucking nuts," Foley said, "before you told Madam Rosa about him or after?"

"The first time he started in on me, like he could read my mind, was at the funeral home. Everyone had left and I was alone in the parlor with him, sitting by the casket."

"Mourning your loss."

"And, you might say, thinking of my own life, the rest of it, what could be the best part of it going to waste, if I don't make something happen."

For the first time this evening Foley began to wonder how Danialle Karmanos saw him, the ghost expert in his free-falling sport coat and spotless jeans, one of the black shirts not buttoned to excess, and cowboy boots from a flea market, old boots, the toes curling up but they took a shine. Foley believed the way he dressed showed confidence, a nice guy being himself. *Hi, I'm Dr. Foley, but you can call me Doc.* In his own way a conservative ghost hunter.

"Tell me when you saw Rosa the first time."

"Months later. I mean from the time he died."

"You told her Peter had an unnatural hold on you."

"Rosa saw it right away. She said, 'You can't breathe, can you?'"

"No matter how much you miss him," Foley said, "you wish he'd stay in the spirit world—"

"And leave me alone," Danialle said. "I refuse to play the grieving widow and wear black the rest of my life. I have de la Rentas in black, but give me a break."

"You want him to know how you feel."

"Even though he'll always be in my heart and I do think of him, I mean a lot. But I refuse to make a career of grieving, like an old Greek woman with worry beads, mourning my way through a boring life."

"But you haven't told him."

"Not yet, but I will."

"What are you waiting for," Foley said, "his permission?"

She didn't answer. He saw she was looking at the rocking chair, no longer rocking.

Now it was Danialle asking, "How did you do that?"

Eighteen

Last night on the way home Dawn said, "the next time you want me to do the chores, let me know beforehand. I'll remind you I don't do house cleaning, even with a spiritual purpose."

Foley said, "I couldn't see myself smudging the house."

Dawn had explained how Foley was to open all the windows and go through the Karmanos home with a bundle of dry sage burning in a smudge pot, "To rid the house," Dawn said, "of stagnant energies." Foley was to recite the words of expulsion, "Begone, negative energies and the spirits responsible," swinging the smudge pot like an altar boy dispensing incense. This was the part that gave Foley trouble, reciting the incantation, talking out loud to a ghost.

"It's only been the accepted custom since the Middle Ages," Dawn said, cruising along Sunset Boulevard toward the 405, her tone only somewhat condescending. Dawn's irritation showed in the way she gripped the steering wheel, like you'd have to pry her hands from it. She didn't look at him when either of them spoke, not giving Foley, alone in the dark with her, even a glance.

He told Dawn about the rocking chair and she said, "Yes . . .?"

"Who was doing it?"

"Who do you think?"

"She said it was Peter letting her know he was there."

"Or," Dawn said, "was it the poor little rich widow?"

"She asked if I thought she was making it move."

"Have you considered," Dawn said, "she *was*, but didn't know she was doing it? How would you describe her state of mind?"

"She's convinced Peter's making her miserable. I told her, let him know how you feel and he'll back off. She thought *I* was the one made the chair stop rocking."

"What did you tell her?"

"I let her believe it."

"Good," Dawn said, "you're catching on," still without looking at him.

"I feel sorry for her," Foley said. "She's doing this to herself."

"It doesn't matter where the energy comes from, as long as you become her savior."

"I don't know," Foley said.

"Why? No sign yet of your charm working?"

"I mean I don't like the idea of faking her out."

"That means you're confident," Dawn said, "your charm *is* working. But you're just a humble bank robber, you don't want to sound conceited, toot your horn."

What was she doing?

A few days ago she'd make fun of him, but with a look of love in her eyes, and she was funny in an easy way. Foley and the psychic who'd found each other dreaming up a score. Even if it was making less sense to him now, he was curious, waiting to hear what Dawn had in mind.

She said, "It's eleven-thirty. Raffish Cundo Rey, the midget lover, will now be standing on his tiptoes waiting for me."

Foley didn't say anything. A few days ago he would've thought it was funny.

At half past ten the next morning a different Dawn spoke to him on the phone.

"Jack, I'm sorry if I woke you. Cundo would like you to come have breakfast with him. If you've already had it, come anyway, I'll make you an espresso." Dawn sounding breezy, Cundo nearby. She said, "Guess what? Danialle Karmanos called. She wanted your address so she can send you a thank-you note. She said for solving her problem. She hasn't heard a word from Peter—may he rest in peace and quit fucking around—since our visit."

"All I told her," Foley said, "was let him know how you feel."

"Well, evidently, she told him off. Wait a minute." Dawn came on again saying, "Cundo wants to know if you told Peter to begone. He can't see you talking to a ghost. I said don't worry about Jack, he's sly, comes up with tricky ideas." She said, "Listen, I told Danialle you're staying right across the canal, feel free to drop by whenever you want—when she gets the wim-wams. She said, 'Oh, really?' I told her you were always home, you're writing a book on identifying signs of ghosts. How to tell when they're watching you take a bath." Dawn said, "Jack, we have to stretch this one out a bit, not make exorcising a ghost look so easy. The next time we visit Danialle you'll have to spot Peter hanging around and talk to him." She said, "Wait, here's Cundo."

"You coming over?"

"I had breakfast two hours ago."

"You don't keep prison time no more? Listen, I told her, I can't see you talking to a fucking ghost, man."

"I don't think I've ever said 'begone' to anybody."

"No, now you say, 'Get the fuck out.' But listen, how does this broad Miz Karmanos look to you?"

"She seems nice."

"Tha's what you want, a nice girl? Listen, I won't stick my nose in your business, you know, your private life, whatever you get going on the side . . ."

"And I don't stick my nose in yours?" Foley said, "something you're gonna spring on me? Can I tell you to get fucked if I don't like it."

Cundo said, "What?" He said, "The fuck are you talking about? You think I won't say to your face anything I want? Tell me what you think I said."

"I got the wrong idea, I'm sorry," Foley said. "I'll be over in a few minutes."

He said it, but couldn't help thinking she was up to something. Dawn. Dawn telling Cundo, "Jack's sly." Comes up with tricky ideas, because she was still pissed off from last night.

He phoned their house. Dawn answered and he said to her, "Hold the espresso, I'm going for a walk."

She said, "Antsy, Jack?"

He went out the front and followed the walk toward Dell Avenue, a narrow street that humped in turn over all four canals. He wondered if he might see Tico hanging out. Two figures stood on the bridge that crossed the canal, one leaning on the low concrete wall, his necktie hanging over the side. Foley knew it was Lou Adams before Lou stood up and raised his hand. Foley wasn't sure about the guy with him, wearing a sport shirt with his sunglasses, relaxed, hands in his pockets, but took him to be a cop. He saw no problem with that and he went up the steps to the street. Lou Adams was leaning on the concrete wall again looking this way past his shoulder. Waiting. If you walk over, Foley thought, he'll think you're wondering what he's up to.

Well, he was, so he walked over.

Lou straightened, turning to Foley.

"Jack, this is Ron Deneweth, just recently retired after going on thirty years with the LAPD. Ron helped me sign Tico as my second in command. Works with me other ways too."

Deneweth said, "How you doing?" without stepping over to shake Foley's hand. "I've been reading about you—good stuff, going back to Angola, man, twenty-two months in that stink hole. I believe you were driving for your uncle Cully, the one got you started."

"Ron looked that up for me," Lou said, "helping me with my book. Now I got notes on you go all the way back to your first communion."

Foley said, "You're writing a book?"

"I thought I told you. I know I told Tico. I have your early life, your prison life, and what you're up to now."

Deneweth was grinning at him. "Lou says he's waiting for you to go down one last time."

"That's right," Lou said, "as the most notorious bank robber in the history of our country, put away for good."

Foley said, "You're writing a book about bank robbers?"

"I mention some others, but it's about you."

"The book's finished?"

"I'm over five hundred pages into it."

Deneweth said, "I told him he ought to number his pages. You know, in case the wind blows 'em all over the floor."

Lou said, "I'll have a girl do that when I'm done, and type me a clean copy. I got a lot of notes written along the margins."

Deneweth said, "And get her to double-space it."

"You say this book," Foley said, "is about me?"

"You've robbed more banks than anybody else, haven't you? By the time I finish you'll be the most famous bank robber in history. I compare you to John Dillinger and Willie Sutton—"

"Willie *Sutton*—you're kidding."

"Today he's more famous'n you, but when I'm done—don't worry about it. I ask my agent and he said yeah, put Willie in it."

"You have an agent?"

"Jack, you don't have an agent you're fucked. How do you think all these writers who don't know shit about dirty guys doing crimes get their stuff sold? My agent once had movie studios bidding on a book not one of 'em had read. The publishing business isn't about writing, Jack, it's about selling books."

"But the book's about me, my career?"

"Most of it's about your life of crime, with a big finish I'm looking forward to."

"But you don't know anything about my life."

"What're you talking about, I got your sheets."

"They don't tell you anything personal, how I wanted to have a charter fishing boat someday, but went to work for my uncle instead, driving for him. You know Cully did twenty-seven years and died in Charity Hospital? I can tell you what it's like to get caught finally. Here I was leading a life of, well, crime and thought I could get away with it," Foley said, shaking his head. "Lou, when you're young, you never think of making a mistake."

"You learned your lesson."

"Going down for thirty years opened my eyes."

"But a little late, huh? I'd like to put that statement in the book, I think near the end. Have it come right after I tell how I busted your ass back to federal prison, I imagine for life."

Foley said, "Lou, the day you die of being a failure, I'll do one last bank in your memory. I'll say to the teller, 'Sweetheart, this one's for that dumb but dedicated Special Agent Lou Adams.'"

Lou said, "Jack, if it isn't a bank . . ." He said, "Let me think a minute. You're the houseguest of the Cuban jailbird who's back of any number of homicides, the kind of heavy-duty ex-con he is." He looked at Ron Deneweth and said, "Tell Jack what you did last night."

"I followed you and the fortune-teller up to Beverly Hills," Ron Deneweth said, "to the home of a Mrs. Karmanos. Her husband died this past winter leaving her a pile of money. Lives up there off Benedict Canyon in a house used to be owned by . . . Lou, what's the movie star's name?"

"Ingrid Bergman," Lou Adams said. "Ron thinks you're trying bunco now, out to swindle the poor woman in some kind of deal. She puts up the money and you disappear on her. I said well, maybe. But if I know Jack Foley he's gonna hit a bank. He can't help it."

The phone rang in the water closet part of the bathroom, the toilet, with the quickest flush in Foley's experience, and a bidet, the two fixtures in there side by side. Foley, out of the shower drying himself, reached in and picked the phone off the wall.

She didn't say hi, this is Danialle Karmanos, she said, "You're home. I tried you a little earlier—"

Foley said he was out taking a brisk walk for an hour, covered about five miles. Danialle said that's what she did, but liked to run. Foley said, "Jog?" No, she'd run it, sometimes six, seven miles. "I could tell you're in good shape," Foley said, "and you watch your diet."

"Oh? You can tell by looking at me?"

Now she sounded like she was coming on to him.

Foley said, "Miss Navarro told me."

"She told *me*," Danialle said, "I could drop in and see you. She said anytime, but I don't want to interrupt your writing."

His writing. He and Lou Adams both at it—and wondered for the first time if Lou was actually writing a book, and had an agent. He said to Danialle, "I've been practicing more than I've been writing lately, as you know. How're you doing?"

"That's what I'd like to talk to you about. Can I stop by, if you're free?"

"Anytime you want."

"I'm in the car. I'll see you in a few minutes."

They were on the sofa now among the throw pillows, a bottle of red on the glass-top table, Danialle sipping hers, saying, "Mmmmm," Foley feeling good, hair combed still damp, Foley smelling of Caswell-Massey No. 6, but not too much, Foley knowing when he felt good he looked good, but was not in a hurry. He'd let Danialle, widowed eight months, show the way.

She started in: "I asked an artist I know, Richard Guindon, if he thought I should wait a year before I start seeing anyone. Richard said, 'What are you, Sicilian?' I said no, but I'd be that kind of Old World widow if I didn't get Peter, God love him, off my back." She raised her glass. "And you made him disappear. It was amazing, and I didn't even see how you did it."

He said, "I thought you were paying attention," and stopped. Foley threw out what he was going to say about his approach to the paranormal, communicating with spirits, and said, "You put his ghost out of your mind and that did it."

She said, "*I* did it?" sounding doubtful maybe but not worried or especially concerned.

Foley took a chance, still looking right at her, and said, "I think you're tired of pretending there's a hex on you, put there by a ghost."

It took her only a moment. She smiled saying, "You caught me," and said, "No, I liked the idea of the hex. It was Madam Rosa I got tired of almost immediately, setting me up to give to her church. For ten thousand she'd get the gypsies praying for me and the hex would be lifted. I sent Rosa on her way and hung on to the hex and Peter's ghost. I'd think of his grandmother and become a scared little girl when I had to play that part." She said, "Are you mad at me, Jack?"

See how easy it was? Foley smiled, he liked her.

"Dawn said you wanted to give my house a spiritual cleansing. I told her the house is clean, Peter's given up pestering me. She said she'd speak to you about it." Danialle raised her glass and said, "Would you like to clean my house, Jack?" looking at him over the rim.

"Any time you say," Foley said, "but I don't do windows," and saw her taken by surprise.

"You're not as serious about it as Dawn, are you?"

"She's real, she's psychic."

"And sort of spooky," Danialle said, "talking about the reality of the unseen world. It exists on a higher vibrational frequency than ours. The temperature's a constant seventy-eight degrees, and there aren't any insects, but there are animals, pets. Everything in this world, you and I, are all made up of vibrations. Did you know that?"

"I wasn't sure," Foley said.

"You believe in heaven?"

"As my reward," Foley said, "for changing my life in time."

"You'll have to handle this with Dawn, tell her I'm a fake, but I'll pay for her time." She said, "Unless you want to keep it going. It's okay with me. But I will pay you, now, for dealing with Peter, you were great." She said, "You're not into the paranormal at all?"

Foley said no and watched her turn a hip to bring a checkbook out of her slacks. He said, "That was on the house. I hope Peter wasn't watching." Now she was leaning over the table writing a check. "I mean it," Foley said. "My first time running ghosts there's no charge." She didn't smile or maybe wasn't listening. He watched her sign the check and turn it facedown on the glass top.

She said, "If you aren't into the occult, what are you into?"

He watched her face.

"I'm a bank robber."

Her lips parted.

"You aren't."

Sitting up straight now in the pillows.

"I don't believe you."

"Yes, you do."

They stared at each other, a few feet between them.

"I've robbed more banks . . ."

"Yes . . ."

"Than anybody in America."

"More than Willie Sutton?"

"Willie *Sut*ton, Jesus Christ—"

She said, "I believe you."

Sounding awed.

"How many have you robbed?"

"A hundred and twenty-seven. The chances are I won't do another one, but you never know."

"Amazing."

"Can I ask you one?" Foley said. "How did you get the rocking chair to rock?"

"I didn't get it to rock, you did . . . didn't you?"

They had a second glass of the Australian red, Danialle wondering if they should ask Dawn about the rocking chair; Foley wondering if they should switch to Jack Daniel's, speed things up while that warm feeling came over them. But thought, No, you better wait.

He said, "Dawn thinks you make the chair rock without knowing you're doing it."

"How could I?"

"I have no idea."

"But I *was* making the whole thing up. Peter never once yelled at me."

"You sounded sure he was rocking the rocker."

"Because I couldn't explain it."

"Maybe he was."

"You think it's possible?"

"There's no way of telling," Foley said, "so I'm not gonna worry about it."

"I think you're right. Peter used to say, 'Don't worry about anything you can't do something about.'" She said, "Why don't you call me Danny, since we're conspiring together, and might want to play this out?" She looked at her watch. "I have to go, I'm meeting with our lawyers again, and again."

He walked with her to the back of the house where her Mercedes convertible, a white one, stood waiting.

She said, "You can come and clean the house anytime you want. Or, we could have a swim and sit by the pool, sip frozen daiquiris . . . What's your favorite?"

Foley wasn't sure if he'd ever had a frozen daiquiri, but said, "Pineapple."

She said, "Mmmmm, me too."

"You don't mind," Foley said, "entertaining an ex–bank robber?"

"I don't know," Danny said, "you're my first."

She brought her hand to the side of his face saying, "You smell good," and kissed him on the mouth and smiled and got in her Mercedes and drove off to Beverly Hills.

Too late he thought of the check on the coffee table, wanting to give it back to her. He had watched her write the check wondering how much she was paying him for conspiring with her, saying they might want to keep it going? What she had said was they might want to "play it out."

Yeah, give her time to realize she had invited an ex-con to the house to go swimming. Though she didn't ask him about prison. He didn't think it was likely he'd see her again. She'd wake up thinking, What am I doing? And he'd mail the check to her or tear it up.

He went through the kitchen to the living room where Dawn was sitting on the edge of the sofa waiting for him, the check in her hand. She looked up at him, Foley on the other side of the coffee table, then at the check. "This is our score?"

"You don't sound grateful," Foley said.

"Why'd you take it? I told you what we're going for."

"She started writing the check—I tried to stop her."

"Well, this isn't going to do it."

"What's the amount?"

"You didn't look at it?"

"She had to leave and I walked her out."

"Something tells me," Dawn said, "you weren't going to mention the check."

"You want it?" Foley said. "It's yours."

"I want a lot more than this. What's the next move? Is she warming up to your charms?"

"She said I could clean her house."

"We'll do that next. But the main thing, she has to be nuts about you, Jack, if we're going to get what I want." Dawn came off the sofa, the check still in her hand. "I'll show Cundo what you're worth as a ghost expert."

"How much is it for?"

"Ten thousand. Actually it isn't bad as a down payment."

Foley said, "Have you ever scored that in a half hour?"

"I've made ten grand, Jack, in less than ten minutes," Dawn said, "that's why I'm directing the show."

She left with the check.

Ten grand. He'd said it was on the house, but Danny was already writing the check he thought would be for a couple of hundred, no more than five. But if he cleaned her house and she knew he wasn't a ghost expert, what would she be paying for? Turn it around. Why was he taking money from her? What was he, like an escort? The woman paying for his company? He wouldn't be *like* an escort, that's what he'd be, a fucking escort. If he gave her back the check that would be the end of the ghost business. No reason to see her again.

But he wanted to see her again.

He wouldn't mind keeping the check either.

Nineteen

"All the time we inside," Cundo said, "I'm thinking when I get my release I go straight to South Beach, two hours away, man, tha's all and return to life there. Get it all done in a few days, everything we talk about inside. The chicks in the clubs are asking each other who that cool guy is. He could be in the movies. On the beach I know some of them get away with not covering their *tetas*. You know a chick don't show them unless she proud of them. Or the ones you see in the Victoria's Secret catalog, these are even of a higher quality and you can look at them all you want if you casual about it. But, I also think of coming here, not stopping in South Beach. Do I want to be the Cat Prince again, go to clubs and go-go? Or do I want to come home and be with Dawn? Of course I do."

"Since you aren't a show-off," Foley said.

"But I was tempted. Pay her back for cheating on me, because I know she did."

Foley kept quiet.

"I say that because there is no chick can go eight years without getting laid when you know she has an appetite for it, man, loves it."

"I imagine though," Foley said, "there might be a few girls who've gone that long without it."

"Yeah, but they got something else turns them on. I don't care, I'm at peace with the universe. I lie here," Cundo said—stretched out in a recliner, holding a flute of champagne on his chest—"and look at stars. They all out this evening, every star in the fucking universe is right there. Heaven, where I almost went, if those fucking emergency guys hadn't found me, I believe is some of the planets up there we can't see, off beyond the stars. It's so they don't have to look at the Earth and think oh, man, am I glad to get out of that place."

Foley said, "You think you're going to heaven when you die?"

"Course I am. I was almost there before."

"You tell me you've killed a few guys."

"So? You ever hear of self-preservation? It's okay if you know they trying to see you dead or put away.

Why do I want to go to clubs and look at bare tits on the beach when I have Dawn here? She does whatever I want, rolls a perfect joint for me, as good as Little Jimmy's. You know faggots by and large roll the best joints, no question about it?"

"By and large," Foley said.

"But what she won't do is cook for me."

"You sure you want her to?"

"Before I went up and since I come home, I say why don't you ever cook? She say because she wants to be with me every moment, not be doing something else."

"I'd leave it at that," Foley said.

"She wears me out being loving," Cundo said. "How you doing with the crazy rich broad, her dead husband holding on to her?"

"There's been a change," Foley said. "I haven't told Dawn, but Mrs. Karmanos, when she came this afternoon to visit? She confessed she was putting the whole thing on 'cause she was bored. Listening to Madam Rosa gave her ideas. She got hexed and ran with it."

"Wait—she made up all the ghost stuff?"

"Everything. I took a guess that's what she was doing and called her on it."

"How could you know that?"

"I didn't, I guessed. She said it was fun for a while, but if we were gonna get to know one another—or she said 'each other'—she'd have to come clean."

"So, you looking into that, uh?"

"She meant get to know each other as friends."

"Of course," Cundo said. "But you say you didn't tell Dawn."

"I haven't seen her since this morning."

Cundo pushed up from the recliner to get his bare feet on the tile floor, still holding his champagne. He said, "Dawn tole me Mrs. Karmanos is hexed, maybe a little nuts in the head, but she's nice, she's timid, and has plenty of money left by her husband. Dawn say the woman is waiting to be taken."

"Not anymore," Foley said. "She's willing to keep playing if I want, but what would she be paying for?"

"You entertaining her."

"Like I'm an escort?"

"Or a bull put out to stud. Come on," Cundo said, "I'm kidding you. I know you better than the fortune-teller, better than Miss Megan the lawyer, better than anybody say they know you."

"You think so?" Foley said.

"You my friend," Cundo said and shrugged and took a drink of his champagne. "You the only man I know I can look in the face and say that."

"Walking the yard like a couple of road dogs," Foley said, "in our blues you had tailored for us— best-dressed prisoners in that dump, couple of old-time convicts. I don't think we ever had a serious argument."

"Only friendly ones. I tell you you full of shit, you tell me to get fucked. Almost three years, man."

"I was sure you'd start talking about a heist, get me working for you," Foley said, "start to earn back the thirty grand you paid Megan."

"Man, I tole you"—Cundo with a pained look now—"I don't want nothing from you. I paid her 'cause you don't want to do thirty years. Like I don't care Dawn wants you fucking with ghosts. They things you do, man, to keep the woman happy, tha's all. But can you tell Dawn," Cundo said, "she's wrong about Mrs. Karmanos? Tell her so she don't get into a rage and destroy my home? Dawn don't like to be tole she's wrong."

"I can try," Foley said.

Dawn joined them under the stars wearing a long black Morticia dress and pearl earrings.

"I thought you were taking me out to dinner?"

"When I'm ready," Cundo said, stretched out in the recliner again. "We been talking about something."

Foley poured her a glass of champagne and she sat down at the patio table with him.

"Well, I know where I'm going with Danny," Dawn said, "once we get through the ghost phase and Dr. Foley, everybody's best pal, Dr. Jack, tells Danny how to get Peter to settle down, find a cause he'd be good at. He's Pisces. Kurt Cobain and Albert Einstein. Danny's a Taurus. George Clooney and Liberace."

"How come," Foley said, "Evel Knievel is a Libra, 'cause he's levelheaded?"

"Dr. Jack," Dawn said, "has been reading about his sign and thinks he knows all about it. What I want to do is tell Danny that events later will have her looking back at this time, happy that she made the right decision. It has to do with Venus, her ruling planet, stirring her emotions. Romance is in the air and she's glad now she listened to Dr. Jack. I'll tell her, go ahead, there's nothing wrong with taking a chance on love."

" 'Here I go again,' " Foley said, " 'I hear those trumpets blow again . . .' "

Cundo's gaze came down from the stars to Foley.

"The fuck you talking about?"

"He's singing," Dawn said. "Once she's in a romantic mood," she said to Foley now, "you tell her not to worry about Peter. Let her know Peter's hanging out at the studio where they have *Born Again and Again* almost ready to go. Did she tell you that?"

Foley shook his head.

"Peter is a Pisces," Dawn said, "the sign of dreams. He's emotional, imaginative, but will have to go along with what they plan to do to his picture. Danny Karmanos won't be in it, they're looking for someone else to play the faith healer. But Danny doesn't care. Do you know why?"

"She's taking a chance on love?" Foley said.

"Yes, she is," Dawn said. "Now it's up to our Dr. Jack to let Danny know he feels the same way."

Dawn paused and it became a silence.

Cundo waited for Foley to tell her. He did, but took his time to find the right words, until finally he said, "I don't think it's gonna work the way you want. I told Mrs. Karmanos I robbed banks."

Dawn stared at him waiting for a punch line. "Yeah . . . ?"

"This was after she told me she was faking the whole thing. She's never heard from her husband's ghost. She made the whole thing up."

Dawn didn't move. She took a few moments before saying, "Really . . ."

Now she was lighting a Slim.

"You know she's an actress," Foley said.

"I know her better than you do, Dr. Jack."

"Well, I believe she made it up."

"Peter hounding her? Got on top of her one time?"

"She mentioned that."

"How did she tell you she was making it up? Just came out with it? 'Hon, didn't you know I was putting you on?'"

Foley kept quiet, waiting for Dawn to get finished.

"Did she say she had a confession to make, that she was lying the whole time? Or"—Dawn drew on the cigarette and let the smoke drift out of her mouth—"did you say something to prompt her."

"I took a shot," Foley said. "I asked if she was tired of pretending she had a hex on her."

"Something told you she was making it up?"

"I thought maybe she was, just maybe."

"And she admitted lying to you."

"Right away she changed from acting depressed to giving me a big grin. She said, 'You caught me.' I could tell she was relieved, glad it was over."

"Her loving husband dies," Dawn said, "and Danialle thinks it would be fun to pretend he's a ghost."

Foley wasn't going to say anything; there was no point in arguing with her. But he said, "She made up her mind she wasn't going to play the grieving widow the rest of her life. She has a sense of humor, and she couldn't say anything funny."

"I know the maids thought she was acting strange," Dawn said. "She told them there was a ghost in the house and they freaked. You know they're Filipina."

"Dawn," Foley said, "Mrs. Karmanos made the whole thing up. She told me. She pretended she was in touch with her dead husband. That's all I know."

"She pretended the rocking chair was rocking?"

Foley paused. "That's different."

"Did she make it stop?"

"She asked me if I did."

"Then who would you say, Dr. Jack, was fooling with the fucking rocking chair as you sat there watching it?"

"I don't know."

"Who do you suspect?"

"Jesus Christ," Cundo said, pushing up in the recliner to get after Dawn, "you're suppose to know everything and you don't get it?"

"I don't get what?" Dawn said. "Dr. Jack doesn't want to be a ghost expert? Doesn't care to walk around with a smudge pot?"

"Tha's exactly what he don't want to do. He's no con artist, he's a fucking stand-up bank robber. Leave him alone."

"I will," Dawn said, "if Jack can tell me who was rocking the rocker."

"He don't *care* who was rocking the fucking rocker, it's one of those things. It starts rocking by itself and nobody know why or gives a shit. Okay?"

There was a silence.

Dawn got up from the table and Cundo said, "Where you going, to cook our dinner?" He looked at Foley, who gave his buddy a tired smile.

"You're taking me out tonight," Dawn said, "why I got dressed for you. But tomorrow night, all right, I'll fix dinner, whatever you want. Have Dr. Jack dine with us."

Cundo said, "Anything I want? How about *camarónes al ajillo*?"

"We'll go Cuban tonight and tomorrow I'll fix you a surprise for dinner, okay? Let me comb my hair and I'll be with you."

She left them and Foley and Cundo had to look at each other, Cundo squinting.

"The fuck is going on?"

"I don't know," Foley said, "unless she wants to poison us."

Dawn raised the eyeliner pencil to the serious eyes staring at her in the bathroom mirror. She began to retrace the line on her eyelid and stopped and put the pencil on the edge of the sink, still looking at herself.

The boys-will-be-boys were beginning to gang up on her, still convicts with their buddy system and the guy-thing: guys were bigger than girls—in its usual application—so they were the boss and the boss was always right. From the beginning she was afraid they might get into a buddy act, hoping Foley was above it, but the guy-thing was part of each guy since birth. He's pulled slippery out of his mother and the nurse takes him and tells everybody it's a boy, hoping he doesn't grow up to be as haughty and arrogant as some of these fucking doctors. Cundo would make a remark and look at Foley to get his approval. He doesn't ever look at you. The one in the mirror said, "The prick."

By now Foley would have no intention of taking Cundo's money. His fortune. He was hanging out with his buddy. Dawn in the mirror said, "How much more time can you devote to the Cat Prince, Jesus, you waited eight years for this?"

On her own now.

The one in the mirror seemed to feel pretty confident about it. She said, "Why not?"

Right. The two buddies weren't the ones with all the money anyway.

Little Jimmy had the keys to the vaults: the payer of Cundo's accounts, owner of Cundo's homes. What he didn't have were the balls to do the guy-thing. And he loved her. Always dying to go to bed and show her some tricks. Or use the sofa, or the top of the television set—reminding Dawn of the porno flick, the girl about to light a cigarette pauses and says to the grocery deliveryman going down on her, "You mind if I smoke while you eat?"

Dawn picked up the eyeliner pencil and the raised face in the mirror said, "Wait. Why not get in the mood. Use the kohl."

The black kohl paste. She traced it over the eyeliner already adding an exotic look, brought the pencil along her lower lid and made the circle again and she was looking at herself with Egyptian eyes for the first time since she posed for Cundo's shots, the blond pharaoh with the eyes of Hatshepsut.

It was Marlene Locklear, the renowned spiritualist, who regressed Dawn under hypnosis to discover that in a past life, an astonishing 3,500 years ago, Dawn was Hatshepsut, daughter of a pharaoh and became a pharaoh herself: kind of a B.C. character who dressed as a male ruler with the *khat* head cloth, the *shendyt* kilt and the king's false beard. She held off the guys with their Upper and Lower Nile guy-thing and the threat of revolt, Hatshepsut playing a lone hand until her death in 1458 B.C.

"That was you," the Dawns said to each other, and thought, If you were pharaoh and a couple of hieroglyph rock chiselers were giving you a hard time . . . What would you do?

Twenty

They got on her again the next day. Foley stopped by as she was fixing breakfast for a change—Cundo saying the fucking eggs were too runny, the coffee was like water; Dawn saying, "Then hire a cook, you cheapskate."

It was an insult to his being a man, the little Cuban still a macho guy. Foley came in, Cundo told him to sit down, have a cup of watery coffee. Foley said no thanks, he came over to get the check.

Dawn said, "What check?"

"The one for ten thousand you picked up."

"You want to endorse it for us?"

"I'm giving it back."

"I get nothing for all the advice and counsel I gave her?"

Foley turned to Cundo seated at the kitchen table.

"Not once," Dawn said, "did she tell me she was faking, and I spent a lot more time with her than you did, Dr. Jack."

In this moment she was thinking she should pull back a little, and Cundo saved her from talking too much.

He said, "Give him the check."

"I *have* spent quite a lot of time on this failure."

"Give him the fucking check."

"You now do whatever Dr. Jack wants?"

"Don't call him that again," Cundo said. "Flip the fucking egg and go get the check."

She said to Foley, "You want me to tear it up?"

"I told you, I'm giving it back," Foley said.

"You think that'll get her pants off?"

"Jesus Christ," Cundo said, and put his hand flat on the table to get up.

Dawn laid the spatula on the range and left them.

"She wants that ten grand," Foley said.

"Keep it for yourself," Cundo said. "I won't have to give you an allowance. Last night she kept telling me the guy's ghost is in the house, whether the Karmanos woman was faking or not. I said to her, 'Honey,' in a nice way, 'will you please shut the fuck up.' Eight years inside I dream about her. I come out, she acts like she's my wife."

"It's none of my business," Foley said, "but I wouldn't let her put the houses in her name."

"She say something to you?"

"No, but I bet it's what she wants."

"The homes gonna stay with Little Jimmy."

"Watch she doesn't get too close to him."

"Last night when she don't shut up I slapped her a pretty good one across the face," Cundo said. "It stung my hand. I was sorry and tole her I try not to hit her again. But maybe I shouldn't have said that."

She came in the kitchen and handed Foley the check folded in half. He felt her hand touch his and saw her smile as she changed from a woman who was always right to a girl with green eyes circled in black, the way she was in some of the photos, having fun, with a serious intent.

"I might as well tell you," Dawn said, "what I was hoping to do with the money, get Cundo some new outfits so he'll look cool at his homecoming party, a big welcome-home blast, and invite everybody on the canal. It's a costume party, you have to wear a mask, since we don't know any of the people anyway. But, what'll make it the Venice party of the year, we have it on the roof."

"Costume party," Cundo said, "so she can do her Egyptian number. You have it on the roof, somebody'll fall off and kill themself."

"We string colored lanterns along the edge," Dawn said, "to show just how far you can go." She said to Foley, "What do you think?"

"About a bunch of masked drunks stumbling around forty feet from the ground . . .?"

"We can have it in the street, anywhere we want," Dawn said. "We *have* to celebrate Cundo's return."

Cundo said, "You want a party, you pay for it."

"We can talk about it some other time," Dawn said. "Remember, I'm fixing dinner this evening for my favorite guy. We want you to be here, Jack, and I've asked Little Jimmy. Oh, and I'm getting Tico to help me serve and clean up." She looked at Foley again. "You're going to see Danny later on?"

"For lunch."

"At her home?"

"Some place in Beverly Hills."

"So you might not make dinner."

"Jesus Christ," Cundo said, "he can keep the check or give it back and go to bed with the broad, it's his money, right? He can tear it up, he can give it to a bum, he can do anything he wants with it, so leave him the fuck alone, all right? Please."

Foley waited for Cundo to finish, said thanks, and asked if he could borrow the car.

"Take it, I'm not going nowhere."

Dawn said, "If you're picking Danny up . . ."

Foley said, "Yeah, at her house."

Dawn said, "She looks at the VW, garage paint on the front bumper—"

Cundo said, "Leave me out of this."

"Where my darling scrapes the bumper now and then driving into the garage—twice a day since he's been home. I see Danny look at the car, she says, 'Jack, why don't we take my Cadillac?' And gives you a half-assed reason why she doesn't want to be seen in a twelve-year-old VW."

"How do you know she drives a Cadillac?"

"Jack, come on."

What she said was, "Jack, do you mind if we take my CTS?"

Asking if it's okay, showing him more consideration than Dawn.

"The valet guys know my license plate. They like to take care of me."

All Foley said was, "Sounds good," without saying why or knowing what a CTS was.

Dawn was right, it turned out to be a Cadillac. Foley liked the interior, with a screen that came up out of the instrument panel. He said, "You watch movies while you're driving?" Danialle said the video screen was in back. This one was a computer; it told how to get where you wanted to go and what was playing on the stereo. Foley said, "Yeah?" It was as much as he needed to know. He was wearing his shades for Beverly Hills, his drip-dry sports jacket over a black T-shirt. He felt good, liking the way he looked. Danialle had on hip-hugger jeans and a man's white dress shirt, the tails tied together in a way that gave Foley a look at her tan midriff and navel.

"You must spend a lot of time in the sun."

"Alone by the pool," Danialle said, "with my grief. Thanks to you I'm beginning to feel like myself again."

"I haven't done anything."

She glanced at him. "Are you sure?" And said, "I was thinking we could go to the Sunset Marquis or the Beverly Wilshire, avoid the crowds."

"Aren't those hotels?"

"They serve lunch, Jack." She said, "I thought of Spago," and brought a cell phone out of her straw bag. "If Wolfgang's there he'll find us a table. I wanted to call this morning, but the girls, my Asian twins—they put their hands over their mouths, fingers straight up, when they're talking about me—they're driving me

bananas, absolutely sure Peter's ghost is still around."
She pressed buttons on the cell and said, "Hi, this is
Danny Karmanos. Let me speak to Wolfgang." She
listened and said, "Too bad. Tell him when he comes
out of hiding he missed his chance to meet America's
foremost bank robber." She turned off the cell. "I'll try
the Ivy."

Foley said, "I'd just as soon people don't know about
me," bringing her check out of his coat, folded, the way
Dawn had handed it to him. "And I'd like to give this
back to you. Not that I don't appreciate it, but I didn't
earn it."

She looked at Foley, stared for a moment, glanced
at the road descending through Benedict Canyon and
looked at him again, not saying a word as they crossed
Sunset and now were going south on Cañon.

Foley got as far as saying, "I remember you were
writing the check—" and she cut him off.

"Shhhh, don't say anything, I'm thinking."

"Where to have lunch?"

She didn't answer and they were both silent all the
way through the busiest part of Beverly Hills, past
shops and restaurants, bumper to bumper from Little
Santa Monica to Wilshire where Danialle said, "That
was Spago we just passed," and turned left saying,
"I've thought of the perfect place," and turned south

on Beverly Drive, "the menu's great and the location's ideal for what I have in mind." She said, "You do like Italian."

"Everybody likes Italian."

"There it is on the left, Piccolo Paradiso. They have my very favorite Italian wine, Amarone, and Norberto the maître d' I think is in love with me." She turned into a lot next to First Bank of Beverly Hills, directly across from the restaurant. They sat in the car while she told him why she had an account at First Bank.

"I was meeting an agent at Piccolo's, the guy dying to represent me, couldn't wait to tell me why I should be with him. I got there first. I'm late, but not nearly late enough; I'm waiting for an agent. So I came over here and opened a checking account. I have one at Citibank too, across from Spago. I got back to Piccolo's and now the agent's waiting with his bottle of water. I say, 'Sidney, I'm so sorry I'm late.' Sidney said, 'Danny, I'd wait day and night for you.' In Hollywood, you never want to be the one waiting unless you can make a story out of it."

Crossing the street to Piccolo's, three empty tables on the sidewalk, she said, "You know who I saw the last time I was here? Billy Baldwin."

Foley took a moment to say, "No kidding."

"After lunch we'll stop in the bank and open an account for you. It'll only take a minute."

By the time they were having their risotto, one with sliced sausages, the other with spinach puree and pesto, and a bottle of Amarone . . .

Dawn was taking her walk, jogging when she wanted to make a show, got to Tico's aunt's house and took off her top. Tico came after her with the towel to grab her from behind, get his young arms around her—God, but he was just right, a horny youth in his prime, slim, a main event, and she told him, "Sweetheart, I want you so bad, but . . . we don't have time. Tonight's the big night."

Tico, moving the towel over her back and around to her ribs, her arms raised, said, "Tonight, uh?"

"What have we been looking for," Dawn said, "trying to decide how to approach the job? Go in with guns drawn or try to be a little more subtle. I was thinking it could be an idea we've already considered but decided no, because it looked too simple. There was one plan we had I looked at again. I remember how easy it looked except for one, well, drawback."

Tico said, "What is it we doing?"

All the ideas she'd whispered to him during the afternooners, and he didn't know what she was talking about, pressing himself against her.

"Tico, what is it we want?"

"Yes, Cundo's fortune. Yes, of course, and you see a way to make off with it?"

"Not take everything but enough."

"Tell me how we do it."

"It came to me—"

"In a trance?"

"Out of the blue. I've been wearing myself out, becoming irritable, trying too hard to think of a foolproof way—"

"Yes, I remember—a way to slip a fortune, you said, out from under the old man."

"I never called him old," Dawn said. "He's old to you, but he isn't old. He pays attention. He has his guys who keep watch over his money, his accounts. He knows how to work things, and he's lucky."

"Tell me," Tico said, "what was it came to you?"

She turned in the towel to look at his face. "I can't believe it isn't the only thing you've been thinking about."

That got his white teeth grinning at her.

"See, I don't know," Tico said, "if you only talking or what. Since I have experience in this kind of business and you never stole anything before."

Still another one shoving the guy-thing at her.

"Tonight," Dawn said, "we take Little Jimmy away from Cundo. That's the first step."

"Yes . . .?"

"Without Cundo knowing we're doing it."

It got him grinning at her again, nodding, trying to look into her eyes. He said, "Yes, I think I know how you going to do it."

"No, you don't," Dawn said.

"I thought it might take a couple bottles of wine," Danny said, "to convince you it's yours," sounding to Foley a little surprised.

Or maybe disappointed, he wasn't sure. He had told her he was returning the check because he hadn't done anything to help her. "Dawn says she's positive there's a ghost in your house, but for all I know I'm working a con game." He held the check in his hand and waited for Danny to insist it was his, he earned it, something like that.

But she didn't. She said, "It's up to you," with kind of a shrug. "If you don't want it, tear it up."

Foley took a moment.

He said, "I've never torn up money before," trying to smile, took a chance and held out the check. "You want to destroy ten thousand dollars, here."

She reached out to take it and he pressed the bank note between her fingers. Her fingers touched the check while she looked in his eyes and she had to smile feeling his grip on the check. To Foley the smile meant she was kidding, she wanted him to keep the check. He thought of saying he'd pay her back, and thought, Why do you want to fuck this up? Tell her thanks. She wanted him to have it because he was . . . fun. All Foley said was, "You win," and put the check in his pocket.

She said, "Good, you got me out of that nutty role I was playing. I was afraid to tell Dawn. I kept thinking if I don't tell the right person, word will get around I've lost it. I knew I could tell you and you'd understand. You didn't seem that interested in what you were doing, though you and I got along fine. But Dawn? I didn't have a good feeling about her."

"I told Dawn the ghost was your own idea and she said, 'Making up a story about a ghost doesn't mean there isn't one in the house.'"

"She believes there is?"

"She'd like to."

"Well, my maids believe it. And you know I believed you were actually a ghost catcher." Danny leaned on the table, close enough to Foley to look in his eyes. She said, "You know, there might be one after all."

"The rocking chair?"

"And other things that don't seem quite normal."

"More paranormal?"

She said, "Listen to the ghost catcher. Have you ever thought of acting?"

He felt her moving in, coming at him now.

"To tell you the truth," Foley said, "I have played a part now and then, when I had to."

She said, "Oh, in prison, yes, of course," still close to him. "The kind of situation—a smelly, hulking convict, tattoos all over him, wants you to be his sweetheart? What do you do, kick him in the nuts?"

"He'd have to be a new arrival. I'd tell him I'm famous, known to the hacks *and* the population as the most artful bank robber in the known world, and if he tries to bend me to his will he'll do ninety days in the box."

"You just gave me the chills. If I told that to Wolfgang," Danny said, "you could get a table anytime you walked in."

"I'm known inside prison," Foley said, "and to some degree with FBI agents, but not the general public." He almost told her about the book Lou Adams was writing, over five hundred pages into it.

But Danny wanted to know if he'd ever robbed a First Bank, like the one across the street.

"I might've," Foley said, "but I'm not sure. I know I've never done that one." Trying to see the bank through the ornamental plants in front of Piccolo's.

"Would you sit here and case it?"

"I'd look it over from a car, not sitting here. Norberto tells the cops, 'Yes, of course I remember him, Mrs. Karmanos says is the most famous bank robber in America.' I'd pass on that bank anyway, the security guy sitting in front."

"I saw him as we got out of the car," Danialle said, "he's just some old guy they hired."

"Yeah, but he's a good kind of old guy. I saw him too," Foley said. "He's over seventy, weighs a hundred and forty pounds, wears white socks with his uniform and has a big .38 revolver on his belt he knows how to shoot. He took this job after he retired from the sheriff's office."

"You're guessing," Danialle said.

"I'll tell you another reason," Foley said. "In the past hour a cop car has driven past four times. One drove into the parking lot to turn around, instead of making a Uey, what he'd do if he was after somebody going the other way."

Danialle said, "There're cop cars all over Beverly Hills, and policemen on beats, and police*women*."

"I've noticed there's a lot," Foley said. "But you're right, I haven't been around here long enough to get local police customs straight."

The check came. Foley picked it up and she let him. He paid with his credit card balance running low.

While he was signing Danny said, "If you want we can go over to First Bank, I'll tell them I have an account, so you won't have any trouble depositing the check."

"What I think I'll do," Foley said, "is deposit half of it and take the rest in cash. I don't walk out of a bank with at lease five grand, I feel like a failure."

Twenty-one

It was the first time Foley could recall going in a bank to open an account. It was a lot different from the times he'd made withdrawals with a note. He was introduced to the manager, another first, a pleasant young man who seemed surprised and then delighted to see Mrs. Karmanos, happy to shake her hand and Foley's, and brought them to a conference room set off behind a glass wall. Across the lobby were the teller windows, security cameras on the wall behind them, four of the windows doing business, customers waiting in line, but no glass separating them from the money. Three other windows showed framed signs that said they were closed. They sat at the conference table waiting for the manager to return with the paperwork and Foley's five thousand in hundreds, fifty of them. He'd told the manager new bills were fine.

"It's nice to be rich," Foley said, "not have to stand in line."

Danny said she was surprised the manager knew who she was. Foley looked at her with no expression and she said, "Really, I've only been here a few times."

"Doing some banking," Foley said, "so you're late for lunch."

"Jack, when your name will open a picture and producers are sending you scripts, you can be on time for lunch. I'm not sure why," Danny said, "but you've made me want to get back to work. I think it's your energy. I can feel it."

"My energy," Foley said.

"I'm ready to pick up where Peter and I left off on *Born Again and Again.*"

"Dawn said they're looking for another actress to play the faith healer."

"Jack, who do you think told Dawn? I said I doubted I'd be working again for at least a year. But then I thought, Why? You've got a hit, keep the momentum going. Offer your friend Jack Foley a part. I see you come up to the front of the auditorium, your head down. I say, 'Look up at me, Jack Foley'—you're kneeling at my feet. I take your head in my hands and look up at the lights, like God is telling me what to do as I rub your head, feeling it, getting in touch with you, and before you know it, you're healed. You grab me around the knees and have to be restrained."

"What's wrong with me," Foley said, "I have leprosy eating away at my nose?"

She shook her head waving him off and her gaze drifted across the lobby to the teller windows. She said, "*No*," turning to Foley again with lights in her eyes, "you have an overwhelming desire to rob a bank, and I squeeze the idea right out of your head. I studied footage of Oral Roberts from the fifties, the way he laid on hands was inspiring. He was so fervent you're afraid one Sunday morning he's going to fracture some believer's skull. *But*," Danny paused and said, "I just had an idea. Instead of healing you and you grab me around the knees, you get me to go along on your next bank job." She said, "I'm serious, I'm going to talk to Peter's writer about it, a young guy who gets a million and a half a picture and a cut of the back end if it makes money. He wrote *When the Women Come Out to Dance*, a fantastic script that was never produced. I'm told studio execs didn't understand it and eventually chewed the script to death. What I'll do, Jack, I'll tell the writer my idea and he'll say you're kidding. At this point in the story I'm beginning to lose my faith, but there's something about the bank robber that fascinates me and I go off with him. What happens during this interlude is the *and Again* of the title. I was born again in the first picture and I'm born again *again* in the sequel."

"You get your faith restored by a bank robber," Foley said. "How does that work?"

"The writer will come up with something."

"I don't want to be in the movies," Foley said. "I like acting like myself."

"That's what you'll be doing, playing yourself. I think you'll even get some movie offers."

"To play another bank robber?"

"The first time you're on the screen you're sitting in a car across the street from the bank. You hold still as a police car creeps past."

"I hold still."

"Jack, you're in a bank right now with no intention of robbing it, you're being yourself. I think you could be good."

"You have the clout," Foley said, "to tell the expensive writer and the new director what you want?"

"There's a good chance," Danny said. "*Born Again* was made on a thirty-million-dollar budget and grossed over two hundred million worldwide. I wear a blouse with a Peter Pan collar and a long black skirt slit up to my knees so I can move around the stage. I'm the star and this is the same part. But it needs fresh ideas, unexpected plot turns. I've been thinking, what if a woman comes up to me before the congregation with a baby in her arms. Jack, the baby's dead and the mother begs me to bring the infant back to life. At this point in the film I'm on the verge of giving up my ministry. If I lay on my hands and nothing happens, I'm out of business. But if I refuse even to try . . . The scene doesn't go anywhere."

"But if you take the baby in your hands," Foley said, "and it begins to cry—"

Danny, shaking her head: "That's way beyond the ability of any faith healer. I'd lose the audience."

"Not if the little nipper's alive, still breathing," Foley said. "The baby cries as you raise it heavenward in your hands. The congregation goes wild and you're back in the game."

He watched her thinking about it.

"Why does the mother believe the baby's dead?"

"I have no idea," Foley said. "Ask your million-dollar screenwriter. Tell him you want to end the movie with it, your biggest miracle yet."

"But I could go to jail."

"For appearing to restore life?"

"For fraud. Taking money under false pretenses."

"All right, you tell the crowd, once they quiet down, the baby was alive. You didn't bring it to life. You didn't even squeeze the child's head. They admire your honesty—even more, your humility—and you get your faith back." Foley was nodding. "The dead baby who isn't dead's a good touch." He said, "We took care of that problem, now tell me where the security guard is. The old guy I thought looked like an ex-deputy?"

She said, "What about him?" her gaze moving to the bank's glass door.

"He isn't there anymore."

Danny said, "He went to the bathroom."

Foley said, "You want to bet?"

Lou Adams got out of his Chevy, left it double-parked in front of Piccolo Paradiso and came across the street to the parking lot where Foley and Mrs. Karmanos were being held, not technically but with a half-dozen Beverly Hills cops standing by with their holsters unsnapped. Ron Deneweth came out to the sidewalk as Lou Adams approached the scene.

Lou said, "Ron, does that woman look like a bank robber to you? She's a *movie star*, for Christ sake."

"She's with Foley," Ron said. "I didn't know she's a movie star. I didn't know it was Mrs. Karmanos till we ran her car."

"I told you he never packs," Lou said. "You got the Beverly Hills police department ready to draw on him."

"I told him to stand by, that I'd called you."

"He get smart with you?"

"He said he was opening an account."

"Who's the old guy Foley and Danialle Tynan are talking to?"

"He's bank security. Tynan," Ron said, "that's her acting name?"

"One she was born with," Lou said. "Who you suppose they're laughing at, you or me?"

They watched Foley say something to Mrs. Karmanos, leaving her with the security guard, Mrs. Karmanos putting her hand on the old guy's shoulder. The Beverly Hills police officers beginning to fidget, not knowing what was going on, Foley walking past them toward the street.

Lou Adams said to Ron, "Tell the cops we don't need 'em, you read the situation wrong."

"It's my fault, huh?" Ron said. "Get it enough times, now you know why I quit the cops," and moved off as Foley walked up.

"You gonna put this in your book?"

Lou Adams seemed almost ready to smile.

"Chapter fifty," Foley said, " 'How I thought I knew everything but fucked up.' "

"Things aren't always as they appear," Lou said. "There's a shot of John Dillinger laid out at the Cook County morgue with a sheet covering him, the sheet standing up a foot or so from his groin area, like he's got a tent pole for a dick. The man's so legendary people believed he could still have a woody when he's dead."

Foley said, "Somebody was pulling a joke?"

"No, it was his hands resting one on top the other under the sheet. Your case," Lou said, "known convicted felon is seen entering a bank, law enforcement's gonna check it out."

"Seen because you're breathing down my neck," Foley said, "the only reason. If I had a terrible urge to stick up a bank, you wouldn't know about it till you read it in the paper."

"All right," Lou said, "let's bet on it. I read about a bank job has your MO all over it, how this sweetheart of a guy made off with five gees, I swear I won't tell the cops or the Bureau or come after you myself. What I'll do is give you the chrome-plated .45 I was awarded by my colleagues for shooting down three Haitian guys that kidnapped a five-year-old kid. They want three hundred large or they chop the kid up and send him home in a bag. I shot to kill, the only guys I felt good about doing it. I'll give you the piece and say, 'You win, partner,' and never bother you again. How's that sound?"

"You're daring me," Foley said, "isn't gonna do it, or giving me your chromed-up rod. Why can't you get it in your head I'm out of the bank business?"

"See, if I accept that," Lou Adams said, "I'd have to believe we're getting closer to something else going down. Jack, you live with felons you're gonna get dirty."

Twenty-two

Little Jimmy waited on his knees in the confessional for the window to slide open. He could hear the faint sound of a woman's voice on the other side of the priest but not her words. The priest's name was on the middle door, MSGR. WILLIAM EASTON. Jimmy had entered the door on the right to kneel here in the dark waiting: Msgr. William Easton, higher up than a priest and maybe was old, having been a priest long enough to be made a monsignor. The next higher title was a bishop. Jimmy had never heard of a bishop hearing confessions. Now he heard the woman's window slide closed. A few moments later his window came open on its tracks and he could make out the priest through the screen leaning toward him, his hand supporting his head, close to Jimmy but not looking at him.

Monsignor Easton said, "Yes?"

Little Jimmy said, "Bless me, Father, for I have sinned," making the sign of the cross as he offered this admission. "It has been twenty-seven years since my last confession." He paused as Monsignor Easton raised his head from his hand.

"Twenty-seven years."

"Yes, Father. Since then I have missed Mass almost fourteen hundred times, though I go to midnight Mass sometimes at Christmas if a friend desires to go, and also on Easter Sunday when I was still living in Cuba, my home."

The monsignor asked Little Jimmy if he was married.

"No, I have never the desire."

"You keep company with women?"

"Not to speak of. Though in the past year I have been more with women than before. I thought to myself, well, as a new experience it wasn't so bad."

"Up to this time you've been chaste?"

"You mean, Father, by dudes? If I like the guy he don't have to chase me."

"You're saying you have relations with men."

"Almost all my life."

"Did you ever tell it in confession?"

"No, I didn't think I was committing a sin. The dude was always willing. You know, a single guy. We fool around, we not hurting anybody."

"Possibly not, but it is a mortal sin."

"Why? They don't say in the Bible don't do it."

"Not clearly, but it's implied," Monsignor Easton said. "Are you involved in the sale of drugs or other illegal activities?"

"No, I hardly touch it. I smoke weed, you know, but only a few times a week to relax my mind. The illegal activities? I'm not sure of this. Some funds have been used to pay prison guards, but it wasn't for me, so I don't see I was committing a sin. It was for my boss when he was an inmate in Florida."

There was a silence, one long enough that Little Jimmy wondered if the monsignor had fallen asleep, bored from hearing the same old thing; though some of the confessions he heard in Venice, man, might be hard to believe.

"Can you tell me," the monsignor said, "why it's been twenty-seven years since you've been to confession?"

"The last time before this," Little Jimmy said, "I was in prison in Cuba for a crime that didn't hurt no one. I was afraid I would die at the hands of prisoners desiring to make love to me in an excessive manner. But I was save by my boss, also in that prison, Combinado, before it could happen."

The monsignor said, "And this time, why are you confessing?"

"I want to be on the safe side, confess to missing Mass fourteen hundred times," Little Jimmy said, "because I'm going to dinner in honor of my boss. There is a possibility he could have the fortune-teller, who's preparing the food, poison me."

Again there was a silence.

"This is the same boss who saved your life the time before, when you were in prison?"

"Yes, I don't think in my heart he'll have her poison me. He would be more likely to have someone shoot me. But there are times, since he's with this fortune-teller woman again, he acts crazy. Is why I don't want to take a chance. You know, if I have sins on my soul."

Again he waited.

This time the monsignor said, "Do you remember how to say the Act of Contrition?"

"Yes, of course," Little Jimmy said. "Oh my God I'm heart'ly sorry for having offended Thee—"

"Wait," Monsignor Easton said. "Let me give you your penance first."

Little Jimmy came out of St. Mark's making a sign of the cross with the hand he'd dipped in the holy water font and approached his Bentley standing at the curb. His driver Zorro, resting against the front fender with his arms folded, took his time turning to open the door.

"You confess your sins? Tell the priest everything you been doing?"

"Everything."

"Some sins he never heard of before?"

"Nothing outrageous."

"What do you do for penance, flagellate yourself?"

"Don't be disgusting. I say ten Our Fathers and ten Hail Marys," Little Jimmy said, "and anything I did to get God pissed at me is forgiven."

By six Tico was sitting in the kitchen of Cundo's home drinking red wine with Dawn who wasn't drinking, quiet for a change, not bothering Tico with situations from his past life, Tico talking, asking why Cundo bought fifteen-dollar wine—the price sticker still on the bottle—when he could afford to pay fifty, a hundred dollars a bottle and serve his guests a vintage they could swirl in their big fishbowl wineglasses and smack their lips over. "Is the man cheap? Let me start over. Is the man a cheap motherfucker? I'm forgetting my heritage, my sweet mama getting out of Arkansas soon as she hears big-city niggas talking, they visiting Tunica, Mississippi, to lay money on the gaming tables. Soon as she understood what they saying she's gone. My mama say to me I'm high-yella with a Costa Rica tan. What I have to do, talk to some of these stone-ass hip-hoppers, get me the latest nigga expressions, so I ain't going around saying, 'How you doing, my man?' stead of 'Sup, bro?' Walk away I say, 'Have a good one.' Foley I bet could teach me how to talk and his speech is mostly pure white. Tha's where you learn the expressions, among the bad boys, the jive-ass gangbangers showing off, dying to get out and shoot some dude, anybody, it don't matter."

They sat at the kitchen table, two ashtrays and the bottle of red on the clean round surface.

"You're rambling," Dawn said. "Is it the wine or your nerves?"

"I'm a ramblin' man," Tico said, wearing a white shirt mostly unbuttoned and a lavender scarf over his black curls. "You hear me ramblin' means I feel good."

"But no rambling at dinner," Dawn said, "when I'm talking to Cundo. I have very specific things I want to tell him."

"This man with the temper, stings you with his talk and slugs you in the belly."

"Slaps my face when he feels like it."

"Be the revenge of the fortune-teller. You see it working?"

"Sweetie, all you have to do is serve, exactly the way I told you, leaving the top on the silver platter you place at Cundo's end of the table. You don't remove the cover."

"Want to keep the food hot."

"That's right. I give you a nod and you take it off."

"I never been a waiter, but I can do it with style," Tico said. "What's Cundo up to?"

"Sleeping off lunch. He had a few La Yumas, what he calls straight rum over ice."

Tico grinned. "He's having a good time being out of prison. What about Little Jimmy?"

"He'll be here."

"You say he scared to death of Cundo. You sure he's coming?"

"I told him not to worry about Cundo, I'll see he behaves himself. Jimmy's in love with me. You know I'm his first woman."

"What about Foley?"

"He's in love with me too, but it's giving him problems."

"No, what I ask, is he coming?"

"I'm afraid Dr. Jack's gonna miss the party."

"He don't want to be here, you cooking dinner?"

"He's trying his luck with Danny Karmanos. If he can't play the ghost expert," Dawn said, "he'll try to dazzle her with close-call situations from his life in crime. Like he's about to leave a bank just as the police pull up in front. Danny can't wait to hear how he gets away."

"How does he?"

"You have to hear him tell it," Dawn said, "lets you know how clever he is. One of his tricks, he says something funny and closes in while you're laughing."

"Takes you by surprise," Tico said.

"With Danny, I can see him trying to kiss her and she stops him cold. Who does this phony baloney think he is? Dr. Jack is not in her league and she lets him know it. Danny's a movie star and he's what, a fucking bank robber."

"She say that to him?"

"In a nice way," Dawn said.

The way Foley told it to Danny:

"The time I almost got caught I was lucky. It was the rainy season out here. I pulled the job in a raincoat and stuffed the money in an umbrella I kept closed. I'm almost out of the bank and there's a black-and-white Crown Vic in front, the two uniforms out of the car stopping people from entering the bank, telling them a robbery's in progress. They waved to us, just inside the door, to come out, and that's how I managed to slip past the cops, with the rain people. As soon as the police stepped inside, I took off. Remember Gene Kelly in *Singin' in the Rain?* That was me splashing along Hollywood Boulevard with an umbrella full of money."

This was earlier, Foley telling true-crime tales on Danny's patio, the two sipping vodkas with lime juice, Danny grinning, shining her eyes at Foley, though Peter was still around somewhere.

Time for a swim. The best time, Danny said, dusk settling in.

Foley now in his low-rise briefs rather than a pair of Peter's trunks—even the ones Danny said Peter had never worn—Foley preferring to look like a Calvin Klein ad in the low-rise grabbers. Danny had a towel around the skimpy bottom of her two-piece, reminding Foley of *Sports Illustrated*, the one with all the chicks in their swimsuits. He always referred to those bits of cloth the girls wore, ones you could ball up in one hand, as swimsuits. His favorite was the chick standing with her thumb hooked in the waist of her panties. They hadn't been in yet but stood holding or wearing towels, Foley hanging his in front, then after a while over his shoulder. Hey, let's go if we're going.

They were standing by the open cabana on the patio side of her California hacienda, looking at the swimming pool as Danny said, "Wait, you're about to see it." She turned, shading her eyes to look at the sun, and brought her gaze back to the pool. "Watch the water. The sun hits it at just the right angle and there's something spooky about it and yet you want to dive in. There! Watch the pool, the way the sun takes its last look and seems to lie there, dark all around before it seems to sink in the water and I start to shiver. Look, I'm shivering right now."

Or putting it on.

"Can you cry when you want? I mean acting."

"I'm not good at crying when I'm overwhelmed with happiness. I have the happy crying scenes rewritten. I told the director I'm a tough born-again but can show little hints that I'm moved by what's happening to me. It's fun." She said, "Last night I took a dip with the pool lights off."

With only the moon, Foley thought, lighting the scene.

"With a dreary moon, dark clouds passing in front. What do you think sneaked into my mind?"

What if Peter *is* here? Foley thought.

"What if Peter *is* here?" Danny said. "Dawn believes his spirit is still in the house, or someone's spirit.

Her manner put me off, the way she judges you with that condescending tone. But I believe most of what she told me. You saw the rocking chair."

"What I do," Foley said, "is not think about it."

"But I live here with it."

"Give it away. Or, if you want, I'll bring a smudge pot the next time I come. Dawn swears it'll run any spirits hanging around. Or, she said if you stand up to the ghost you can get rid of him. Tell him to get out, you have a new life about to begin."

She said, "Do I?" unwrapping the towel, ran to the pool and dove in.

The scene from a number of movies: the girl says the line and runs out to dive in the ocean, not a swimming pool, and the guy either waits or goes after her. Foley, with some reluctance, followed her, did a nice flat dive from a run and scraped the bottom of the shallow end. He did a few underwater strokes and came up to stand with his chin above the surface. Danny, floating in the deep end with effortless moves, said, "Why don't you come and talk to me?"

Foley didn't believe he could talk and tread water at the same time. He was honest about it and said, "I'm not much of a swimmer. I think because where I've been lately they don't have pools."

"But you like to dive," Danny said, "and jump off high places, don't you?" She seemed to know that, not waiting for an answer, and said, "Peter and I didn't care much for diving, why there isn't a board. He'd swim a few lengths to relax, come out of the pool and say, 'There. I can read the fucking script now without tearing it apart.'" Danny smiling now. "He meant ripping it up with his hands."

"You ever see him do it?"

"No, he was reminding himself he had to be tough. He had no patience with screenwriters who tried to make scene descriptions sound literary. Peter called them 'Look-at-me-writing' scripts. He'd say, 'Now look at the Coen brothers screenplay of *No Country for Old Men*. It's spare but it's all there, without one extra word.' He'd allow the studio to give him predictable stories like *Born Again,* and he'd put his writer and DP on it and come up with scenes you'd swear were for a documentary. Peter loved realism, and Terry Malick. *Days of Heaven* was Peter's favorite picture."

She said, "I'm serious about his ghost in the house. Or whoever it is." She said, "But not serious enough to do anything about it. Aren't you tired of talking about ghosts?"

They came out of the pool and she said, "Don't move. I'm going to take off my suit and put on a robe. Are you all right? Help yourself to the bar in the cabana. I'll get some dry undies. New ones," she said, "still in the package. I remember buying them for Peter."

He said, "You're kidding, aren't you."

She paused before saying, "If you don't want to wear them, don't."

Foley sat on the patio smoking a cigarette. Not anxious to show off in her husband's underwear. He realized he should never've told her she had a new life about to begin. She said, "Do I?" in a coy way, because she knew it was her line. "Do I?" Playing the part. But that could be all it was, a reaction.

She could be feeling Peter's presence, not as a ghost but on her mind and she wasn't ready to let go of him, whether she knew it or not.

Foley believed he could make the premoves and if she softened her eyes it was okay, they'd keep going and in time they'd be acting like they were in love or on their way. Giving it a try because they were comfortable with each other.

Or, she was already into her new life; she could do what she wants and not hold back. It came down to does she or doesn't she.

He believed Peter's underwear could be the key, if he put them on and they didn't fit or they looked funny.

Or, she might not even bring them.

He was patient. Waiting, wondering if Dawn had fixed the little guy something Cuban, one of his favorites, though he wouldn't bet money on it.

He looked up to see Danny in her bathrobe coming out of the cabana with a pair of men's white underwear in her hand.

Twenty-three

Dawn watched Tico setting the oval table in the dining room, a chair with arms at each end, a chair without arms on each side, white linen covering the table.

"You can seat ten people here," Tico said, "even twelve. Four people like this are too far apart from each other."

"It's the way I want it," Dawn said.

"What if Foley comes?"

"He does, he's losing his touch."

"He comes he can take my seat. I be in the kitchen but keeping an eye on Cundo, the other end of the table."

"From the kitchen," Dawn said, "you'll be looking at his back. Cundo always sits facing the room. You could watch from only a few feet behind him. But remember, after you place the platter on the table and remove the cover, stand to one side. Don't go back to the kitchen, I may need you."

"Yes, I see that—he don't like what you tell him. Where did you put my pistol?"

"You won't need it," Dawn said. "If he goes bananas hit him with something, a frying pan. I'm hoping he behaves himself." She said, "The other thing, what about Little Jimmy's driver?"

"You want to feed him?"

"I want to know where he'll be. Does Zorro stay in the car?"

"I don't know," Tico said. "Maybe he sleeps, maybe likes to walk around."

"But he has to stay close," Dawn said, "in case Little Jimmy wants him."

"Or he's ready to go home," Tico said. "What is it worries you?"

"Nothing," Dawn said, "but I hate surprises."

Foley's bottle of Old No. 7 was on the kitchen table. If Dawn had a glass or two of bourbon she didn't show it. She was always cool.

Cundo stepped out of the shower to see Tico waiting for him with a tall drink that looked like a collins, decorated with a cherry on top. Cundo took most of it in three swallows, a collins made of bourbon, and told Tico to get him another one of these, he was dying of thirst. He shaved around the tuft of hair beneath his lower lip he had grown in the past few days. He was thinking of growing a beard but held off because of all the gray bristles he shaved from his jaw. He liked his soul patch, it was dark.

Cundo went in the bedroom where Dawn had laid out a white shirt for him, on the bed with a pair of black silk pants, part of a suit he hadn't worn in eight years and slipped on a pair of sandals. He sat at the vanity and Dawn appeared behind him to stroke his hair with a brush and refasten the rubber band holding his ponytail. She stepped back saying, "There," to his reflection. "You're perfect."

"There's no pocket in this fucking shirt."

"You don't need one."

"For my cigarettes."

"It would ruin the look. I paid two hundred dollars for the shirt, out of my allowance."

"You think for that much they give you a pocket."

He lighted a cigarette with his Bic lighter, a black one, stared at himself in the mirror, leaned forward a little and blew a perfect smoke ring at himself.

"We'd go out," Dawn said, "you'd wear the black Palm Beach suit, a black shirt, that thin yellow tie and you'd carry a yellow Bic."

"The lighter was yellow, yes," Cundo said, "but the tie was a shade of ochre. I never saw an ochre Bic. I wouldn't mind having a few."

He stared at himself with dreamy eyes. Dawn called them his bedroom eyes. She said, "You know how people look at you?"

"What people?"

"Ones who know about you. You're famous, the last of the Cocaine Cowboys. Now you're back. They see you and wonder what you're up to."

"Nothing," Cundo said.

"They would never believe that. They see how you live, in the same house. They see you buy me a car."

"You leading up to something I don't want to hear, so don't say it. Tell me what you cooking."

"It's a surprise."

"Let's see, what are you? Dawn Navarro—you Spanish by way of Puerto Rico sometime back but don't look it. You gonna fix Cuban rice and beans?"

"You'll never guess," Dawn said.

"Why won't I?"

"I don't want you to."

"Why don't I smell nothing cooking?"

"I haven't put it on yet. I'll start when everyone has a drink. We sit at the table, we'll have wine with dinner, Tico the lavender gangbanger serving. He looks like a male escort this evening, a little rouge on his cheeks. But you're the guest of honor, the main man. I still think we should have the roof party. No hurry, sometime when you're in the mood."

"Since I like so much to go up on roofs."

"What I want to believe more than anything," Dawn said, "you really have retired from a life of crime, so to speak. You're not simply resting between rounds."

"So to speak," Cundo said.

"We'll go out once in a while, of course. But this time you won't be competing with all the Tony Montanas in their white suits, their collars spread open. You'd come along vamping in your all-black outfit and ochre tie. I'll never again say it's yellow, and I'll tell anyone who asks you'd like to be left alone, to your own devices."

Cundo was still seated at the vanity. Dawn leaned close to kiss him as Cundo said, "Foley thinks I should go to Costa Rica with him."

Dawn kissed his cheek, lingering for a moment before she straightened and looked at him in the mirror.

"Really?"

"One time he mention it to me."

They had drinks in the sitting room, vodka martinis because, Cundo said, the ones made with gin caused you to be drunk too soon. Little Jimmy asked Cundo if he was angry with him for something he did. Cundo said, "If you tole it in confession I also forgive you," and blessed Jimmy saying, "*Absolvo te*," Cundo making the sign of the cross in the air.

Tico watched Dawn. She excused herself and was gone for almost half an hour. When she returned and said, "Let's go sit at the table," Tico saw she had made up her eyes in the fashion of a royal woman of Egypt.

He poured wine, though only Cundo and Little Jimmy were seated at the table, took the empty bottle and pushed through the door to the kitchen. Dawn stood at the range, where two saucepans were on simmer. She said, "You'd better open another bottle, and put the baguette on the table, if you will, please." Sounding so nice this evening, even with her eyes made up like that. "And the butter. It's in the fridge."

Tico pushed through the door to the dining room and placed the bread and the plate of butter in the middle of the table—Cundo and Little Jimmy talking about point spreads—and draped a napkin over his shoulder and unscrewed the cap from the fifteen-dollar bottle of wine Cundo, the cheap fuck, had bought.

In the kitchen again he saw the lids off the saucepans and the platter standing on its short legs by the pans, its silver cover in place.

"Not a word," Dawn said.

Tico was anxious now. He picked up the platter by its little silver wings sticking out, reached the door and turned his head to see Dawn coming with another silver platter. Tico knew what he was serving, but had no idea what Dawn was bringing to the table.

She came behind Tico who used his hip to hold the door for her. Tico placed his dish at Cundo's end of the table and watched Dawn set hers down in front of her place at the other end. Tico thought it could be more of what he was serving. Dawn sat down in her chair with arms. She looked at Tico waiting by the table, gave him the nod and turned her eyes on Cundo as Tico the gangbanger lifted the lid and stepped back with it to watch Cundo:

Cundo staring at the platter of macaroni and cheese, some of the macaroni sticking out of the creamy melted cheese that had too much color to be something good to eat. It looked more like imitation macaroni and cheese, if there was such a thing.

Dawn waited for Cundo to look at her.

He wasn't smiling.

She said, "You don't think it's funny?"

Tico started laughing. Little Jimmy grinned. Cundo stared at Dawn until gradually the table was silent.

"I know I told you," Dawn said to Cundo, "the ruling planet for Scorpios happens to be Pluto, the reason your personality is dark and you tend, much of the time, to be so intense. Mine's Jupiter. It's why I'm not only optimistic, I'm lucky and, as you will agree, have quite a cheerful nature. I like doing favors for people. Our colors are sort of close. Yours burgundy and mine purple, dating back to my pharaoh days when I was Hapshepsut and ran both ends of the Nile. Your symbol, the scorpion, is secretive and of course deadly. But the part of the body ruled by Scorpio are the genitals, an area I thought might work just right for us, since I'm a fun lover and you're more like an animal in bed."

She watched Cundo light a cigarette.

Tico stepped over to move an ashtray closer to him.

"Let's see," Dawn said, "Scorpio rules insects while Sagittarians rule horses. Not much of a link there, but I thought we could work it out. You're strong-willed, I'm easygoing. You like my style but don't care to hear about me enjoying myself if you're not around. So when you come right down to it, Cundo, we're not at all emotionally suited to one another. You want me fawning over you all the time when I'm not cooking. You kept asking if I'm being a saint. Remember? 'Are you being a saint for me?' I'm playful about sex. You're so intense you have to dominate. You'd keep me in a cage if you could. I mean, come *on*. During the eight years I waited for you I hardly fooled around at all. Eight years, Cundo, is a long time."

Cundo said, "You fucked Jack Foley, didn't you?"

"You already hit me for that, hard. What else do you want to do? Foley's a Libra, so his ruling planet is Venus. He can't help it if he likes to be sociable, it's the way he is. I knew if I stepped out on a Scorpion I could get my butt stung. The problem is, you think the only way to handle me is to lock me up, let me out at bedtime. But I won't stand for that."

"You won't, uh?" Cundo said.

He looked at Little Jimmy.

"You believe this?"

Jimmy didn't nod or say a word, struck dumb.

Cundo said to Tico, "Where are you in this? You fucking her too?"

Tico said, "Who me?" but with a grin, on and off.

"Is Jimmy the only one who knows you I can trust? Jesus Christ, or you get him in bed too? This woman say she loves me so much?"

Cundo drew on his cigarette and stubbed it in the pile of macaroni and cheese and looked up at Dawn:

Dawn standing at her place now. She set aside the cover of the serving dish in front of her and brought out Tico's pistol, the good-looking Walther PPK with the silencer attached, and pointed it at Cundo.

"Jesus Christ," Cundo said, "you want to leave, go, get out of my sight. I won't stop you."

Dawn said, "I'm not leaving, you are," aimed the pistol at Cundo's white shirt without a pocket and shot him three times in the chest, the silenced pistol sounding no louder than a BB gun.

"There," Dawn said, "I'll never have to fuck that dwarf again."

Tico lifted Cundo's head by the hair, holding it at arm's length like a game kill, a trophy, Tico saying, "I think he's still alive."

"Not this time," Dawn said, seated again, smoking one of her Slims, using a napkin to wipe her prints from the gun. "Close his eyes and you won't think he's watching you. How does the back of the chair look?"

"Clean," Tico said. "The shots didn't go through, they still inside him. Tha's good, uh? No blood to clean up."

"But there's some on the tablecloth. Take it off and soak it in cold water with a little vinegar."

Tico grinned. "You know the secrets of a good housewife and how to shoot somebody. I could not believe it. You take the gun from the platter—*pow pow pow,* he's gone to the other side. Can you see him over there?"

"Not yet. He must be having trouble gaining admission." She said to Little Jimmy standing by the table staring at Cundo, "Sweetie, will you start clearing, please? Take the macaroni and cheese to the kitchen and dump it. Cundo ruined it with his cigarette."

Tico watched Jimmy move through the door to the kitchen. "He looks like he's in a trance."

"He's thinking," Dawn said, "how did I get into this?"

"He's more afraid of you," Tico said, "than he ever was of Cundo. Man, you were ready. I could not believe it, you make a speech and shoot him. *Pow pow pow.*"

"With your gun," Dawn said, "the one you used on the guy at Saks."

Oh, now she was threatening him, but in a nice way. "You get caught, you say no, it wasn't me, it was that guy owns the gun." Tico grinned at her. "I can tell you, you be sorry you ever do that."

Dawn said, "Darling boy," a little surprised, "you're my *numero uno*, I couldn't begin to pull this off without you." Jimmy came into the dining room and she said, "Jimmy, I want you and Tico to understand, the three of us are in this together. We rely on one another. We share what comes out of this and not have to worry about Cundo." She said to Little Jimmy, "He'll never be mean to you again. But you can't tell Zorro what we did, he's not on our side. All right? You promise?" Little Jimmy nodded his head and Dawn said, "You promise as God is your witness you'll never tell a soul about this?"

"Yes," Jimmy said, "I promise."

"Not Zorro or anyone?"

"Yes, I promise."

"As God is your witness?"

"Yes, as God is my witness."

She thought of Cundo, the way he asked if she was being a saint.

Tico watched Dawn put her hand out to him. Jimmy went to her and bent down so she could kiss him and pat his cheek. "Tomorrow," she said, "we'll look at the books, okay? One of the first things we'll want to do is put the homes up for sale, then decide where to go from there. Okay?"

Jimmy nodded without saying a word and left, going out the back way.

Tico said, "You don't worry about him?"

"I know he's a risk," Dawn said, "but we can't keep him locked up. If Zorro finds out he might make Jimmy pay him, you know, to keep quiet."

"I could take care of Zorro."

"You could?" Dawn said.

Like a helpless woman now, after drilling Cundo three times. Tico smiled. "It would be easy," he said. "Hand me my gun."

It was on the table where she sat, resting after the execution. She said, "Foley's another problem. He'll want to know where Cundo is."

"What if he came for the dinner?"

"Well," Dawn said, "I'm not sure anyone would miss either of them. Barely out of prison."

"You shoot Foley too?"

"I'd have to, wouldn't I?"

"You could do that?"

She looked at him with her made-up eyes and said, "Or you could."

He watched her draw on the cigarette and exhale a long slow stream of smoke.

"Did you get the ice?"

"Sixteen bags. The car is in the garage backed up to the freezer, where I put the ice."

She was shaking her head. "Cundo goes in first and we lay the bags on top of him. If they don't fit you can empty enough bags to cover him. The thing is, love, if I sell the houses in the next few days, we'll have to chip him out of the ice and arrange a quick burial at sea."

Tico, grinning, said, "You remind me of my mama."

"I look like her?"

"The way you talk. You funny the way she is. My cool mama, Sierra. Mr. FBI say he charge her for drugs I don't help him. Tha's the kind he is even bullshitting. Sure, I help him, I get in here where it's happening."

Dawn turned her head to stare at Cundo in the chair, his head against the backrest. "I thought you closed his eyes."

"I close them. They must have come open."

"Did you feel for a pulse?"

"You say he was dead."

"He must be," Dawn said. "We have to get him out, but I don't want to touch him."

"I carry him," Tico said, "like a baby."

"My lover man," Dawn said. "The rouge doesn't go with your body, the muscles under there." She picked up a napkin from the table, touched it to her tongue and gently stroked his cheek with it. She said, "Why don't we put the little monkey on ice before we finish up here?"

Tico liked the way she touched his face, looking at him with her Egyptian eyes. Man, but it scared him too.

Twenty-four

The way Foley looked at his chances with Danny Karmanos, sitting on the patio waiting for her, if she wasn't grieving for a whole year and it was clear her time was almost up, he was in.

If she was still grieving but would go along because she'd given him signs and she wasn't a tease, he could take advantage of the situation.

Well, he could if he wanted to.

No, not if he felt that's what she was doing, didn't have her heart in it, was going along to get it over with. In that situation it wouldn't be cool of him to press it—even if in the act she saw fireworks going off.

When she did come out in her bathrobe she was holding a pair of white underwear. She handed them to Foley standing now in his wet Calvins sticking to him and said, "Why don't you change first? In the cabana."

Foley thanked her for the underwear and walked to the cabana thinking, Why didn't he change *first*? Before they did what? She'd said she was taking off her suit and putting on a robe, and that's what she did, she was wearing a robe. Maybe just the robe. But she didn't work her eyes on him as he thanked her. Then, when he got out of his Calvins and put on the brand-new pair, he had to pull them up over his stomach so they wouldn't droop in the seat. He didn't feel good in Peter's underwear and wrapped a towel around his waist. He walked across the patio wondering if she'd ask how they were, if they fit all right.

She didn't. He sat down with Danny at the table, Foley looking at the pool lights showing in the dark. She said, "I've been thinking. I might be rushing my return to the world."

So much for his changing *first*.

He turned to look at her and said, "I know," nodding, showing he was wise as well as patient. He thought he might as well continue once he started, get it all out, and said, "I understand." He said there was no reason to hurry, it would work out or it wouldn't. They liked each other and they'd get to it one day. The way he said it was, "We'll express our love one day," and thought

290 · ELMORE LEONARD

he should have said "show our love," but didn't like that either. He should've said, they'd get to it, with a grin, and let it go at that. But, he explained, it wasn't a good idea in the long run because his past would catch up with them and she'd see it wasn't going to work. She could announce, "This is my dear friend, convicted felon and former bank robber . . ." but people close to her would already know he was an ex-con, they'd read about him in the *National Enquirer.* Bank Robber Steals Danny Tynan's Heart.

She kept saying at first, "No one has to know."

"You want to keep me a secret?" Foley said. "I think I'd stick out."

That's what it was about.

"I don't see myself playing golf at the club every weekend. Or any of the members playing no-rules basketball with me. I might even rob another bank."

She said, "But you wouldn't have to."

He said, "That's a reason right there."

He got home a little before midnight. He'd watched *Born Again* with Danny. It wasn't bad. They talked some more, kissed good night and Foley said he'd call her. She said, "You promise?" He said he promised. She shined her eyes at him, wet with tears, he believed because it was expected of her, doing the scene. Or, she couldn't help it.

Lights showed in the house across the canal, lamps on downstairs. He could go over and talk to Cundo, tell him he was sorry he missed dinner, he got tied up. Cundo would say yeah, with the widow. Foley would say they didn't fool around, they watched a movie. Cundo would say yeah, you watching a porno flick? You watch them be*fore*—Foley could hear him— the girl saying oh, oh, oh, saying oh, daddy, the girl keeping it up for, oh, fifteen, twenty minutes. Oh, oh, breathing as hard as she could. Like that, Cundo would get onto something else, not interested in how he did with Mrs. Karmanos, and it would become the conversation. What was the best porno flick you ever saw? Foley would ask him what Dawn fixed for the dinner. Ask him who was there. Little Jimmy, who else? Cundo never went to bed before 2 A.M. He drank and made speeches. Sometimes he listened to the music of Cuba.

Dawn had waited eight years to shoot him, living on a hundred thousand a year. She had her own snub-nosed .38 bought and licensed for her protection. Tico came along with the Walther and she went for it in a second, a gun already used in a homicide. She fired two loads practicing—thank God for the silencer—and knew she could hit him down the length of the dinner table. When the time came she was tense, but picked the gun out of the serving dish and put three in him dead center. If Foley had been at the table, seated on her right, she would have shot him first. He was more of a threat. Shoot him twice, put the Walther on the little rascal and shoot him twice. Save three shots in case either of them gets up.

She would still have to do Foley.

Or have him done.

Put him in the freezer with his buddy.

She'd waited eight years. When Cundo told her about Foley she was sure he was her guy. Comes out of prison broke looking for a score. They talk about taking Cundo, cleaning him out but not *how*, Dawn expecting Foley to say, "Shoot him. How do you think?" She'd look at Foley with her psychic vision; he would not stand still. "When was the last time you took your clothes off with a woman?" Expecting him to say it's been years and years. But had to change her mind fast as she looked at him and said, "It's only been five *days*?" And he said, "Actually it's been, four."

Her psychic vision was out of whack. Why was he so fucking hard to read? She met Cundo for the first time and told him he was going back to Florida to stand trial for second-degree murder. Told him before he was even arrested. She told a man the day and time he would die. She was trying to give a talk and he was heckling her, called her a fraud. It flashed in her mind. She closed her eyes for effect and said, "March third, declared dead at three P.M." Two months away.

They said he died at three-twenty. Dawn said, "By the time you looked at the clock it was three-twenty. But he died within thirty seconds of three o'clock."

He died on the day she told him he would. Did that make her a witch? It's what they called her in a feature story in the paper, trying to be funny with a straight face. She kind of liked being a witch, and simple people who believed in omens, bad luck and curses, became fans. It got her a lot more work—even among curious people with money who wanted to know about their future. She was Reverend Dawn to all comers from then on.

Now she'd have to shoot Foley.

This was not like her at all, to be thinking about shooting somebody. She was a true psychic, she engaged in bunco schemes once in a while or she'd be living in a one-room apartment on La Cienega above her store-front shop. If one of them told her she'd be shooting people before too long, she'd say don't be ridiculous. Well, she'd do one, yes, Cundo, a hard-core criminal who showed moments of being a fun guy, but somebody was bound to shoot him, say, over a busted deal. And Foley was the same, an incorrigible ex-convict.

It wouldn't surprise anyone to find them dead. Better though if they were never found.

Unless he goes to Costa Rica.

No, she'd come this far. She knew the second day after they met Foley was wavering, not convinced he was willing to score off Cundo, not after three years of a buddy act. He was in it as her partner but still in the center of things. She would have to shoot him. Do it without thinking about it too much. He comes across the footbridge—it's night—she steps out of the tropical cover pointing a gun at him and says . . . "So long, Jack," and plugs him. Something on that order, but so-long-Jack wasn't bad. Keep it short.

It was eleven, no lights on across the way. She placed the loaded Walther in the drawer of the table where the CD player sat. Now she picked out a few numbers, starting with some Cundo liked, cueing up "Candela," "El RincÓn Caliente," and everyone's favorite, "Chan Chan." She turned up the volume to use the old Cubans as lures.

It worked.

She said to Foley, "He was listening to the Buena Vista Social Club and fell asleep. I woke him up and made him go to bed."

They were in the sitting room where the CD player sat on a small table. She went to the player to lower the volume. "Too bad you missed dinner. You want to know what I served?"

Foley said, "Can I guess?"

"If you want."

He thought, Cockroaches and rice . . . and it came to him and he said, "Macaroni and cheese."

Her face went blank. "How did you know?"

"Cundo hates it."

"I was being funny."

"Then what did you serve?"

"That was it, macaroni and cheese."

"You *were* being funny."

"It got a smile, that's all."

"He's not mad?"

"Maybe disappointed. He settled into himself again."

"You and I haven't talked," Foley said, "since Cundo came home. What's going on? Have you figured it out?"

"Not yet," Dawn said. "I'm going to live with the little darling and be nice to him till I see a harmless way to walk out, hopefully a rich girl. Maybe all I'll have to do is ask. What are you up to?"

"Well, I've got ten thousand—"

"You kept the check. I knew you would."

"And I'm going to Costa Rica."

She jumped on it. "When?"

"When I have enough to buy a house on the beach."

"You couldn't give it back, could you?"

"Danny Karmanos said, 'If you don't want it, tear it up.' I told her I can't do that and offered her the check. I said, 'If you want to destroy ten thousand dollars, here.' But she wouldn't take it."

"That was close. But then you're lucky, aren't you? You knew she wouldn't tear it up. So now," Dawn said, "you've got a stake. Maybe someday, if you don't fuck up, you'll get to Costa Rica. But I kinda doubt it."

"Concentrate," Foley said. "You don't see a sandy beach in my future?"

She paused to stare at him and said, "No . . ." and made a face, a frown, that Foley took to mean she was having a tough time reading him, not sure of what she saw. Dawn smiled and said, "Not tonight, I'm tired. You want to hear the old Cuban guys? What's your favorite?"

Foley said, "I think you've got '¿Y tú qué has hecho?'"

She turned to the table saying, "Yes, I'm sure. Why don't you go out in the kitchen and pour a couple of Old No. 7's while I find it?"

"I'm gonna pass," Foley said. "I've had enough for one day."

"I've got 'Y tú' right here."

"No, I'm going to bed." Foley started for the open door and stopped. "Who was at your dinner party?"

"Just Tico, Little Jimmy and myself."

"And Cundo."

She said, "And Cundo, the guest of honor," staring at Foley like she was trying to read him again.

"Tell him I'll see him tomorrow."

Foley let her stare a few moments more and left.

Gone by the time she got the Walther from the drawer, a full load and the silencer in place ready to fire and went after him to shoot him and push him in the canal, Jesus, get it over with.

Then talk to the police as they fished him out of the canal. It could be done. She'd say she barely knew the man. He was only here a few days. Since Mr. Rey came home. Don't mention prison, but they will, they'll know and try to trap you. Tell them you're Mr. Rey's house-keeper. Then why are those photos of you on the walls? Jesus, it was harder to make up an alibi than read minds. And thought, Why didn't you see Foley lying dead, in the canal or the morgue? In her vision he was in the sitting room of her house, where they were moments ago when she was trying to read him. But he looked different. Something about him . . . They would have to get

Cundo disappeared for good. Tomorrow. Tico lines up a boat and takes the little fella to sea tomorrow night.

No, Officer, I can't imagine where he could be. If it came to that.

This was in her mind as she stepped outside the house. By now he should be across the footbridge on his way home, almost to the pink house. But he wasn't; or not in plain sight, foliage holding the walk in darkness. She moved along the walk on her side of the canal to place herself opposite the pink house. She squinted in the darkness feeling she was wasting time. Where was he?

She looked toward the footbridge, then the other way and saw him on Dell Avenue where it began to rise over the canal. Foley was on the bridge—Dawn sure that's who it was. Now another figure appeared, coming over to the rail, she watched Foley approach him.

Twenty-five

Last night Foley walked up to the kid on the Dell Avenue bridge, a black kid about fourteen, and asked him, "You know who I am?"

He wore a baseball cap set two inches crooked to shade one eye, a white T-shirt and black jeans slung low, belted around his skinny butt. The T-shirt hung out to cover what Foley believed was a piece stuck in his waist, the boy wanting him to notice it.

He said, "Hey, you the bank robber?"

"That's right, the guy you're supposed to be watching. You know I could go out the back, you'd never see me."

"They somebody be there," the kid said. "How many banks you rob?"

"Couple hundred. What do they call you?"

The kid said, "T.B."

"I knew a T.G. in the joint, grown up but still called Tiny Gangsta. But T.B. What's that, Tiny Babe, Tiny Boy?" Foley said, "No, I bet it's Tiny Banger. Still a kid but made it as a gangbanger. You shoot somebody?" The kid was nodding and Foley said, "You're almost grown, you don't mind being called Tiny? Or there's nothing you can do about it."

"Was O.G. gimme the name."

"Old Gangsta. There was an O.G. the fall I took up at Lompoc. That Old Gangsta was twenty-five. He and I shot baskets and pushed each other around. He was pretty good. Tell me how come you're packing."

"So no *cholo* try and jack me. He step up in my face I smoke him."

"Has Lou Adams been around?"

"Don't know a person that name."

"He'll take the piece away from you," Foley said. "Son, you're working for the FBI and don't know it. Who's your shot caller, Tico? Where's he?"

"How do I know. Wha' chew mean I'm working for the fucking FBI?"

"It's how it is," Foley said. "Lemme have your piece."

"For what?"

"Keep you out of juvie hall," Foley said. "So you can grow up to be a famous bank robber."

"You teach me?" the kid said, bringing out his cell and then a Glock he handed to Foley.

In the morning Foley had his breakfast and at ten went over to the big house—the way he thought of it—to have a cup of coffee with Cundo. If he called it the White House he'd see President Obama cleaning up Bush's mess. He didn't see Cundo all day yesterday and missed talking to the little Cuban. It surprised him, a feeling he'd never had before.

Dawn told him Cundo was still sleeping off a killer hangover. Foley said that was something new. Cundo claimed he'd never had a hangover in his life.

"He's been lying to you," Dawn said. "He has a cold beer and then opens his eyes. But this is heavy, diarrhea and he keeps throwing up. It might be the dinner last night."

Foley said he'd stop by later.

Dawn said, "I'm still thinking of a party, a big blowout on the roof. My darling said it was okay with him if he didn't have to do anything. I told him I'd get Tico to hang the balloons and string the party lights."

Foley looked at his watch. He said, "I still have the keys to the VW. Mind if I use it?"

She told him no, go ahead. "See if it needs gas."

Foley said, "I'm not going far."

She watched him go out, thinking of the Walther in the drawer again, but now was not the time, there were neighbors outside, a guy washing the windows of the cool, all-glass house next door. Meanwhile the little Cuban had to be taken out to sea and deep-sixed. Tico's job. Have him stop at the lumberyard and pick up a few cement blocks, and make sure he had rope. What else? She had to see Little Jimmy today. Have him sign the houses over to her and she'd put them up for sale. Take care of Foley. Get him to disappear. It would be so simple if he wasn't hanging around watching. She didn't think he was suspicious. He comes back later she'd tell him Cundo's still throwing up, the poor little guy. She gave him Kaopectate but it didn't seem to be helping. It was that fucking Cuban dinner. But how long could she keep Foley from seeing the man who wasn't there? It sounded like a movie.

It came to her in the next few moments, a way to remove Foley from the picture without shooting him, without endangering herself, and it was brilliant.

Get him up on the roof, with Tico.

She phoned him at his aunt's.

Tico said, "I call the guy has a boat at Marina del Rey. He say I can use it, yeah, for five hundred dollar."

"Hon, that's cheap."

"I think he believes I want to throw something over-board."

"Don't worry, I'll give you the money. You think this guy would do the whole job, dispose of Cundo?"

"Cost about five thousand, then you got the marina guy to worry about."

"You mind taking care of it, hon? You could do it tonight. Roll him up in that horrid orange and brown rug in the guest bedroom, tie on a few cement blocks—all there is to it."

"I never dropped a guy in the ocean before."

"Be sure to bring a fishing pole and bait. Come back with tomorrow's dinner while you're at it. If you know how to clean fish." Dawn said, "Hon, one other thing you might do. I told Foley we're getting ready to have a party up on the roof."

"You serious?"

"For Cundo, to welcome him home."

"Yeah . . .?"

"Foley, I know, will come back this afternoon to see Cundo. You're here, you tell him I've taken Cundo to see a doctor. And you have to go up and measure the roof so I'll know how many balloons to buy, party decorations."

"You want me," Tico said, "to get him up on the roof."

"And push him off."

"Push him off the roof," Tico said, "in the daylight and somebody sees me?"

"Both houses," Dawn said, "are higher than any others on the canal. Trust me, you won't be seen. And, Tico?"

"Yes?"

"Push him off the back end, so he lands in that brick patio. The bamboo trees give it privacy."

"Then what do I do?" Tico said, "take Foley out in the boat with Cundo?"

"You might as well," Dawn said. "Save you making an extra trip."

Twenty-six

Zorro was in his room on the third floor watching the History Channel, learning about UFO hunters, army sniper teams, how they built the Golden Gate bridge, mining for diamonds, while looking at the *National Enquirer*, catching up on movie stars seen at the beach getting fat or in trouble doing drugs.

The last action he was into, Cundo phoned and told him to steal Jimmy's Bentley. Then Cundo calls Jimmy to tell him his car is gone and what it will cost him to buy it back. Teach him to quit skimming so much, Jesus Christ, enough to buy a Bentley. He went to prison in Cuba for skimming and would have been sodomized to death if Cundo didn't save him. Little Jimmy looked like an easy mark, Cundo said, and had to be protected from wolves, dirty guys, as well as from himself, his *avaricia.* Zorro asked what Cundo would do to punish him and Cundo said, "Scare him to death, tha's all. The Monk has been loyal to me for twenty-seven fucking years, man."

Today he walked in Jimmy's office and saw something had Jimmy by the throat. It was the same as last night driving him home, he wouldn't say a word. "You have a good time?" Nothing. "It was a good dinner?" No answer. Zorro asked him what was wrong, can he be of help. Jimmy said he couldn't talk about it. It wasn't business, business was good. Zorro had the feeling—it was like someone had made Jimmy promise not to say a word about something that happened or something he saw, under pain of death. He wouldn't sit down. Kept walking to the window. He wouldn't answer the phone. It rang, Zorro had to pick it up and say he wasn't in the office. The guy Foley called, asking where he was. Zorro said he was out. The same thing Zorro would say when Jimmy used to put his nose in the powder. Zorro believed he could help him if he knew what was wrong.

Or could it be Cundo scaring him again?

Or past scaring him. Cundo in a rage this time over something Jimmy did. Cundo wanting Little Jimmy cut up with a chain saw and dumped in the ocean. Cundo through with him. Could that be?

Foley came up the stairs and Zorro stopped him, spread his hand open on Foley's T-shirt.

"Jimmy don't need you bothering him today."

"What's wrong, he's sick? I hear Cundo's laid up," Foley said. "Might have ptomaine from eating some Cuban dish. Is that Jimmy's problem? I'd like to know where they ate and stay away from the place."

"Jimmy didn't go out to eat. I brought him home from Cundo's."

"Cundo went out—"

"I don't know. You told me one time," Zorro said, "you don't want nothing to happen to Jimmy."

"I meant I'm on his side. I said I didn't want nothing to happen to him and you said, 'It won't.' If I'm gonna believe you, you have to believe me."

"I can tell you," Zorro said, "he's ascared to death of something can happen to him. He won't talk to me. He went to confession so he's in the state of grace his life comes to an end. He knows I'd go out and shoot whoever is scaring him. He has papers on his desk today, and his desk is always clean."

"Legal papers?"

"I don't know, maybe. Or they deeds to property. The only thing he said to me, 'I'm so tired.' I said, 'Go to bed.' But it wasn't that kind of tired."

"What happened last night?" Foley said. "Dawn served macaroni and cheese, she said to be funny. Then after they took Cundo—Dawn and Tico took him out to eat Cuban and today he's sick as a dog. That's according to Dawn."

Foley looked right at Zorro, the little mustache on the face like a fox; Zorro a young-looking fifty. "We go in," Foley said, "I'd like you to stand up with me and we'll get it out of him."

Little Jimmy stood back of his desk looking out the window. Gray out there today: looking at the bar across the street where a man was stabbed with a screwdriver the other day. He looked around as Foley came in with Zorro, took their time but came right up to the marble desk, their stares pinning Little Jimmy to the window.

"I hear you're having a nervous breakdown," Foley said. "Have you thought it might be booze?"

"I can't talk to you," Jimmy said.

"Who said you can't?"

"I tell you, you'll try to talk me out of what I have to do."

"But you want to tell me, don't you?"

"I have to see the properties, the houses, this building, are put in Dawn Navarro's name." He looked at

Zorro. "You call her the *bruja*," and said to Foley, "She told him she knows he's my boyfriend, why I keep him close by."

"I don't get it," Foley said. "You don't sign the properties over, she tells everybody you and Zorro are getting it on?"

"No, but is what she said. We never like that. Zorro is a devout Catholic. He's going to shoot her she says that about us."

"Then what's the problem?" Foley said. "If you don't want Dawn to have the properties, don't give 'em to her. You hold the deeds, don't you? Cundo told me that himself."

"Yes, but I don't think I can deny her if she wants the houses."

Foley said, "You mean 'defy her,' don't you? You're afraid not to give her what she wants. She put a hex on you? You don't give her the houses she'll turn you into a fairy? I mean a real one, with a magic wand." He began to smile and Jimmy showed a grin.

Jimmy said, "She's surprised, she thought I would want her to have the properties."

Foley said, "This isn't Cundo's idea."

Jimmy said, *"No."* Then took time to say he didn't think so. "She has the right as his common-law wife, you might say."

"Or you might not," Foley said. He watched Jimmy turn in profile to the window again and stood looking at the gray sky, no life in it.

"You know what it sounds like you're telling me?"

Jimmy turned his head. "I don't know. What?"

"Cundo's dead."

Jimmy stared at Foley and Foley waited, but Jimmy turned to the window again.

"Tell me if I'm right or not."

Foley waited.

"What happened last night?"

Waited and said, "At the dinner."

Jimmy shook his head.

"Cundo was there, wasn't he?"

"I'm not talking to you," Jimmy said.

"You can always run. Go to Vegas and spend some of Cundo's money. Or you can stay."

"And tell her," Zorro said, "to forget what she wants."

"The day before yesterday," Foley said, "I told Cundo I would never let Dawn have the homes in her name. He asked if she'd said something to me. I said, 'No, but I'll bet you a dollar she'll sell the homes out from under you and take off.' Cundo said, 'No, the homes stay in Little Jimmy's name.' You can have that notarized," Foley said, "and I'll sign it."

Zorro nudged him.

"Why are you afraid of her? You've got Zorro here. Zorro's pledged his life"—and could feel Zorro looking at him—"not to let anybody take advantage of you. Or take a shot at you, some guy Dawn knows will do it for her." Foley said, "Jimmy, you gotta man-up this time."

Zorro said, "We only dealing with a woman."

Jimmy said, "Yes, but she has a gun."

"She still only a woman," Zorro said.

"Jimmy, whose gun is it?" Foley waited. "Or is it hers, she's always had it?"

"I don't know," Jimmy said. "A gun is a gun and she has one. Wha's the difference whose it is?"

"Look at me," Foley said. "Jimmy, don't give her any of the properties, nothing."

He was looking out the window again.

"I don't see her," Jimmy said. "Maybe she'll go away."

Twenty-seven

Foley put the VW in the garage, pulled it up to the freezer; it was on, making a humming sound. He crossed the back patio to the kitchen and thought about going in. He would have if Cundo was alone. Or Dawn, if she was by herself. It was different now. He walked along the side of the house to the front and looked in through the open door. They left doors open out here and there were never any bugs or flies in the houses. Something Foley couldn't understand. There were no sounds from inside this afternoon. No Buena Vista riffs. Cundo liked the Social Club when he could listen to the music and wasn't having a conversation. Foley called Cundo's name through the open door.

Tico appeared on the second-floor balcony.

"The man is not doing so good, still throwing up. Dawn took him to UCLA Medical."

"When'd they leave?"

"Wasn't too long ago." Tico said, "Listen, if you not doing nothing, you want to help me measure the roof? Dawn don't know how many balloons and lights we need."

Foley, looking up at Tico. "You have a tape?"

"I do, but I need someone to hold the end. I bet you good at holding a tape measure. I'll find you a beer when we through."

Foley asked himself if he wanted to go up on the roof with Tico.

Yes, he believed he did.

Foley followed Tico upstairs to the third floor and then to the metal stairs on the side of the house, like a fire escape to the roof, Tico bringing along a volley-ball.

"The one I have being a Mikasa Competition ball, forty-nine ninety-nine. I had a chick walk out of the store with it under her top looking eight and a half months gone. I play the game on the beach, get any-body wants to try me."

They were on the tar-and-gravel roof now. Nothing in the way of the gray sky hanging over them.

"I say to Dawn, 'How 'bout we put up the net for the party? Choose up teams among the neighbors and play us some volleyball.' She don't think much of the idea. But I bet when the party gets going I bring out the net? They people gonna want to play." He lobbed the ball to Foley and backed up a few feet. "You think?"

Foley bounced the ball, said, "Maybe," and caught it on his sneaker, standing on one foot with it till he put the ball in the air and caught it on his other sneaker, put it in the air again and this time kicked it to Tico.

"Tha's pretty good you can do that." He held the ball straight out to the side in one hand, flipped it to his shoulders and let the ball roll along his other arm to his hand. "You like that?" He backed up again, getting closer to the edge of the roof.

Foley said, "Dawn told me about the macaroni and cheese."

Tico grinned. "The old man didn't think it was funny. What he did, lit a cigarette and stuck it in the cheese food."

"He was pretty mad?"

"She was just messing with him."

Foley watched him start to grin.

"And you went out after?"

Foley waited.

"We did, we went to a Cuban place."

"What'd he eat made him sick?"

"I believe *camarón,* shrimp."

"You brought him home?"

"Yes, I put him to bed. Laid him out . . ." Tico serious now. He said, "Hey, want to play a game? Roof ball. From Costa Rica." He turned around, stepped to the edge that looked down on the brick patio in back, and turned again to face Foley. "You suppose to be drunk when you play it. One man stands here, his back to the edge of the roof. So you can feel they's nothing behind you. I'm already here, I can be the first one. What you do is throw or kick the ball at me. You do it three times, the first one from five paces, say fifteen feet. The next one from ten feet, and the last throw you closer still, from five feet. You want to play?"

"How do you win?"

"The other man can't handle the ball."

"Anybody ever fall off the roof?"

"Tha's the one loses. Man, this is a serious game. You playing or not?"

"Let's loosen up first, play catch."

Tico said okay and they threw it back and forth, Tico left-handed. After a minute Foley said, "I'm ready."

"You're good where you are," Tico said, and threw the ball to him.

Foley tossed the ball underhand in a high arc, letting it roll off his fingers. He said, "You drove Cundo home?" to Tico looking straight up before moving in a step to catch the ball.

"Man, I never saw that kind of throw before, looking at the sky. What you do in roof ball—I'll tell you this one secret—you throw the ball high and hard, wing it right above the man's head. He throws up his hands and can lose his balance."

"Did Dawn take care of him?"

"What?"

"When you got home."

"Yeah, she gave him something, put him to bed."

"I thought you did."

"Yes, both of us. Move in and throw another." He said, "Yes," nodding, "about there is good."

Foley threw the next one hard at Tico's feet.

Tico did a dance step and kicked it back to him.

"You didn't catch it."

"No, you have to handle it is all."

Five feet in front of him Foley threw the ball straight up with both hands, as high as he could and stood looking at Tico's head bent back, his feet moving, then planted and bent back to catch the ball above his head.

He said, "All *right,* I took your best shot. Now is my turn. Come here and stand on the edge."

Foley took a minute to stretch and twist his body one way and then the other, Tico patient, the ball under his arm as he watched.

"*Listo?* You ready?"

"I guess so."

"You on the edge? Your heels have to touch."

"I'm on the edge."

And Tico drop-kicked the ball at him, hard, and Foley caught it with his forearms at his midsection doubled over. He brought the ball up with one hand gripping it and tossed it back to Tico.

Tico said, "Man, you quick for an old dog."

This time Tico bounced the ball twice and used his foot to press the white ball against the black tar-and-gravel roof. Now as he stepped to kick Foley said, "You check on Cundo today?" Tico tried to hold back but his foot topped the ball and it rolled to Foley.

"That's two," Foley said.

"You kidding me? That wasn't my shot?"

"You kicked the ball, didn't you? But you didn't answer my question. You check on Cundo today?"

"I was busy."

He was annoyed too.

"When Dawn asked you to get me up here . . . help you measure, weren't you at the house?"

"When she told me? Yeah."

"You see Cundo?"

"He was getting in her car."

"How'd he look?"

Tico said, "You want to cheat me, okay, I take my third shot."

"I asked you how he looked."

"Sick, man, how you think?"

He rolled the ball with his foot, playing with it, rolled it toward himself and scooped it up with the toe of his slender brown shoe, caught it and shoved a pass at Foley. This time he got his hands up to stop the ball and it bounced back to Tico.

"You didn't handle it that time, I get to do it again. Huh, where you think I'm gonna shoot it at you?" Tico faked a shot and grinned. "Not that one." He faked another and shoved a two-handed bullet at Foley, high. Foley turned his head and the ball sailed past him and they heard it bounce in the patio below.

"Man, you still don't catch the ball. Now you have to go get it," Tico said, stepping closer to Foley, an arm's length, moved in another half step and put his hand on Foley's chest. "You want to go down the stairs," Tico said, "or you want me to help you?" He gave Foley a gentle poke with his finger. "Tell me how you think about it right now, how you find yourself."

Foley said, "I think you're giving me a bunch of shit, Dawn taking Cundo to the hospital."

Tico said, "Oh, is that right?"

"I think he's dead," Foley said. "I can't see Dawn shooting him or clubbing him over the head at the table—come up behind him from the kitchen—but I can see you sneaking up. She make you do it?" Foley said, and felt the fingers move on his chest, saw Tico begin to turn to get his shoulder into the shove, and Foley took a finger from his chest, twisted it and saw Tico's mouth come open and saw him rise straight with the pain, and Foley went down, rolled into Tico's legs and pulled him by the finger in his grip to sail into space this gray afternoon, Tico's scream cut off as he hit the patio.

Foley crawled around to wrap his fingers on the edge of the roof now, still scared, *more* scared looking down at Tico lying on his back looking up. Foley could tell he was dead.

He knelt down next to Tico looking at his bloody eyes, felt his throat for a pulse; he didn't find one. The young man from Costa Rica, former Mayan spear-chucker in another life, had left for the other side, his lavender scarf still cinched to his head. Foley thought of pressing his eyelids down, but thought about it a few moments and left him staring at nothing.

He phoned Jimmy's office from the house across the canal. Zorro answered and said, "She stop by just now."

Foley said, "Alone?" Wanting to be sure.

"All by herself. I tole her Jimmy was out, don't know where he went. Maybe to have his lunch."

"Good, she'll look for him."

He told Zorro about playing roof ball with Tico.

Zorro said, "Man, tha's some game. I'm glad I never play it. Listen, you want me to move the body away from there, I will."

"He isn't our problem," Foley said. "We'll let Dawn figure out what to do with him."

Twenty-eight

Dawn drove home and eased her Saab into the garage next to the VW. Foley was back and Tico, with his cheerful innocence, had lured him up to the roof. She hoped Tico was still here, inside having a drink, Dawn dying to know how he worked it. One push and a huge problem would be solved. Foley would be in the freezer now with Cundo, his buddy. She didn't look forward to seeing Dr. Jack stretched out cold, but not frozen, not quite yet. The freezer was padlocked, the key should be in the kitchen. But she had to pee, bad. If she did look at Foley one last time—her dream partner no more—she'd do it later. First have a drink and put k.d. lang on, loving her natural, barefoot style. Fall into a deep chair and light a Slim. It was a shame Foley hadn't worked out. Foley too close to his convict buddy to see the score.

Little Jimmy was the only possibility of a problem now. She should have kept him around. Now the sweet little son of a bitch was hiding, his bodyguard lying for him.

Zorro could be her other mistake, not warming up to him along the way, a stand-up guy with kind of a long nose but dreamy eyes she should've looked into to see who he was and what he liked. He wasn't getting it on with Jimmy; she made that up. Was he married? She didn't know but it wouldn't matter. He'd called her a witch. If he believed it, good. She could do something with it, tell his fortune and watch his eyes glow. She might want to keep him around.

Little Jimmy took an oath before God he would not tell what happened, and in Jimmy's case it sounded like it would be enough; though she couldn't count on his promise keeping him quiet forever. As soon as she got to talk to him and the properties were signed over, Little Jimmy might have to go.

Leaving Tico.

The Costa Rican seemed to like the way this was working out. But if Tico didn't accept whatever she'd offer, if he insisted on at least half the score, she'd be facing another problem.

After eight years of planning how to snare the little guy's fortune, after all the waiting, rejecting Foley as a partner and taking on Tico, she jumped at the idea of shooting Cundo, always a possibility in the back of her mind. With Tico's gun—don't forget that. It was so simple and she was so fucking anxious to get it over with, she didn't look at the odds and ends that would have to be cleaned up. Well, she did, but maybe not closely enough. Foley, she knew for some time would have to go. The others she felt she could deal with in time. If she wasn't confident she wouldn't have come this far.

The brick patio looked wet in places.

Still drying.

Falling from way up there—Dawn looking up—could leave a mess, a lot of blood, depending on how he hit the bricks. Tico must've hosed down the patio, cleaned up after himself like a good boy.

Dawn opened the screen door to the kitchen.

Then why was he asleep on the table?

In a chair but slumped, sprawled over the bare surface, arms stretched out in front of him, Dawn looking at the top of his head from the doorway.

She said, "Tico? You're drunk. You look like a bum." He didn't move. She said, "Please tell me you've passed out, okay?" She said, "Jesus Christ," in a solemn voice and walked to the table where she could look past his arm to see his face, his bloody eye staring at her.

The phone rang, the one on the kitchen counter.

The timing—he couldn't be watching her, and yet she knew it was Foley.

The question was, how much did he know? One thing she was sure of, he was an experienced convict, he'd know enough not to call the police.

She let it ring and ring before she picked up.

What Foley did, he got Tiny Banger to go over to the big house with the phone number written on a fifty-dollar bill and told the kid to call him the moment the Saab pulled into the garage. He gave Dawn time to come in and find Tico.

It rang nine times before she picked up and said, "Dr. Jack, how can I help you?"

"Your friend fell off the roof."

"I see that. He lost his balance?"

"Lost a game of roof ball. He's your problem, so I left him for you."

"It must've been an accident," Dawn said. "You'll testify to that, won't you? Talk to the police?"

"Dawn . . . where's Cundo?"

After a few moments Dawn's voice said, "All right, last night at dinner"—sounding resigned—"I hoped

I could keep you out of it. I did tell you what I served and Cundo didn't think it was funny. When he's drunk he tends to get mean. I was laughing, I couldn't help it, so were Tico and Little Jimmy. Of all the things we could serve . . . Cundo put his cigarette out in my lovely entrée, got up and started slapping me, really out of control. He would not stop until Tico came to my rescue. He shot him."

There was a silence.

"Three times, in the chest."

"Like that. At the table?"

Foley sounding as though he wasn't sure.

"Cundo's dead, Jack. He was beating me up. Tico said it was the only way to stop him."

"Shot him three times?"

"He's a kid, he started shooting . . . I don't know, maybe he got a kick out of it."

Foley didn't say anything.

"It's the same gun Tico used once before. On a case they can open again in five minutes."

"Where's Cundo?"

There was a pause.

"In the freezer, the one in the garage. Jack, I was afraid Tico would make a deal with the police and implicate me somehow, the victim. Jack, Cundo lost it completely. I'm thinking, Tico's been up enough times he knows how to work the system. But I can produce Cundo's body, the bullets still in him fired from Tico's gun."

"Where is it?"

"Jack, you don't need to know all this."

"Where's the gun?"

"I have it hidden away."

"How did you get it?"

"I told Tico I'd hide it for him. I'm sure some detective will ask why I didn't produce it right away. Why? Because as long as Tico was alive I was scared out of my wits." Dawn's voice said, "Jack, I can't imagine you'll have a problem. I don't know anything about roof ball, but all you'll have to say is Tico tripped, or he was showing off, walking along the edge, and fell. You can say you tried to grab him if you want. But I wouldn't overdo it. He fell." Her voice said, "Aside from all that, what would be wrong with us getting together again?"

"I don't know," Foley said. "Maybe."

"The payoff is still the same. We get Jimmy to assign the properties to me, or to you if you want, I don't care. I trust you, Jack."

"You make it sound easy."

"We sell the houses and disappear. Leave the building with all the business in it to Jimmy. What do you say we get back together?" Dawn's voice said, "Jack, the whole time I was with Cundo I was scared to death. But if I told you, I knew you'd have a talk with him and that's all it would take. He'd imagine we were cheating on him again. I was so afraid this time he'd have you killed. One phone call, that's all it would take. And if we did keep seeing each other, I know he'd find out sooner or later. We were too intense, Jack. Remember?"

There was a silence.

"I have to think about it," Foley said. "Two guys I know are dead and I just got out of the can. I want to see if any surprises could jump out at me."

"Come on over," Dawn said, "we'll look at it together."

"Let me see where I am in this, okay? I'll give you a call."

Foley hung up the phone.

He stood at the counter remembering Cundo at different times. He saw him every day for three years. He could say to Jimmy it sounds like Cundo's dead. But he wasn't thinking of him *being* dead.

What he had to think about now was Dawn with a gun.

Lou Adams came up to Tiny Banger in the alley behind the house Foley was in. He said, "You still working for me, or you working for him now?"

"I do a favor for him and he pays me, the only difference."

"What'd I tell you? When we're through here, or I don't have to fire your ass and send you home, it's payoff time. But now I catch you fuckin' off on the job. You work for me or him?"

"I work for you," T.B. said.

"Then what're you doing for the guy you're suppose to be watching?"

"He axe me to tell him when the lady come home's all I done. And he paid me."

"You're in deep shit," Lou said.

He walked along the side to the front of the house and went in. A lamp was on in the sitting room though it wasn't dark yet. He called out "Foley!" as loud as he could, and called a few more times before Foley came down the outside stairs in his T-shirt and Levi's, stood in the doorway and said, "What?"

Lou came around.

"You paid one of my guys fifty bucks to tell you when Dawn Navarro gets home?"

"Yeah . . .?"

"He don't run errands for you when he's working for me. You understand?"

"But I'm the one he's watching. Where's he out of line? He knows where I am, I talked to him on the phone. How'd you find out?"

"I hadn't heard from him. They don't call I look into it."

"Lou, you've been running a surveillance on me since I got out, and I'm standing here talking to you. Does that make sense? Maybe when you started out it looked like a good idea. You'd made up your mind sooner or later I'd rob a bank. You still think I will?"

"It's all you know," Lou said.

"I've got some money now, I don't need to steal any. You saw me, I was in a bank the other day, setting up an account and making a withdrawal. The young lady and I came out, there you are on the job. I'll tell you something, you didn't look yourself, Lou, you looked tired. I would think you'd be bored out of your fucking mind. At one time, if you felt any excitement about your plan—"

"You're trying to throw me off what you're doing," Lou said, "and then start up again."

"I've learned banks," Foley said, "aren't the way to do it. I think it's time for you to get back to being an active special agent, and I'll find something in my retirement to keep me busy. Doesn't that make sense? Quit the Mickey-Mousing around with the home-boys, call 'em off and get back to going after real bad guys."

Lou Adams stared. He looked worn out.

"Let's go out to the kitchen," Foley said, "and have a beer. You can tell me about your book."

"You go straight," Lou said, "I won't have the finish I want."

"Be patient," Foley said, "I'll see if I can get you an ending."

Twenty-nine

Maybe telling Foley his buddy was in the freezer was a mistake. He seemed to know already Cundo was dead but didn't act like he believed it, or didn't want to. He turns up in a homicide and the police look at him with hard eyes. But Foley wasn't dumb. He'd know when to talk and when not to talk. The whole thing would gradually blow over: the cloud passes and the sun comes out again to shine down on your mess, Dawn thought. Here were the problems:

She could not see giving Foley half of what she'd make from the houses. She would do whatever necessary to make him disappear instead.

But she needed him to get rid of the bodies. Both were in the freezer once she dragged Tico to the garage, had to remove bags of ice to get him to fit inside and poured loose ice over him. She could see there wasn't room for three. It was a shame the way fate was fucking with her again. But she was not going to split the take after waiting eight years to get it. He wasn't part of the job anyway, he was off playing hide the weenie with the actress. Setting her up was work. The mistake was introducing ghosts. She should've made Foley some other kind of expert. One who deals with simple hexes and can work things out on the other side.

She thought, What if she let him have the two-million-dollar house and she kept the one worth four and a half?

Why? He didn't do a goddamn thing to help. She was letting Foley in bed persuade her. He *was* getting better. If she wanted to she could make him a star.

Or make some other guy a star. Six million was better than four. Do a blood oath thing with Little Jimmy and let him keep the building full of business. It occurred to Dawn, if she seduced Zorro she could get him to take the two bodies out to sea. No remains of the dead, no bodies, no case. No court appearances to worry about. Foley, the simplest way would be to shoot him and dump him in the canal. Not the one that ran between Cundo's houses, a different one. Drop him in from a street that crossed the canals. In fact, all three could be dumped in different canals. It would be a kick to follow the investigations. Hmmmm, are they related? Three bodies, two gunshot victims and one that fell off a building.

The Walther was in the drawer again, the silencer screwed on. But she wouldn't be playing Cuban music for him this time. If he ever decided to come over. She could place the gun in a drawer in the kitchen. Dawn was sure she could get him out there for a drink.

Or get him in bed, her nude painting on the wall. He's having his after-the-furor cigarette. Reach into the drawer . . . *Pow,* or *ping,* and wrap him up in the covers, Jesus, and drag him to the car.

Eight years ago she never once saw it as physical labor. Drop all three from the bridge and be in Vegas when she got the call from the police. Or Nevada deputies knocked on the door. What? You mean they drowned?

No, taking them out to sea was the only way to avoid an investigation. She'd have to come up with a way to do it. Put her three lovers in the car and take them to Marina del Rey. She had the name of the guy with the boat. Or take them out to the desert and scatter them around. All three are convicts, with enemies.

Now it was starting to rain, getting dark early.

She could sit here waiting for Foley to call. Or, she could put on Cundo's raincoat with the deep pockets and drop in on him.

Foley and Lou Adams were in the sitting room drinking beer, trying to decide on an ending for Lou's book, Foley asking him about actual cases he was on, one Foley might've read about.

"You mean how we developed evidence?"

"I was thinking more of arrests," Foley said. "Tight spots you were in. Like one time I was in a bank, somebody pushed a button, the cops are already outside not letting people in, hurrying the ones coming out."

"And you and the five grand in the umbrella are hustled out. The cops never heard of a bank robber carrying an umbrella, the dumb fucks. That wouldn't work if I was there, I recognize the famous Jack Foley—no, the infamous Jack Foley—and bust his ass as he's coming out."

"You know about that one?"

"You told me about it one time I'm trying to get you to list your bank licks. I said gimme the ones I can close and you shut up."

"What page are you on?"

"I told you I got between five and six hundred, around in there."

"You came to see me at Gun Club," Foley said, "told me you're from the Big Easy. I'm suppose to tell you all the bank jobs I've pulled, since we're both from New Orleans."

"Tell me for my book and I won't bother you no more. The number of banks."

"A hundred and seventy-six."

"Jesus Christ, in twenty-five years?"

"Take off for time served, it would be close to fifteen years. That's eleven and a half a year. Take off for Christmas, the Fourth of July and holydays of obligation, it's close to one a month. Five grand a month, sometimes more, spending my time at the seashore. But I miss being married and having a family. I blew that one. Unless she's still a young girl when I marry her. I should be looking at a certain age. You think?" Foley said, "But you're not in any of my bank jobs. You need one where you step up and do the job, a tough situation, where you could get shot."

Lou said, "I was in that kind more'n once. We go in to make an arrest on a guy we know is a looney-toon believed to be armed. We confront him in the kitchen of his girlfriend's house. Her name was Louise. The guy has a drawer open and is reaching in. It looked like a knife drawer. I tell him to take his hand out of the fucking drawer. He says, 'I'm

getting a Kleenex, I gotta blow my fuckin' nose.'
His hand comes out of the drawer with a Kleenex."
Lou paused. "Actually it was a Puff, another kind of
tissue."

Foley waited for him.

"His other hand is trying to get a Smith out of his
pants. He never got to blow his nose."

Foley said, "You saw the gun in time."

"Once we laid him out and went through his
clothes." He looked at Foley and said, "Hey, he was
going for it."

"I was thinking," Foley said, "you could put me in
one of your cases, only I never carried a gun. Once or
twice I might've referred to having one, to the teller,
but I never packed. It would be, you know, in a humor-
ous way. We're gonna have to keep thinking to get you
an ending."

Lou Adams got up to leave. He said, "Swear you'll
never rob another bank and I'm outta here."

"I can't do that," Foley said. "It could be years
from now when I'm old and broke. Can you wait that
long?"

"Forget it. I'll make up an ending," Lou said and
left.

Foley got up from the table, the empty beer bottles,
the ashtray full of butts, went to the phone on the counter and called Jimmy Rios. Zorro answered.

"I'm about to see the lovely Dawn," Foley said. "Tico's out of the picture, so Jimmy's safe, nothing can happen to him and he'll never see Dawn again. Tell him that and put him on."

He waited, looking out at the weather, almost dark now, fog setting in.

Jimmy's voice said, "Jack, tell me how you going to handle this with Dawn."

Foley wasn't sure. In fact, he had no idea.

He said, "First tell me what happened last night.

Dawn's hands were in the pockets of the raincoat, Cundo's, her right hand gripping the Walther without the silencer. It didn't fit, part of her hand would be out of the pocket. It was all right with Dawn; she wanted to hear it this time. But she'd bring it just in case, the silencer in her left hand in the pocket.

Cundo's black raincoat buttoned up came almost to her knees. Dawn stood in front of the full-length mirror in the bedroom. She looked great in black with her dark hair and Egyptian eyes, seeing herself as Hatshepsut, the queen who became a king. The Dawn in the mirror said:

"Hi, Jack, I was in the neighborhood and thought I'd drop in."

She said, "You're kidding, right? You thought you'd drop *in*? Just take out the fucking gun and shoot him."

She wasn't thinking of doing it right away. She thought she might have some little girl–type fun with him first. Turn him on.

The gun was ready?

She checked it. Loaded, cocked, ready to fire.

You haven't pulled it out of the coat yet.

She brought it out. The hammer caught for a couple of seconds on the hem of the pocket. She released the hammer and drew the Walther again. Good—it came right out. She'd fire without cocking it. Unless she might have a few things to say first. Then cock the gun for effect, just before she says, "So long, Jack, it's been . . .

"Fun?

"A ball?

"It's been nice knowing you."

She said, "It's been nice *knowing* you?"

She said, "It *was* nice taking showers with you."

She was making it hard, trying to think instead of just saying it. How about, "I love you, Jack, but you're no six-million-dollar man." That wasn't bad. He'd get it.

She said to her image, "Did you ever think you were greedy?

"Not really.

"You ever think of yourself as a cold bitch?

"When I have to be. But I'm never really cold. You think? When you've put in eight long years living by yourself—

"Poor you.

"Well, it's true. I waited eight fucking years for something to happen and had to do it myself.

"Poor, poor you.

"Shut up.

"You ready?

"Let's go, girl."

She left through the front door, hands in her pockets, one gripping the Walther, the other holding the silencer. She reached the sidewalk to go to the footbridge and stopped. A figure was on the walk across the canal, moving toward the bridge. In a light, shapeless coat. Foley. It had to be . . .

"Jack?"

And knew it was a mistake. He hadn't seen her.

He stopped. He said after a moment, "Dawn? What've you got on? I can barely make you out."

If she had the silencer screwed on . . . There was still time. She said, "I'm wearing Cundo's raincoat, it just fits me," turned as if modeling the coat and screwed the silencer in place. She faced him again, the Walther at her side. What she wanted to hear was a plane coming in to LAX. They heard planes all the time, the airport just seven miles south of Venice. She said, "Where are you going?"

"I was coming to see you."

There—an airliner coming in and she raised the Walther. Dawn said, "And I was coming to see you," and fired, heard the BB sound, the *pop*, and saw him turn. Saw him stop then and look at the house behind him.

He said, "What was that? Like glass breaking."

No lights on in the house, no one coming out.

Dawn said, "I didn't hear anything."

It wasn't going to work, shooting at him in the dark, too foggy. No more than sixty feet away and she missed.

She said, "Go home, I'm coming over."

She'd have time to unscrew the silencer and go back to the original plan. Get him in the mood looking at her navel, and shoot him.

Foley thought about the sound of the flight coming in to land, loud overhead, and the sound of glass breaking and wondered if one caused the other. He told himself to wake up, it was a gunshot. It was Dawn firing Tico's piece with a silencer, or everybody on the canal would have heard it. She missed and hit a window in the house where he was standing.

He had a gun, the Glock he took off Tiny Banger. Try to explain that: an armed convicted felon shoots a girl he said was trying to kill him.

He heard her call his name and came out from the kitchen with a fifth of Jack Daniel's and a couple of short glasses, a dish towel over his shoulder. He said to the well-mannered girl waiting in the doorway, "Black's your color, you make it work."

"I look good enough to eat?"

"If you weren't here on business. Let me have your coat."

"It's all right, I won't be here long." She was unbuttoning the raincoat, both of her hands out of the pockets. Foley took the moment to pour a couple of doubles. Dawn came over, took one and drank half of it and put her glass on the table again.

Foley said, "The FBI was here."

She seemed to pause. "Really?"

"Lou Adams called off his dogs. I'm helping him think of a new ending for his book."

The coat hung open now, Dawn's hands in the pockets again holding it against her hips. Foley took a look at her slim-cut underpants and a shorty T-shirt that hung almost to her navel. He said, "Tell me what it is about a girl's navel? It catches the eye and won't let go."

"I suppose," Dawn said, "because it's right in the middle of the playground. You didn't call. I took it to mean we won't be getting back together. But if I'm on my own, Jack, I get both houses."

"How do you take over the deeds?"

"Little Jimmy loves me. He'll do what I ask."

"I'll bet he won't."

"Jack, believe me, okay?"

"Jimmy's changed," Foley said. He picked up her glass, offered it and she took it in her left hand.

"I don't see any way you'll get the properties."

"You don't know him. Little Jimmy gives me the houses and I let him keep the building."

"You know what Cundo would say about that?"

Dawn finished the drink and handed Foley the glass. She put her hands on her hips inside the raincoat, giving Foley pretty much the whole show. "I'm his heir, Jack. I put in eight years waiting for him. He comes out and beats me up."

"You have to be Jimmy's heir, he owns everything."

Foley moved closer and put his hands on the curves of her shoulders and felt her stiffen and gradually relax. "You tried to shoot me a while ago, missed and broke somebody's window."

"You think I should pay for it?"

"I think you ought to learn how to shoot, you want to kill me." He felt the barrel press against his stomach. "The thing is, you don't have any reason to shoot me. Jimmy's showing his manhood now. He said he watched you do Cundo and then you made him clear the table. He's breaking his word, but doesn't care. Zorro told him you're a witch, so he doesn't have to keep any promise he made. You can shoot me—you understand I'm only making a point—but it won't get you any closer to Jimmy. You can put his little face between your jugs and purr, Jimmy won't give up the houses. He says he'll die first. And you say, what? He may have to?"

"No, what I say, I'll swear I saw you throw Tico off the roof."

"You can't even put me there," Foley said. "I hate to say it, but it looks like you're out of business."

"Jack," her voice soft, "you don't mean that."

"I'll give you the name of a lawyer, if she can practice out here. Your problem, you've been thinking about doing Cundo for eight years. Still, I bet Megan'll see you get no more than twenty-five to life." Foley telling her in his natural way. "Jimmy said you put on a show at dinner. He had no idea what you were up to."

"Jack, don't do this to me."

She let him lift the raincoat from her shoulders to slip down her back and fall with a thud as the gun hit the floor. He brought Tiny Banger's Glock out of his back pocket, stooped to lay it on the cocktail table and picked up the pack of Slims. Dawn took one and Foley struck a match and held it for her.

"You know I could never shoot you," Dawn said. "I wanted to scare you, that's all."

"You did."

"Get you to help me. I aimed over your head."

"Help you do what, get away?"

Giving her the idea, and she picked up on it.

"Yes, vanish."

"But what did you learn?"

"I was too impatient." She looked up at him getting a plea in her eyes. "Jack, we think alike. We could disappear together, change the way we look—"

"Grow beards?"

"We're the Psychic Doctors. You'll have to make up another name, something more exotic than Foley. I've got all the lying-around money we'd need, close to a hundred thousand. We go to Costa Rica and decide what we want to do. A *bank*," Dawn said, smiling at the idea. "I've never robbed a bank. But we'd go for the vault, not one of the tellers. We'll go big-time for a change."

He watched her in her little white panties sink into the sofa and pour herself a drink and place Old No. 7 on the table again, close to Tiny Banger's gun.

Foley noticed, Foley telling her, "Buddy, my old partner, and I thought of going big-time, just the two of us get into the vault. Buddy said, 'You want to go in, scream at everybody to hit the floor and then wait, looking at our watches for the vault to open? That's what you want to do, with all the things can go wrong?' I told him he was right and we never went for the vault."

"Jack, that kind of a heist, you have to plan every step, know what to look for. I'll bet I could visit a bank a couple of times and know how to make it work."

Foley said, "Is it a robbery or a heist?"

"Don't make fun of me, okay?"

Foley said, "You want to go for six and a half million in houses, you give me up for a punk, a guy plays roof ball. For what? Keep the expenses down? Stick to bunko, getting it off of rich women." Foley said, "I was ready to take a chance on you. Sometimes I have weak moments. But you sneaked up on Cundo and shot him for a couple of houses. That's your style, not mine."

"Because you know him?" Dawn said. "You had nothing in common with him. I told you, think of Cundo the way you see a bank you're gonna rob. It's nothing personal."

"We jailed together almost three years," Foley said. "He thought I was still watching his back and I was playing ghost doctor."

"But he wasn't like you at all. He was vicious, he killed, he beat hell out of me."

"You had it coming," Foley said. "I did too. He could've shot us and felt okay about it, but he didn't. In his macho way he laid it on you."

"The guy-thing," Dawn said. "I can't believe you two were friends. It's beyond me."

"I didn't judge him," Foley said. "We walked the yard and kept our eyes open."

She didn't understand that or ever would.

So he brought it back to what was important.

"You think you can vamp Jimmy out of the house? You won't even get close to him."

"What does that mean," Dawn said, "you're blowing the whistle on me?" She placed her glass on the table, picked up the Glock and put it on Foley.

He said, "You don't hear 'blow the whistle' so much anymore. One I like, you ask if I'm gonna put the stuff on you. I say no, I've never ratted out anybody in my life. It's how the law gets you in their sights."

Dawn held the Glock in both hands aimed at his chest.

"You want to shoot me?"

"I don't *want* to, but you're standing between me and my retirement. I've got enough trouble, Jack, without worrying about you."

He said, "You think the gun's loaded?"

She raised it to his face and stared at his eyes to read him.

"If it was," Foley said, "you think I'd leave it on the table?"

Now she wasn't sure. He was so fucking hard to read.

"What am I suppose to do now," Dawn said, "lay it down? You were ready to pull it out of your pocket, shoot me if you had to. It's why you acted so cool." She brought the pistol down to his T-shirt again at arm's length and delivered her line:

"So long, Jack."

He didn't move, didn't hunch or turn away as she squeezed the trigger and heard the empty sound, a click, and yanked back the slide and let it snap closed, squeezed again and got another click, but no sounds after that when she squeezed and squeezed a few more times. Dawn said, "Shit," and eased back in the cushions.

"I didn't think you'd believe me," Foley said. "Now where are you? Gonna dye your hair red and wear dark glasses? Go ahead, I won't tell the cops. You're none of my business."

She said, "Jack . . .?"

He said, "You have anybody in your world can hide you? Or they all dead? That's what you should do, look at the spirit world, talk to some women died in prison, get an idea what it's like."

She said, "Jack, couldn't you help me? Get me out of town? I'll pay you."

"How much?"

"Ten thousand."

"I make that stirring up ghosts."

"Jack, come on, help me out."

"A minute ago you said, 'So long, Jack,' expecting to kill me. Where'd you get that, the movies? I told you there weren't any bullets in the gun. All you had to do was believe me. Dawn, you're psychic, you're suppose to know the gun was empty."

"I did, but it didn't make sense. Why would you carry a gun with no bullets in it?"

"You have a gun, I know I can take it away from you. I don't need one. Two weeks ago I was a convict. I don't want a gun. You understand? Now you're trying to bribe your way out of doing time."

"What's wrong with that?"

"I can't say I blame you. You'll go nuts inside."

"So help me out," Dawn said. "You know what I see in your future? In *ours*, the best time of our lives coming up, on a beach in Costa Rica."

"And one night you shoot me in the head while I'm asleep. You know what I see in your future?" Foley said. "Fences topped with razor wire. Bunch of hefty broads standing around looking at the new girl."

"You're no fun," Dawn said, and took a few moments before pushing up from the sofa. "That's it, huh?"

"It's what happens," Foley said, "in the life. You go down."

Thirty

O nce the bodies were released, Cundo and Tico were given separate parlors in LoCicero & Sons Funeral Home in Santa Monica. Jimmy Rios testified as an eyewitness to Cundo's murder: shot and killed by Dawn Navarro one night while Jack Foley was visiting a friend in Beverly Hills, a famous film star, who said yes, it was true, Jack Foley was helping her accept her husband's death.

"If Jack had been here for the dinner," Jimmy told the police, "Cundo, like a father to me, would still be alive."

Tico Sandoval, they believed, fell to his death while measuring the roof for Cundo's welcome-home party.

Dawn Navarro, who had hidden the bodies in a freezer, was the prime suspect in Cundo Rey's death. The pistol used in his murder was found in the canal in front of his house.

Sierra Sandoval came to mourn her boy. She stared at him in the casket, Tico wearing his lavender scarf around his neck like an ascot. Sierra stayed an hour, watching the boys from the hood passing through to look at Tico, Sierra imagining one of them on the roof with her baby, playing that game.

Mike Nesi came, his left arm in a cast, his right hand sticking out of his open shirt, the rest of the arm taped to his body. He said to Foley, "You owe me nine bills for the hospital and two bills the Cuban squirt owes me." Foley and Zorro threw him out the front door of the funeral home.

A photo of Foley with Jimmy Rios appeared in the *Los Angeles Times* over the story of the bodies found in the freezer. He wondered if Karen Sisco saw it and might give him a call. It would be up to her; he wasn't making any moves in that direction.

When Lou Adams and Ron Deneweth dropped in, Lou stood looking at Cundo waiting for his eyes to open, his lips to come unglued and tell him Foley was in on his death. Lou would turn Foley around on the spot and cuff him and he'd have the ending for his book. Lou waited. Cundo refused even to blink.

Lou went up to Foley and said, "I'm going back to Miami and you're on your own. You'll hit another bank 'cause it's your nature. Go ahead, I don't give a shit what you do."

"You have an ending for your book?"

"Not yet, I can't wait for you, I got to think of something."

"How about this," Foley said. "Because of the awful pressure you put on me, I've given up robbing banks for good."

Lou squinted as Foley told him, "Don't ever doubt the power of prayer. I asked God to help me stay out of banks. I prayed to find honest work I could do, and the next day Jimmy offers me one of his homes. I can take my pick, the white one full of pictures of Dawn and a painting of her bare naked. Or I can have the pink one."

"He gives you a million-dollar house *free*?"

"Jimmy feels he owes me for standing behind him. He said, 'Jack, I love you, man. You save me from that bitch wanted to take my homes and kill me. Which one you want?' I took the pink one worth four and a half mil," Foley said. "I had to, it's my favorite."

"It's the pressure I put on you," Lou said, "turned you away from a middle-age life of crime. That's not a bad ending."

Every half hour Jimmy played a recording of *"Alto como la luna,"* done in a slow tempo for the warmth of it, Cundo Rey's favorite.

There were women who came to kneel by the casket and look at Cundo. They made the sign of the cross, kissed the tips of their fingers, some of them, and touched their fingers to his lips glued shut. There were more women than Foley imagined Cundo had known, Foley looking for a girl with dyed hair wearing dark glasses.

HARPER LUXE

THE NEW LUXURY IN READING

We hope you enjoyed reading
our new, comfortable print size and found it
an experience you would like to repeat.

Well – you're in luck!

HarperLuxe offers the finest in fiction and
nonfiction books in this same larger print size and
paperback format. Light and easy to read, HarperLuxe
paperbacks are for book lovers who want to see
what they are reading without the strain.

For a full listing of titles and
new releases to come, please visit our website:

www.HarperLuxe.com